PEN
ITE
NCE

Jude Williams

The Book Guild Ltd

First published in Great Britain in 2019 by
The Book Guild Ltd
9 Priory Business Park
Wistow Road, Kibworth
Leicestershire, LE8 0RX
Freephone: 0800 999 2982
www.bookguild.co.uk
Email: info@bookguild.co.uk
Twitter: @bookguild

Typeset in Bembo Std

Printed and bound in the UK by TJ International, Padstow, Cornwall

ISBN 978 1912881 260

British Library Cataloguing in Publication Data.
A catalogue record for this book is available from the British Library.

For my mum and dad, with love and gratitude

CHAPTER 1

She stared, incredulous, at the tiny, ugly, puckered face protruding from one end of the writhing bundle the midwife thrust at her. It had been only hurriedly cleaned and she noticed that there remained a couple of minuscule, slimy threads of blood, all fibrous and gleaming, smeared across its fleshy, lobster-red cheeks. The baby was protesting noisily, furious to have been heaved out of its warm, dark refuge into this harsh, neon light. She could understand why it wanted to be back there again. Its whole chicken-like, vernix-smeared body shuddered with the effort of crying, gasping for frantic breaths in between piercing shrieks. Its limbs flailed wildly, tiny claws grabbing aimlessly at fistful after fistful of air.

'Well, don't you want to hold her, Emma, darling?' Her mother's excited voice startled her and portrayed only the merest hint of anxiety. Unperturbed, the midwife was still waiting for her to take the baby. Obediently, Emma held out her arms and the baby was dutifully, almost ceremoniously, placed into them, but instantly recoiling from the warm mass she was holding, Emma in turn held out the screaming baby to her mother. 'You take it, Mum. I'm tired.'

Her mother paced round the delivery room for a while, jogging the small bundle up and down in her arms, as though the last time she had done this was only yesterday, instead of nineteen years ago. As the yells slowly subsided into whimpers, out of the corner of her eye Emma was aware of her mother stealing worried glances in her direction from time to time.

As the baby gradually forgot forever about the sanctuary she had come from and her traumatic passage into this strange, complicated new place, the rocking motion lulled her, irresistibly, into an easy sleep. Emma's mother cautiously lowered herself onto the edge of the bed. After a few moments, she began, wordlessly, to stroke her daughter's dishevelled hair. The midwife had left the room now, summoned no doubt to deliver yet another tiny, determined life into the world. After the earlier racket, the delivery room seemed conspicuously silent.

They remained like this for a while, the two mothers; the older gently stroking the younger's hair with one hand, while cradling her sleeping granddaughter in the crook of the other arm, and the younger slightly reclined on the bed, staring impenetrably ahead of her.

Again, her mother's voice startled her. 'So, have you thought of a name for her yet, darling?' Her voice sounded unnaturally bright.

Emma shook her head wearily. 'No, not yet.'

Her mother tried again to engage her in some sort of exchange, tried to force Emma to take notice of her daughter, tried to make her voice sound casual, like it didn't matter to her, when Emma knew full well that it did. 'She's beautiful, isn't she?' Her voice faltered a little as she raised it self-consciously at the end. Emma responded with an almost imperceptible movement of her head, her eyes still fixed straight ahead of her, refusing to do what she knew her mother was desperate for her to do, which was at least to *look at* her baby daughter.

With a barely concealed sigh, her mother evidently decided to give up for the time being. 'Why don't you try and rest a bit while she's asleep? You look exhausted, darling.' After a few moments, Emma shut her eyes gratefully.

She felt as if the night were suffocating her. Almost horizontal sheets of rain whipped the stationary car. A relentless, deafening pummelling. Onto the windscreen, which was streaming with water, the slither of a moon cast strange, menacing shadows of the trees at the side of the road. As their branches were buffeted about in the squally wind, spindly, watery fingers clawed frantically at the windscreen. Her heart was racing as her own fingers fumbled with the key, trying desperately to insert it into the ignition. She cursed as she dropped it into the blackness. Now she was groping about on the floor beneath the driver's seat, her terror mounting with every second that passed. 'Please, God, please, God.' At last her fingers found it, her knuckles closing around it with relief. Again, with shaking hands, she struggled to insert the key. And then, finally, it was in and she was turning it. Nothing happened. She tried again. She was breathing quickly, practically panting. She felt her heart thumping. Nothing. Another time she turned it and depressed the accelerator pedal repeatedly as she did so. And again nothing. As she desperately turned and re-turned the key, even though she knew it was futile now, she noticed that the rain splattering onto the windscreen seemed to have become thicker, less transparent. And it was no longer colourless, but had taken on a rusty appearance. She stopped turning the key to watch, horrified, mesmerised, as the rusty colour turned crimson. When she realised that it was blood, not rain, falling out of the sky, she instinctively opened her mouth to scream. But the sound was swallowed up by the night.

Her heart was still pounding when Emma woke up, even though the recurring nightmare had become familiar to her now, give or take a few details. She remembered with a start where she was and stole a glance at her mother and the baby. Her mother, looking weary herself now, continued to cradle the little girl, who was still sleeping peacefully. Emma closed her eyes again, unwilling, for the time being at least, to confront the unfamiliar scene before her. Her own fitful sleep had not refreshed her in the slightest and she felt too fragile to submit to more well-intentioned questions and kindly concern from her mother.

She lay there for a few minutes, her drowsy mind swimming indolently in the peacefulness of the room. Her overwhelming relief to have got that alien thing out of her body had quickly given way to a feeling of numbness, of not knowing what or how to feel.

She had met him at a friend's house party last summer after her A levels, the summer, *that* summer, that she was poised to take up her place at Bristol University to read English. But, of course, that wasn't going to happen any more, now that she was lumbered with this baby. It had been a one-night stand, a drunken, fumbling, sordid encounter and one that she would rather have shut out from her mind completely. She had told her parents that she had been with him for a few months, this guy whose name and face eluded her memory, because she felt too ashamed to admit that she barely knew him. She knew that she would disappoint them enough with her revelation that she was pregnant without twisting the knife even more through the addition of further details that there was no need for them to know.

And indeed this single piece of news in itself had been more than was needed to break her father's heart. He had always doted on her. He had been so proud of his little girl who had earned herself a place at university, who had achieved what he had never had the chance or ambition to achieve himself. To his boundless delight and to her own not insignificant embarrassment, he had basked in her reflected glory, tirelessly mapping out to his friends and acquaintances the dazzling future that surely lay ahead of her. He had always loved her with an uncontained passion, demonstratively and, she thought, unconditionally.

However, she remembered his slumped posture in his chair, as the three of them – Emma and her parents – sat at the kitchen table while she tearfully, courageously revealed her predicament, his crumpled face in his weathered hands, and then, like a child who hasn't got its way, the slammed door, the angry thud, thud, thud as he ran up the stairs and the seemingly endless sulking, skulking in her parents' room as reality painfully sank in.

Their relationship had never been the same since that black day. Her father decided to move out. She knew it wasn't all her fault and repeatedly reassured herself that she had simply been the catalyst that had made him do it sooner rather than later. But she couldn't help feeling that she had let him down and not kept to her side of the bargain. Her father had been threatening for a while that he was going to leave. The rows between her parents had reached fever pitch, becoming more frequent, more heated, her mother's voice becoming ever shriller and ever more grating, her father's behaviour more childish. And the things that triggered a row became more and more trivial. It was as if her parents were constantly lying in wait for the slightest excuse to vent all their fury on each other, fury that was restlessly simmering deep down inside them, like a bottle full of fizzy drink that had been shaken too violently, ready to explode at any moment. The threats to leave would often be made at the height of an argument, left to float clamorously in the sodden, ringing air after her father had made his usual melodramatic exit from a room, slamming the door behind him in a self satisfied way, but neither Emma nor her mother had ever paid any heed to them. Neither of them believed for a moment that he would ever have the guts to go ahead and do it. He would stay put because that was the easier option. He would do anything for an easy life.

So it was with much surprise and incredulity that Emma and her mother received the news from Emma's almost apologetic father one drizzly February day that he had just signed up to a six-month lease on a flat in the nearby town. 'Just till I find something more permanent,' he mumbled, his face turned towards the wall, as he peeled off his gloves, hung up his heavy coat which smelled of the rain and wiped his tired-looking, prickly face on the sleeve of his jumper.

Emma's mother looked up at him from her ironing, eyes like saucers, struggling to absorb what he had just said. 'But you can't; I mean, you could have told us; I mean, not now, what with Emma and the baby due in a few weeks. You can't leave us now, Colin. Give it a few more months at least. Think it over. Please, Colin, not now. Think of Emma,' she continued, motioning towards their daughter's rounded form. Emma looked away, fiddling with the buttons on her cardigan.

'I know, I'm sorry, love. The timing's not brilliant, you're right. But what's done is done. I've signed the contract now. It's too late. I've made up my mind. Don't worry, things will work out fine, you'll see.' He forced a weak smile.

'How can you say that – don't worry? How can you do this to us? To Emma? What about your family, your grandchild? There you go again, you're so *selfish*. It's always you, you, you, isn't it? You don't give a damn about anyone else. Well, go on then. Clear off. See if we care. We'll be better off without you anyway.' She carried on ironing, pretending that he wasn't still standing there awkwardly, pretending that she hadn't just heard his horrid news, although the furious, venomous movements she made back and forth with her hissing iron made the extent of her hurt painfully apparent to husband and daughter, who looked on apprehensively.

After a few moments, her husband's voice cut through the steam. 'Well, it's not my fault you've driven me away, is it? I'm only doing what any sane man in my position would have done a long time ago. What with your incessant nagging and scolding, who can blame me for not putting up with it? You'd try the patience of a saint, you would.'

Emma's mother could keep silent no longer. She stood the fizzling iron up, fist clenched round its handle as if it might come in handy as a weapon. '*You* put up with *me*? Huh, that's rich, that is.' The sole spectator of some grotesque comedy, Emma watched with mild curiosity her mother's features contorting along familiar lines etched by the accumulation of years of marital bickering as she spat out her words malevolently. 'I've wasted twenty-one years of my life with you, you pathetic, spineless bastard, twenty-one long years hearing your constant whinging and whining, waiting for you to make something of yourself. All those grand ideas, the big house, the flash cars, the fancy holidays…' She exhaled audibly, shaking her head slightly as she did so, eyes narrowed, nose wrinkled disdainfully. 'Well, what have you got to show for yourself at the end of it all? Where are all the millions you said we'd be rolling in? I don't see them, do you?' Her voice was rising steadily. 'Well, where are they? Well? Well? Where, Colin?'

He was looking at the floor. Emma could see his temples pulsing. He looked defeated, exhausted. She wanted to go and wrap her arms around him and tell him everything would be all right. She wanted his forgiveness and she wanted to tell him that she forgave him too, for all his failings, for all the times that he had let her down. But her courage deserted her and in any case, she wouldn't have had time before the next onslaught from her mother.

'I'll tell you where they are. They're at the Dog and Partridge, that's where. Every time you have a few quid, off you go. Oh, it does look posh now, doesn't it, now it's all refurbished? Well, you should feel proud, you should, 'cause *you* paid for that, you know. And they're in that beer belly of yours and that liver and those decaying lungs. Let's hope those millions finish you off. 'Cause I for one certainly wouldn't miss you, *that's* for sure.'

In a self-satisfied way, she resumed her ironing with brisk, angular movements, her chest moving in and out rapidly. Apparently too consumed by anger, she paid little heed to the items she was ironing.

Emma was expecting a similar retaliatory tirade from her father, but instead he merely fixed his wife with a stare brimming over with loathing, muttering, 'I should have done this years ago.' Then, without even bothering to take his coat, he opened the front door wide and strode back out into the rain which was so fine that it looked like glitter falling from the leaden sky.

Neither Emma nor her mother heard anything from her father for a couple of months after that. He furtively moved himself out, waiting till the house was empty to come and collect his belongings. The house seemed strangely quiet, although its two remaining occupants tried to retain a sense of normality, strained though it was.

And of course there was the baby. Throughout the day, Emma's mother seemed to think about nothing else. She seemed to have forgotten all the disappointment with which she had received the news of her teenage daughter's pregnancy. She busied herself in her spare time with knitting baby bonnets and bootees and had taken it upon herself to sort out things the baby would need such as a cot and a pram. To be fair, she had asked Emma whether she wanted to be involved in the decision-making, but when Emma declined the offer had more than readily set about it herself. And with her friends, it was all baby talk. When they came to the house or spoke on the telephone, she must have driven them round the bend with her inane wittering on. It was almost as if she was proud now to have a teenage daughter who was pregnant, to be the first among her friends to be a grandmother. How her attitude had changed! But sometimes Emma wondered whether her mother's determined excitement, her optimism, were all a facade and whether when she was alone in bed at night, the mask fell away to expose feelings of anguish and desolation.

Emma's musings were interrupted by the sound of the baby starting to whimper, pathetic little noises which, after only a few attempts, developed into wholehearted shrieks that were impossible to ignore. With great reluctance, Emma lifted her heavy eyelids, only to be confronted by the overpowering glare from the delivery room. Once her eyes had become accustomed to the brightness again, she could see her mother who had stood up now and was frantically bobbing the screaming little creature about. 'I think someone's hungry.' She smiled.

'Will you do it then, please?'

'But she needs you, darling. Breastfeeding is much better for her, you know.'

'Not now, Mum, please. Can't you just ask someone for a bottle this time and then I'll do it next time? Please, Mum, I'm just so tired.'

'Well, babies *are* tiring, darling. You're going to have to get used to feeling tired all the time, I'm afraid.'

The baby's shrieks were becoming louder and more frantic. They sounded like a dentist's drill grating in Emma's head. 'I know, Mum, but I just can't face it at the moment. Please…'

Her mother relented. 'Oh well, all right then. It's your decision. She's your baby. Here you are then. You hold her while I go and try to find a bottle from somewhere.' She handed the red-faced, screeching creature over to her startled-looking daughter and hurried out of the room before there was any time for her to object.

Oh my god, thought Emma, as she regarded her daughter properly for the first time. *You're so loud. And so ugly.* The baby was putting all her effort into crying, working herself into a frenzy. Emma felt the tiny body shudder with each new ear-splitting shriek. She had probably forgotten the reason she had started crying in the first place, so intent was she now on making as much noise as she could with as much energy as she could possibly muster as if her very life depended on it.

Emma sat there, holding the baby awkwardly, wishing she were anywhere else but there in that depressing room with that stupid, noisy baby. She kept glancing over to the door, wishing her mother would return to take it from her and feed it, or whatever needed doing to it. She felt sore and exhausted. She wanted this nightmare to stop.

After what felt like hours, her mother reappeared carrying a bottle of milk. The baby was still wailing frenetically, oblivious to anything else. 'Sorry, I had to wait for the nurse to finish with someone else. God, she's a determined little mite, isn't she? I could hear her at the other end of the corridor.'

She took the baby from Emma and proceeded to feed her. After some gentle coaxing with the teat and much spluttering, it wasn't long before the baby got the hang of what she was supposed to be doing and was glugging contentedly, eyes closed, worn out from all her exertion. The room was once again peaceful.

'Isn't she lovely?' Smiling, her mother looked up at Emma expectantly, waiting for a response that didn't come. Satisfied that the baby had stopped drinking now, her mother, careful not to wake her, placed her gently into the transparent cot next to Emma. 'I'm just going to pop out to phone your dad. I suppose I'd better let him know he has a granddaughter.' She rolled her eyes at Emma. 'Unless you want to tell him yourself, of course?' Emma shook her head. 'I won't be a minute then.'

Left alone once again with her daughter, Emma turned to look at her, finding it hard to believe that she was looking at the same baby. Her little chest was rising and falling rapidly, almost imperceptibly, her arms folded upwards so that the pink, pudgy palms of her tiny hands were upturned next to her shoulders in a gesture of total submission, which gave her a look of vulnerability. She looked so relaxed now, so comfortable, like she didn't have a care in the world. Her sleep was an easy one, untroubled by anxiety of any sort. Hers was the sleep of the innocent.

'There was no reply so I left a message.' Emma's mother bustled back into the room. 'No doubt down the pub.' Her mother gave Emma one of her artificial smiles, emitting a little light-hearted sigh as she lowered herself into the plastic chair next to her again, as if she felt obliged to stave off silence. 'Still asleep I see...' She nodded towards her new granddaughter. 'Any nearer with a name for her, darling?'

'Sophie.'

'Oh sweetheart, that's lovely!' exclaimed her mother far too enthusiastically, flinging her arms round Emma who hugged her back woodenly, thinking to herself that whatever name she had chosen, the relieved, exuberant reaction would have been the same.

Following her little outburst, her mother sat herself down again and the two women spent an awkward half hour or so together, a half hour punctuated by tiny snuffling and shuffling sounds from the sleeping Sophie and subsequent silly coos and exclamations from her grandmother.

Eventually, a nurse appeared at the door to tell them that Emma and Sophie were to be moved onto a ward and that once she had settled Emma in, her mother should really leave, as visiting time had now finished. Soon afterwards, Emma found herself being wheeled along the corridor, together with the still-sleeping Sophie in her cot, her mother following behind with Emma's belongings.

The maternity ward seemed surprisingly calm to Emma, who had been imagining it to be filled with activity and the noise of screaming babies. She surveyed her new surroundings warily. While some babies slept, others lay peacefully in their mother's arms or were feeding contentedly. The other mothers eyed up the newcomer with brazen curiosity and ill-disguised disdain. They all looked much older than Emma. They seemed so self-assured, she thought, so confident in the way they handled their babies. She stole envious glances at them. Serene and unflustered, they seemed to be taking the new experience of motherhood in their stride. They all looked so happy. She thought to herself gloomily that she could never be like them.

Left alone and dreading the long night ahead, Emma suddenly wished with all her heart that her mother was still there with her, notwithstanding the fact that she found her presence irritating. She would rather feel mildly irritated, she thought to herself, than be overwhelmed by feelings of loneliness and desolation.

Her eyes wandered to the huge smeary window at the far side of the ward. Darkness was falling now and the multi-storey car park opposite the maternity wing was suffused with an orange glow from the electric lights which had switched themselves on. A small trail of people was heading along the illuminated footpath towards it and Emma thought that she could make out her mother among them, fumbling for something in her handbag, her car park ticket perhaps. A tiny, indistinct silhouette in the distance.

Emma looked down at her daughter, who continued to sleep, tiny chest rising and falling steadily. She envied her being able to sleep like that – peaceful, untroubled. She knew that if she managed to get any at all, her own sleep on the ward that night would be broken continually by babies wailing, hushed voices and the soft padding to and fro of the nurses' rubber-soled shoes, not to mention the usual terrifying nightmares that caused her to wake up screaming sometimes, breathless and sweating, her heart filling her chest with its thumping. From time to time, her screams had woken her mother who would stagger, bleary-eyed, into Emma's room to sit on the edge of her crumpled bed, stroking her damp, dishevelled hair to soothe her back into a turbulent sleep. The nightmares had started the previous summer and her parents had put them down to worries about the pregnancy. Her mother would frequently try to allay her concerns, endlessly reassuring her that everything would be fine and that she would be there to help with the baby, but the nightmares continued as before. Emma knew only too well that they were nothing to do with being pregnant.

Her night in hospital passed much as Emma had imagined it would. Exhausted, she had drifted off into a brief, fitful sleep a couple of times in between all the disturbances of the night. When Sophie had woken up screaming, the nurses had tried hard to persuade Emma to have a go at breastfeeding, assuring her that the earliest breast milk was the most beneficial for her baby, but after a feeble, unsuccessful attempt at it, Emma had refused to try any more. As well as being frightened by the idea of breastfeeding, she secretly found it slightly repulsive. By the third time Sophie needed feeding, the busy nurses had given up trying to persuade Emma and had just brought a warmed bottle straightaway. With their help, she had at last managed to give Sophie her feed. It was with relief that Emma saw the watery light of day beginning to seep around the edges of the paper blinds at the window.

That morning, Emma and Sophie were discharged from the hospital and Emma's mother came to pick them up. The day had dawned sunny and bright, but the early-morning cotton-wool clouds were quickly accumulating and darkening, blotting out the sun now and again on the journey home and threatening some early April showers. Emma had been looking forward to getting home, but at the familiar crunch of the car wheels on the gravel driveway in front of their house, her heart sank. She looked up at her bedroom window at the front of the house, saw her jaded fairy lightshade that had dangled from the ceiling since she was at primary school and the faded print of the dusty curtains that had hung at her window for as long as she could remember and the thought suddenly struck her that she would never be able to return to her old life. She would never again be the same carefree teenager who had burst into fits of giggles with her friends at the silliest things, laughing and spluttering hysterically until they were doubled over, staggering helplessly, barely able to breathe, ecstatic tears streaming down their flushed cheeks as others simply looked on with mild irritation, wondering what they could possibly find so amusing. The teenager who had enthusiastically made plans with her friends as to where they should go on a Saturday night, tittering excitedly as they compared notes on which boys in their class they considered the best-looking, while they all got ready to go out together, her bedroom a sordid jumble of make-up and discarded clothes and the air thick with perfume.

On hot, balmy summer days when she and her best friend, Tara, used to wander around the local town where they had come by bus on one of their jaunts, they would stand still for a few moments and look up together at the interminable azure expanse of the sky, the lines of the ancient cathedral sharp and distinct against it. Then, whooping with laughter and intoxicated by the sheer gloriousness of the day, they would pretend to try to swallow the sky. It was a crazy, preposterous idea, they both knew, but there they would stand on the uneven cobbles, which had been polished by the countless pairs of feet that had trodden upon them through the ages, taking great gulps of the warm, dry air. Their mirth, however, was overshadowed by a certain gravity that they both failed to acknowledge out loud. Jesting and levity aside, they both knew deep down that this was in part a stupid, vain attempt to hold onto their youth and childhood innocence forever. Oh, those heady, halcyon summer days, rendered more poignant now by the relentless passage of time! Unsullied, treasured memories that were like a thin sheet of highly polished glass, so fragile, so brittle, and it suddenly felt to Emma as if it were shattering into thousands of minute shards, tiny daggers inside her which were stabbing deep within her heart.

Her mother unfastened Sophie's seat from the back of the car and carried her, fast asleep, thanks to the lulling ride home, to the back door. Unlocking it, she walked through to the kitchen where she set the seat down on the table. Emma followed them inside slowly, her overnight bag slung over her shoulder.

'Ooh, it's quite chilly, isn't it?' Her mother rubbed her hands together briskly. 'I'd better put the heating on, I think. We don't want our gorgeous little girlie getting a chill now, do we?' Smiling, she nodded over at the car seat where Sophie continued to snooze blissfully. 'Shall I put the kettle on?'

Emma slumped down wearily onto one of the wooden chairs and watched as her mother went through the well-oiled routine of making tea. She handed the steaming mug to Emma, who took it gratefully, blowing into it and clasping it with both hands to warm them.

'Your dad said he'd drop by later.' She sat down opposite Emma. 'He said he's dying to meet his little granddaughter.' Emma didn't know whether to believe this or not. Since moving out, her father had hardly seen her. He had become a different person almost overnight. She had sometimes suggested that she come over to his new flat to see him, but he usually managed to come up with some lame excuse or other, so in the end, she had all but given up trying. He seemed to be spending even more time now at the Dog and Partridge, drinking with his workmates every evening, frittering away what little money he had. The pub and his drinking mates were his home and his family now. She felt as if she were no longer a part of his life, as if he had closed a heavy door on her. She couldn't help feeling that he didn't really love her any more, that he had still not forgiven her for falling pregnant and scuppering all his neatly laid-out plans.

Sophie had started shifting slightly in her car seat and grunting, as likely as not gearing herself up for her next feed. Emma couldn't help groaning inwardly. Stretching, Sophie screwed her little face up and flicked her eyes open and shut a few times like a plastic doll with movable eyelids, as if trying to work out whether it was worth waking up or not. But in the end, the call of hunger was evidently more urgent than that of sleep, as the grunting turned into crying.

Emma could feel her mother's eyes boring into her. 'Well, darling, don't you think you'd better lift her out? I expect she's ready for some more milk. It's been four hours since her last lot, after all.' Trust her mother to have made a mental note of the time she was last fed. 'You get her out while I get her bottle ready. Well, unless, of course, you want to try breastfeeding her again, that is.'

Emma shook her head listlessly. Apparently expecting that answer, her mother had already jumped up and started busying herself like an automaton with bottles, steriliser and powdered milk. She seemed to know exactly what she was doing, Emma thought, as if she had been programmed. Emma wondered how such a tiny thing, merely by crying, could have such power over everybody, commanding them to do what it wanted. Sighing to herself, she leant across to the car seat on the table in order to unfasten the straps. Once undone, she managed to slide Sophie's flailing arms out from underneath them, gingerly, for fear of hurting her, then she slid her own hands behind Sophie's arching back and scooped her out before manoeuvring her self-consciously into a cradling position on her lap. She was aware that her mother had been watching her all the while out of the corner of her eye.

'Here you go, then.' Her mother handed her the bottle once it had warmed up enough. Emma took it wordlessly, surprising her mother who had no doubt expected some sort of protest. While Emma fed Sophie, her mother wittered on inanely about how her friends were all dying to meet her pretty little granddaughter and how she must buy more formula milk and nappies when she next went to Tesco and how she should phone to book a check-up for Sophie with the GP, with Emma only half-listening, absorbed in her own thoughts.

And so began the ceaseless monotony of feeding and nappy changing, of putting something in and then removing what was left of it, and of disturbed nights and constant tiredness, drudgery to the most dedicated, enthusiastic mother, let alone to an uncommitted nineteen-year-old who had been used to doing as she pleased, who had been used to a frivolous world which had up until now always revolved around her, and for whom motherhood had belonged in a hazy, distant future, not in a gritty here and now.

Emma's father didn't show up that day. She couldn't help feeling a little disappointed. She hadn't expected him to, but had been secretly hoping that he might. And there was no word from him either.

However, the following afternoon, he dropped by. Emma's mother answered the doorbell. That he came to the front door and rang the bell now, waiting dutifully to be admitted on the handful of times he had visited since his departure, seemed odd to Emma. It served to confirm his estrangement from them, making her realise once and for all that he no longer belonged there and probably never would again.

Her legs tucked underneath her as she sat on the sofa in the lounge beside a dozing Sophie, Emma watched in the smeary mirror on the lounge wall the very slightly distorted reflection of her father taking his coat off in the hall and hanging it up, following a cool reception from her mother. He was unshaven and had obviously not put a comb through his unkempt hair in a while. Under his coarse stubble, his face looked pasty and drawn and the skin under his sunken eyes was the colour of mustard.

'They're in here.' Her mother led him into the lounge, a less-than-welcome guest now in his former home.

Her father came over to the sofa and gave Emma a peck on the cheek. He smelt of stale cigarette smoke. 'All right, love?' She nodded half-heartedly. 'So this is my little granddaughter, is it?' He motioned towards Sophie, who was still sleeping peacefully, palms upturned towards the swirl-patterned ceiling. 'Well, she is a beauty, isn't she? Looks like you did when you were a baby, you know.'

Grunting loudly, he lowered himself gratefully into the armchair opposite Emma, the one that he had claimed as his a long time ago. His imprint was still on it, probably, as nobody had sat in it since he had left. He slouched back in it, plumping up the familiar, worn cushions around him as he had done countless times before. He certainly looked at ease there, as if the chair knew instinctively whereabouts to yield and its springs just how much to stretch. 'So, how are you then, love, all right?' he asked her again. Again, Emma nodded. 'Did the birth go OK? Did she fly out like a champagne cork?' He chortled to himself at this, which, in turn brought on one of his coughing fits. 'Well, she certainly is a pretty little thing, isn't she?' he resumed, once he had finished coughing, without giving Emma a chance to answer his question. 'A real corker,' he announced with a knowing smirk. There came another explosion, his chest heaving as he wheezed uncontrollably with laughter.

Emma obliged him with the ghost of a smile, wondering whether he had already been to the pub at lunchtime. 'So, what was it you're calling her?' he asked, once he had recovered.

'Sophie.'

'That's nice, love. I used to have an Aunt Sophie. Wasn't a very common name back in them days. Owned a sweet shop, she did. Have I told you about her?' Emma nodded again, but her father took no notice and carried on. 'We would always call round after school and she'd give us some treat or other. Me and your Uncle Dave loved it in there. And it smelled so good – mm, I can still remember that smell now.' He closed his eyes and inhaled deeply, as if he was back there once again in the sweet shop. 'And Aunt Sophie would have all the tall glass jars lined up neatly on the shelves filled with every kind of sweet you could imagine. All the colours of the rainbow they were, in all different shapes and sizes. Then out we'd both come, me and your Uncle Dave, pleased as Punch, grinning from ear to ear, with liquorice laces dangling from our mouths or sucking on giant gobstoppers, which made us dribble like anything and shut us up for the rest of the walk home. We'd try to finish them before we got back otherwise your gran would get cross and say they'd spoil our tea. We used to worry that she'd tell Aunt Sophie to stop giving us sweets on our way home from school.'

Her father seemed in good spirits today. Emma hadn't seen him this jovial for a long time and wondered what had made him so cheerful. She dared not hope that it might be because of his new granddaughter. He had probably had a couple of beers… Or a win on the horses…

'Go and ask your mum to put the kettle on, will you, love?' He winked at her. 'I'd murder a cup of tea. She probably won't do it if I ask her.' Emma got up from the sofa, casting an uneasy glance at Sophie. 'Don't worry, I'll watch her for a second.'

In the short time that it took Emma to go and ask her mother, her father had taken possession of the remote control and switched over channels on the television, dragged over the faded faux leather pouf on which his feet were now squarely planted and had helped himself to the newspaper, deep within the sports pages of which his tousled head was now buried. 'Thanks, love.' He didn't look up, as Emma re-entered the room.

She slumped down again wordlessly and looked out of the front window. Her father's worn-out red van was parked on the drive, rusty paint flaking off round its wheels. The stencilled letters of his name on either side of the van had started to peel off. It had seen better days. Overhead, a couple of birds were wheeling in a brisk April sky, one mirroring the other's movements, in such perfect alignment and synchronicity that Emma almost began to wonder whether she was seeing double. The sun was playing hide and seek among the lily-white clouds in a shimmering expanse of blue that seemed to go on forever. The living room suddenly seemed stuffy and oppressive. Emma felt like a caged bird waiting for someone to unlatch her door so that she could unfurl her beautiful wings and float up on a thermal to join those other birds, soaring weightlessly, high above a troubled world.

Emma's mother having brought their mugs of tea, her father proceeded to take great, grateful slurps of it, still immersed in the paper except for every so often when applause would sound on the television and he would peer over the top to check the score of the darts match that he was following half-heartedly. When he had finished his tea, he put the mug down on the coffee table beside him and leaned his head back against the top of the armchair so that it lined up perfectly with the greasy stain on the fabric left by his head. A memento of him after he had moved out. 'That's better.' He yawned. Within a few minutes, his eyelids had started to droop intermittently and his hands had started to jerk each time he every so often almost dropped the dog-eared newspaper he was still holding, as he lazily fought off sleep. However, soon his jaw had fallen and, with his mouth agape, he was snoring unashamedly. Seeing her father installed in his chair having forty winks in front of the television, it felt to Emma like old times again, when he was still living with them. She found his somnolent presence comforting; she was cocooned in the lounge with him in a time warp that had swallowed up the present. She closed her eyes and allowed herself fleetingly to imagine that she was a schoolgirl once more and that none of the hurt and trauma of the past year had ever happened. And before long, she, too, dozed off gratefully, for she had had little sleep over the last few days and nights.

Her relief was short-lived, however, since no sooner had she been lured down the beguilingly delectable slope into sleep than the nightmare held her fast again in its stealthy clutches and she was back in the car on that night, frantically trying to start the engine as the rain turned to blood which splattered relentlessly onto the windscreen. She felt all the same emotions, the terror, the panic as raw as the very first time she had had the nightmare, despite having lost count now of how many times she had experienced it. The essential elements were the same each time, although the details would sometimes vary a little from one time to the next. This time she woke up, heart pounding, after the windscreen wipers had started up by themselves, slightly sluggish as they smeared the viscous liquid across the screen. Through the thin film of blood, Emma could make out a child's face, its features contorted by anguish, its beseeching eyes boring into the darkest, innermost recesses of her soul.

She shivered, despite the tropical heat in the lounge, now that her mother had fiddled with the heating controls so that it was on pretty much constantly. She felt exhausted, drained of all vitality. She looked across at her father enviously, who was still snorting, mouth wide open.

Sophie, on the other hand, was starting to fidget and make snuffling noises. Emma disappeared into the kitchen to make up a feed for her which would be ready for her to have when she woke up. By the time she returned with the milk, her father had woken up, no doubt disturbed by Sophie, who had by now started to complain more loudly.

Emma, her movements becoming a little less clumsy now, scooped her up and sat down with her in her arms.

Her father made a show of yawning and rubbing his eyes. 'I'd best be off,' he grunted, glancing at his watch.

'But don't you want to hold her? I'll just give her a bit of milk and then you can give her a cuddle. It won't take long.'

'No, I'd better not, love. Sorry. I told Stu I'd meet him at four.' Her father stood up and smiled apologetically. 'Next time, hey?' Emma wondered when that might be. He walked over to the sofa. 'She really is lovely, though. Got a good pair of lungs on her, hasn't she?' He forced a laugh, trying to make light of the situation. 'See you soon then, love.' He stooped to kiss her on the cheek and then gave Sophie a peck on the forehead, screwing his face up a little as it encountered her flailing limbs.

'Bye then.' He walked out into the hall and Emma watched him in the mirror as he put his coat on. The reverse performance of his arrival. She heard the click of the door as he opened it, then the dull thud as he pulled it shut, followed by the faint crunch of his trainers on the gravel outside. She watched him through the net curtain as he got into his van. She heard it shudder into life and then the sound of the engine pitch getting higher as it reversed out of the drive. Her father had to wait at the end of the drive for a couple of cars to pass before he finally backed onto the road and drove off, the van protesting slightly as he shifted up the gears to drive away down the road.

Emma sat there feeding Sophie, who was glugging away contentedly now. Her father had left the television on and Emma stared at the flickering colours of the screen blankly without seeing, without comprehending, her brain refusing to make the necessary step to process the information and transform it into a rational image. The present had returned and with it, a bleak-looking future and Emma felt its monstrous weight on her shoulders. She felt an overpowering sense of loneliness and of disappointment that her father hadn't taken more of an interest in his granddaughter, evidently finding meeting his mates in the Dog and Partridge more important. She felt inadequate, as if she had somehow let him down once again, automatically blaming herself without stopping to consider that it might be he who was at fault.

CHAPTER 2

As the weeks slowly unravelled, Emma gradually became more accustomed to the monotonous routine of her new way of life and, little by little, her reluctance towards her newly acquired status of motherhood began to dwindle. Now she didn't bat an eyelid at most of the things that had previously seemed alien and daunting to her, like changing Sophie's nappy or giving her a bath, and she performed these tasks with an assured fluidity that belied her initial indifference to her daughter.

A few weeks after Sophie's birth, her mother returned to work at the salon where she was a hairdresser, having taken time off to help Emma. It had been a moment that Emma had been dreading to start with, but the prospect of looking after Sophie by herself no longer seemed quite so formidable.

As the days lengthened and the daffodils drooped their brittle, wilting, russet heads which yesterday, lavish and dazzlingly golden, had pranced back and forth like flamboyant puppets whose strings were pulled by the unpredictable squalls of early spring, and while the world filled with exquisite scents and fresh colours, Emma would take Sophie out in her pram. Pushing her along tree-lined pavements, she would watch as her daughter, wide-eyed and excited, contemplated the gentle, playful movements of branches, heavy with fragrant cherry blossom as they bobbed in the soft breeze overhead. Emma didn't worry about bumping into any of her old classmates, as she had used to. Many of them had left for college now anyway or had found jobs locally. Sometimes, if she was feeling particularly courageous, she would take the bus into town to visit her mother in the salon, who would be over the moon to see her granddaughter and who would make a tremendous fuss of her for the benefit of all her colleagues, who would never tire of cooing over Sophie, and of the salon's customers, who would reward her efforts with an indulgent smile or lingering glance in her direction. Emma, slightly embarrassed, would hover awkwardly at the side of the room, watching her mother make the most of her brief time in the limelight.

A couple of times she had ventured as far as her father's flat on the other side of town. On the first occasion, he had been out, or at least had not responded to the doorbell, and on the second, he had answered the door, but had taken a while to do so, and had appeared somewhat flustered and eager to get rid of her.

'Oh, hello, love. Now's not exactly the best time actually. I was just about to pop out. I'm running a bit late. Sorry, darling.' He smoothed his hair down nervously. Emma could see the outline of the label of the T-shirt he was wearing under the neckline below his stubbly chin. It took her a second to register that it was on back to front.

Despite appearing distracted, her father suddenly noticed Sophie peering up at him. He bent over the pram for a second to tickle her under the chin with his rough, hairy forefinger. 'How's my lovely little granddaughter then?' Sophie obliged him with a gurgle.

As he did so, Emma happened to glance over his lowered back into the small, untidy lounge where, she noticed with a start, in the midst of all her father's clutter, a floral scarf was draped over the back of the sofa and a denim-coloured shoulder bag was lying on the floor. She maintained her composure, her face impassive, her body language giving away not the slightest hint of agitation, as her father straightened up again.

'Come on then, Sophie. We'd better let Granddad get ready to go out,' although Emma guessed he wasn't going anywhere apart from back to the owner of the scarf and handbag. She turned the pram round. 'We'll call in some other time then, Dad. I'll phone you first to check it's convenient.'

'See you soon, love. Thanks for coming anyway and sorry today wasn't a good time.' He closed the door and Emma, crestfallen, started her long trudge back across town to the bus station. The wind had got up and before long, dark, swollen clouds rolled in over the miniature mountain ranges formed by the rows of rooftops and as the clouds blew across the sun, buildings and pavements all of a sudden lost their luminescence and, with the absence of shadows, everything became monotone and drab. Then the first few bloated drops of rain began to plop onto the ground, quickly increasing in number until it was raining steadily.

It took Emma a few minutes to notice the rain, so absorbed was she in her own thoughts. Then she stopped to pull her own hood up and struggled to pull the rain cover over the pram. It was the first time that she had needed to use it and so it took her a while to work out how to make it stay up. Having finally succeeded, she carried on pushing the pram, a fascinated Sophie peeping out between the raindrops which pooled and trickled in front of her face, their pitter-patter on the plastic cover like the crackling sound of fire.

It was a lot to take in. Questions flooded her head. Who was this woman? How long had it, whatever "it" was, been going on? How had they met? And what about her mother? Would she tell her? After all, if her father *was* seeing another woman, he was doing nothing wrong. He and her mother had separated and were free to live their own lives as they chose now. *Weren't they?* So maybe that was why her father seemed to have little time for her at the moment. And she had been worried that she had been the one who was somehow to blame. On the one hand, it was a relief that it was not her fault, but then, on the other hand, it hurt to think of her father focussing all his attention on another woman. But then, was she jumping to conclusions? After all, she was only assuming that her father and this woman, whoever she was, were carrying on together. She had no real proof. *Did she?* This woman might be visiting her father for a totally innocuous reason. But then again, what about her father's back-to-front T-shirt? Emma's head was swimming in a dizzying whirlpool of persistent thoughts and questions that kept surfacing relentlessly.

By the time she had arrived home, soaked and shivering, she had made up her mind to keep what she had seen that afternoon to herself for the time being at least.

A fortnight went by and Emma didn't see or hear anything else from her father. Then, late one evening, having stayed at home to look after a colicky Sophie, Emma heard her mother burst in particularly violently from her weekly shopping trip to the supermarket in town. She slammed the back door behind her, something that her mother would often scold Emma for doing, and threw her bags down on the kitchen floor, including the one containing the fruit which she normally took inordinate care over, with such vehemence that the lid from a plastic punnet of raspberries got knocked off, causing half of them to cascade rebelliously across the lino floor.

Emma stood in the doorway apprehensively, holding Sophie, who had started to bawl again. Emma, becoming quite exasperated herself, had been wandering about from room to room aimlessly with her, bobbing her up and down. The motion seemed to placate her a little, but then every time Emma stopped, she would resume her screaming at full volume.

Unusually, Emma's mother took no notice of Sophie's distress. 'You won't believe what I just saw at Tesco's!' With a face like thunder, she started, furiously, mechanically, to empty the shopping bags and put things away in the kitchen, flinging cupboard doors open, thumping tins and jars down hard on shelves, banging doors shut again.

Sophie's crying was getting louder. 'Your dad arm in arm with some young tart, bold as brass, parading up and down the aisles, all cock-a-hoop, that's what!' Emma swallowed hard. 'She can't have been much older than you, you know! What does he think he's playing at, making a ridiculous spectacle of himself like that? People will think he's her dad!' She whacked a glass bottle of olive oil down on the worktop so ferociously that Emma was surprised it didn't smash. 'Well, I can tell you now, it won't last!' Her voice was becoming increasingly irate and in the background, there was the considerable noise of Sophie's incessant, manic screeching as well as her own banging and clattering. Emma's head was pounding. 'That little hussy's welcome to him, anyway! See if I care!'

But it was obvious she did care. Her angry reaction to what she had seen lay bare her deep-seated jealousy. Her feelings for her husband, which she was usually at pains to keep hidden from view from the rest of the world, her own daughter included, had come to the surface, exposing her vulnerability. Emma knew that her parents' separation had hit her mother hard, even though she tried to put a brave face on. Although apparently delighted at the presence of her new granddaughter, who in turn adored her doting grandmother and who helped to occupy her during her evenings and days off, there were nonetheless times when Emma had noticed her mother becoming increasingly introspective, retreating into herself as if absorbed in her own sombre thoughts.

Finally defeated, Emma's mother leant against the kitchen sink, her back crumpled, as if crushed by a terrible weight, and gazed out at the dusky garden which was bathed in the warm orange glow from the kitchen. In the mirror of the window pane, Emma saw the shining tears that had been welling up in her mother's eyes at last brim over and cascade silently down her flushed cheeks. After a long time, she took a huge intake of breath, her body shuddering with the suddenness and violence of it. And then she was sobbing uncontrollably. Like a baby. Like a river bursting its banks. And with a sort of reckless abandon. Like she was experiencing incalculable anguish, but the very process of crying was purging her of it.

Emma sidled up to her, still holding Sophie, who had calmed down a little now and whom she shifted into the crook of one arm, leaving her other arm free to plant round her mother's waist self-consciously. She could feel the sobs reverberating like waves through her mother's body, crashing against her own. It felt as if her own body were absorbing her mother's pain, taking it away from hers. She clung onto that thought as she hovered next to her mother, unsure what to do or say, and it stopped her feeling entirely useless. For she had never been in this situation before. She had never played the part of comforter where her mother was concerned. It had always been the other way round. It had always been her mother comforting *her*. The times when she was a little girl and had fallen over and grazed her knees. When she was ill. When she had lost her new Barbie that she had got for Christmas. When she had started her periods. And more recently, with the nightmares. But now, she was at a loss for words. So shocked was she by the vehemence of her mother's anguish. Up until now her mother had always been at pains to keep her feelings under wraps. Emma was therefore all the more frightened now by this lapse, by this unexpected and violent exposure of her mother's vulnerability, her weakness, her inability or unwillingness to hold it together any more.

So she said nothing. She just held her until the sobs slowly subsided. Until she felt like she had absorbed all her mother's pain. Until her other arm holding Sophie felt like it was about to drop off. Until her mother had no more energy left to cry. And at last the kitchen was quiet again. Sophie had worn herself out with all her crying and was now sleeping angelically, blissfully oblivious to the affliction of her grandmother who now just stood there, still bent over, spent, staring towards the floor.

'Are you OK now, Mum?' Emma ventured finally.

'I'm fine thanks, darling, fine,' sniffed her mother, although it was obvious that she wasn't. She looked up at Sophie with bloodshot, empty eyes and stroked her downy sleeping head. Then she started to continue putting the shopping away as if nothing had happened, gently, this time, wearily. And Emma laid the sleeping Sophie down softly in her bouncy cradle and wordlessly set about gathering up the fallen raspberries. Because she didn't know what else to do.

CHAPTER 3

Neither of them ever mentioned the shopping incident again. It was glibly swept under the carpet to join the pile of other incidents and arguments that had accumulated there to gather dust over the years. They both carried on as normal, slotting back like magnets into their daily routines, her mother flitting between home and the salon, Emma looking after Sophie. And she had to admit that motherhood was growing on her. With every dimpled smile or ebullient chuckle, whenever she heard Sophie's soft, melodious voice coo enthusiastically as she lay awake looking at the morning, with every tiny milestone, Emma loved her daughter a little more. The once despondent girl in the maternity hospital had come at last to accept and, indeed, at times embrace, her status of motherhood.

And yet there were still of course times when Sophie was screaming blue murder in the middle of the night and Emma would have to force her unresponsive body to rise out of the bottomless depths of sleep several times in a single night and stumble downstairs bleary-eyed to warm Sophie's milk, or when she was changing Sophie's nappy for the third or fourth time in an hour, when she would hanker after her former carefree way of life, a time when she had no one to consider but herself and when her main preoccupations were school and going out with her friends. Her "friends" who had one by one deserted her after she had told them she was going to have a baby. Like it was something contagious. Most of them wouldn't have thought twice about having an abortion had they been in her predicament and in fact a couple of them had actually done so, like it was something as straightforward as getting your nails done, but Emma hadn't got the guts to tell them that she had been to the hospital with the intention of having one, but had chickened out at the last minute because she knew that she couldn't take a life, *another* life.

Even Tara, her so-called best friend, had started to exclude Emma from social gatherings once she was looking more noticeably pregnant and there was a risk that she might cramp her style, although she would still call her up on the odd occasion, all bright and breezy, and smoothly invite Emma to accompany her to a bar or a nightclub with the ulterior motive, Emma knew, of getting her to drive Tara into town and back to save her the taxi fare, and Emma, too kind to say no, would spend a miserable evening watching Tara and her friends knock back glass after glass and make a spectacle of themselves, but in the end any calls and texts dwindled altogether. And Emma couldn't be bothered to contact Tara herself and suggest meeting up only to be fobbed off with excuses and lies that fell easily off Tara's silvered tongue. She missed Tara, the two girls having always been inseparable through school when they would spend their free time eagerly anticipating and excitedly planning the next weekend or school holiday they would spend together.

Emma had felt particularly let down just before Christmas when she had dropped by Tara's house to give her a present – they had always exchanged presents in previous years and Emma had spent a long time battling with swarms of Christmas shoppers, trudging wearily between the crowded shops blaring out the same old Christmas tunes, before finally settling on a much too expensive pair of earrings – and the door was opened by Tara's mother, who, looking a little sheepish, apologised that Tara was out and thanked Emma, as she took the little box neatly crisscrossed with shiny festive ribbon that Emma held out to her. And Emma hadn't received any sort of thanks or acknowledgement from Tara afterwards, let alone a present of her own. Nor had she received anything from her, not even a text, when Sophie was born, although she was sure that she must have heard the news, Tara having stayed at home after A levels to take up a place at the college in the nearby town to train to become a beautician.

Tara. The most popular girl in the school. She was just one of those girls who always had a circle of friends and admirers around her without having so much as to lift her little finger. They would always be there, like moths jostling to get to the light. The girls and the boys. Oh yes, definitely the boys. They went crazy for her, like dogs after a bitch on heat, tongues lolling, nostrils flared, a stirring in their crotch. Yes, she was pretty. Very pretty. But she didn't half know it. With her blonde hair swishing about her slender waist and her sky-blue eyes and her long, tanned legs. And with a flick of her hair, a flutter of her big, mascara-drenched eyelashes or a flash of her gleaming smile, she would have the whole world eating out of the palm of her perfectly manicured hand. And she would lap it all up.

Emma didn't know why Tara had singled her out, taciturn, diffident Emma, when girls were virtually queuing up to be Tara's best friend. But she was flattered and grateful. It made her feel special. Invincible. With Tara beside her, she could take on the world. And without her, she was just plain old Emma again.

One Friday afternoon in July, one of those sultry, oppressive afternoons when the blistering air is still and stagnant, Emma was pushing a tetchy Sophie along in her pram in the park down the road. Turning into a shady avenue lined on either side by lush, leafy trees, Emma was startled by the beep of her mobile phone in the hush of the breezeless afternoon. It rarely sounded these days and she fumbled about in the tray beneath the carriage of the pram amidst spare nappies and clothes and sun cream to find it, startling as she did so a fat bluebottle, which buzzed away aimlessly, frenetically through the torpid air. She struggled to make out the words of the text in the dappled light. A bolt from the blue. It was from Tara. *Will b at V 8pm tonite. Hope 2 c u xx.*

Emma spent the rest of that afternoon debating with herself whether or not she should go. 'V' stood for Venus, a lively bar in the nearby town and favourite haunt of the local school and college students, and of the two friends in Emma's pre-pregnancy days. She was nervous about going out again and, if truth be told, of seeing Tara again. It had been a while. And yet at the same time she felt an irresistible urge to see her. She couldn't manage without her. Deep down, she had to admit to herself that she needed Tara more than Tara needed her.

As she stirred the grainy sugar round in her mother's mug of tea she had made for her when she returned from the salon later, Emma asked tentatively, 'Mum, would it be OK if I left Sophie with you tonight? I was thinking I might go out with Tara.'

'Oh, so she's back in the picture now, is she? She's decided you're her friend again, has she?' Her mother raised her eyebrows at her.

Emma handed her the steaming mug. 'She texted me earlier. Don't worry if you had other plans though. I'm sure I'll be able to go another time,' although Emma was sure that she wouldn't. She knew it was now or never. While she was Tara's flavour of the month again.

'No, that's fine, darling.' Her mother had evidently decided to be more amenable. 'Of course you should go. It will do you good to get out again. You don't want to be cooped up with your boring old mum all the time.'

'You're not boring. Well, only sometimes.' Emma grinned. 'Thanks, Mum. You're the best.' She leant over and planted a kiss on her mother's cheek.

'Go and enjoy yourself and don't you worry about us. Me and Sophie will be fine together, won't we, my little poppet?' Her mother smiled down at Sophie in her bouncy cradle as she kicked her chubby little legs excitedly and pawed at the colourful rattles on the bar in front of her.

Later that evening, as her mother gave her a lift into town, Emma felt a swarm of butterflies amassing inside her, fluttering against the walls of her stomach, desperate to get out. It was less than a year since she had last done this, but it felt like a lifetime. So much had happened and she felt like a different person now. It was as if she had never done this before. She had forgotten what to do.

Her mother turned and smiled at her. 'You look lovely tonight, darling, by the way.' And she was right, although Emma would never accept that she was. With her glossy auburn curls dancing at her shoulders and the little spray of pale freckles peppering the bridge of her dainty nose and the dress she had dragged out from the back of her wardrobe to put on. It was one of her old ones that she used to wear before she was pregnant. She was fortunate in having lost all the weight she had gained during pregnancy virtually overnight and the dress accentuated her willowy figure, its colours bringing out the striking olive-green hue of her eyes. Despite her walks in the sunshine with Sophie, her skin remained pale, having a delicate, almost translucent quality, like a waxwork.

'Have a good time!' Her mother raised the window back up and sounded the horn cheerily as she drove away from the pedestrianised part of town, where she had dropped Emma off and from where it was a short walk to Venus. But it felt to Emma like a walk to the scaffold, as she walked up the street towards the familiar neon sign, which was hard to read in the blaze of the warm, sunny evening, her heels on the pavement tapping out an ominous tattoo.

As she neared the bar, the thud of the music from inside got louder, urging her to walk in time to it. She recognised the tune. It was one of the songs in the charts at the moment. A rabble of noisy youngsters crossed the road in front of her, their heads no doubt brimful of hazy plans for an indolent summer that stretched out ahead of them now that their studies had finished, their high-pitched shrieks and laughter filling the warm, humid evening and drowning out the music and the sound of Emma's heels. They headed into Venus excitedly, a burst of music blaring out suddenly as the glass door opened, and then fading again as it swung shut behind them.

She was right behind them but she didn't go in yet. As they had opened the door, it had released a waft of air from the bar out onto the street. She could smell it. She remembered that smell. A sickly mixture of perfume and alcohol and sweat. A heady cocktail of anticipation and promiscuity and sex.

The bar was busy. It always had been on Friday nights. She could sense the buzz of animation from outside. She wished that she had arranged to meet Tara somewhere else beforehand so that she could have gone in with her. But she hadn't, and it was too late now. Taking a deep breath, she pushed the door.

Inside it was deafening, what with the music thumping out of the speakers and the lively hubbub of voices, each striving to make itself heard. Occasionally it was possible to distinguish one voice over all the others because it was louder or more strident, or to hear a girl's shrill peal of laughter rippling across the crowded room. And then there was that stale, nauseating smell again, which hit her like a slap in the face now that she was inside.

She started to make her way to the bar. Past bare-armed girls in short dresses with glossy red smiles and smoky eyes, who tittered appreciatively at what lascivious boys were saying in their ears, the boys leaning towards them, brushing their cheeks against the girls' scented hair, tentatively placing a clammy hand on their waist and gauging the reaction. Past tattoos and armpits smelling of stale deodorant, past fake tan, painted nails and aftershave, finding it difficult to make herself heard as she asked people politely to move out of her way.

As she was halfway across the room, a ginger-haired boy happened to step back as she was passing. He was wearing a stripy T-shirt and busily chatting up a Barbie-doll blonde caked in make-up and wearing a low-cut fuchsia-coloured dress which, Emma noticed, matched the colour of the girl's lipstick exactly. She was laughing inanely at something he was saying. As he stepped back, he bumped roughly into Emma, which caused some of the beer from the almost-full glass he was holding to spill down his front. He swung round angrily to find out who had knocked into him.

'You idiot! Look what you've done!' Orange freckles splattered his face.

'Um, sorry, but you stepped back just as I was walking past.' Emma tried in vain to make her voice sound commanding.

'You should've been looking where you were going, then, shouldn't you?' His breath reeked of alcohol and Emma tried not to inhale. She noticed that the fuchsia girl standing beside him was still smiling mindlessly at whatever joke or anecdote Freckles had just told her, and that she had a tiny smear of fuchsia lipstick on one of her front teeth. Emma suddenly felt the urge to tell her.

But instead, she answered Freckles. 'I was. I told you, it wasn't my fault. You just stepped back at the wrong moment. It was an accident.' She twirled a lock of hair around her finger self-consciously as she cast her eyes down at the wet, sticky floor.

'It wasn't a fucking accident. It was your fucking fault.' His voice was becoming louder. A tiny droplet of saliva landed on Emma's bottom lip. She brushed it away surreptitiously with the edge of her finger.

'Well, there's no need to speak to me like that.'

'I'll fucking speak to you how I fucking want.' The fuchsia girl was still smiling.

'If you're not going to accept that it was an accident, that's up to you, but there's nothing I can do about it now. I'm sorry it happened. What else do you want me to say?'

But just as Freckles was about to open his insalubrious mouth to say something still more offensive, another voice chipped in.

'Why don't you just leave her alone?' Emma turned towards where the voice was coming from and saw that it belonged to a man now standing next to her whose most remarkable feature was his mop of lustrous, conker-coloured hair.

'And who the fuck are you? Her dad?'

'I don't know her, but I saw what happened. It was like she said. You stepped back. It was *your* fault. And I think you should give her a break.'

'Oh, you do, do you? Well, this will fucking teach you not to get involved in things that don't fucking concern you.' And, without warning, Freckles suddenly swung his clenched, speckled fist slap bang into the other lad's face. The lad lost his balance and was knocked backwards for a couple of seconds, then righted himself, one hand clasping his nose. Between his fingers, Emma noticed a thin trickle of blood running slowly, but purposefully towards his upper lip. The lad flung Freckles a malevolent look before heading off towards the back of the bar, still clutching his nose. Freckles remained standing there, grinning stupidly, his fist still loosely clenched, until a couple of bouncers, who had noticed the commotion and come over to see what was going on, took hold of each arm and escorted him, still smirking, out of the front door of the bar. Amid the chaos, Emma noticed that the fuchsia girl had stopped smiling. Around about, despite the pounding throb of the music, a hush had descended as people nearby watched the spectacle appreciatively, all agog, mouths agape, as if it had been put on specially for them. Once the bouncers had disposed of Freckles outside and had returned, stony-faced, to their positions inside the door, the noise level increased once more as people resumed their unfinished, and mostly trivial and inconsequential conversations.

Emma looked over in the direction the guy with the conker-coloured hair had gone and spotted him leaning against one of the wooden chairs round a table where a group of his friends were sitting. She saw one of the girls at the table offer him a tissue from a small pack she produced from her handbag and the guy with the conker-coloured hair take one and start dabbing at his nose with it. Slightly annoyed with herself, Emma wondered why she hadn't thought to do that. But it had all happened so quickly and she had been in a state of shock and the guy had disappeared before she had had chance to regain her composure. She watched him now as he gesticulated animatedly before his surprised audience who hung on his every word. His hair bobbed about a little as he moved. Notwithstanding the subdued lighting inside the bar, she could discern his slightly swarthy complexion. Observing his profile even from a distance of several metres, his eyelashes were long enough and thick enough to be perceptible. A couple of the other lads at the table suddenly jumped up, pushing their chairs back aggressively, and made as if to head for the door, presumably to go after Freckles, but the guy with the conker-coloured hair leaned forward to stop them. After some heated discussion amongst the occupants of the table, the boys at last sat back down peevishly.

Remembering Tara, Emma dragged her gaze away somewhat reluctantly from the guy with the conker-coloured hair and his friends and started to scan the sea of youthful faces filling the room. Eventually she spotted her sitting at one of the tables at the other side of the room with a couple of girls she recognised from Tara's college course. She was laughing, flicking her long blonde hair over to one side as she threw her head back, in that ostentatious way she had of doing everything.

Emma headed in her direction, cautiously, lest she bump into anybody else. As she approached, Tara happened to look up and notice her. Beaming her pearly-white grin, she stood up and walked over to greet Emma, wrapping her tanned, slim arms around her shoulders. Then she stood back and looked at her. 'Wow, look at you! You look amazing! No one would believe that you had a baby a few months ago.' Tara was speaking so loud that Emma looked around quickly to see if anyone was listening. 'How is she by the way? Sophie, isn't it?'

'Yeah, Sophie. She's fine, she's gorgeous. You'll have to meet her.'

'Yeah, I know, I kept meaning to pop round, but I've just been so busy with college exams.' The excuse rolled off Tara's tongue easily.

'I've been waiting for you since eight. You've taken your time.' Emma looked at her watch. It was quarter to nine.

'Sorry, I got a bit held up'. And Emma proceeded to tell her friend about Freckles and the guy with the conker-coloured hair.

Tara's eyes were round. 'Wow, sounds exciting! Trust you to make an entrance. How come all the exciting stuff happens to you?'

'Well, I wish it didn't.'

'So where is this bloke then? The one who stepped in to the rescue, the hero? Is he fit?' Trust Tara not to beat about the bush.

'Not bad. He's that one over there in the blue checked shirt and jeans.' Emma gestured discreetly.

'Mmm, he's a bit of all right. Guess he must have been watching you, if he saw what happened, mustn't he?'

'Doubt it. Probably just a coincidence. I expect he happened to look over just at that moment.'

'Maybe, but even so, he still bothered to step in and stand up for you. Anyway, I think you ought to buy him a drink to say thank you. It would be rude not to.' Tara raised her eyebrows suggestively at Emma.

'Well, maybe I should, but I need to have a drink first before I can pluck up the courage.'

'Oh, you're pathetic. I'll go and get you one then. What do you want? Your usual?'

'Yes please. Thanks.'

'Why don't you go and join the others?' Tara gestured vaguely in the direction of where she had been sitting. As she did so, she tucked her hair behind her ear with the other hand. She was wearing the earrings Emma had bought her for Christmas. 'Back in a minute.' Tara smiled at her. And Emma felt like a million dollars.

And in that instant she forgave Tara for everything. Just as she always did.

She watched her old friend wend her way confidently towards the bar, turning a few heads as she always did and inciting the odd nudge, or lewd comment, which she ignored, carrying on resolutely, her lovely head held high. Emma had always envied her her self-assurance, her supreme composure at all times, no matter what was going on around her. She always exuded an aura of serenity and imperturbability. No one messed with her. Whereas she, Emma, timid, bashful Emma, without even doing anything, just always seemed to be asking for trouble.

She looked across apprehensively to where Tara's friends were sitting. They were tittering away to each other behind cupped hands, no doubt about some guy or other, raising a smeary glass to their glossy lips between sniggers. She wasn't sure whether they would even remember her. Just as she was about to make her way over to them, she was aware of someone approaching her and a voice directed at her. She recognised the voice and knew whose face she would see when she raised her eyes. She was suddenly aware of her heart thwacking against her chest.

'I just came over to check you were OK.' Emma looked up. The eyes of the young man with the conker-coloured hair expressed genuine concern. The irises were dark amber pools of melted chocolate, which Emma drank in voraciously, irresistibly, for a split second before answering.

'Um, yeah, I'm fine, thanks. How are you, more to the point? How's your nose?' She tried to control herself, tried not to let her voice wobble.

'Oh, it's OK now, thanks. It was nothing.' He touched it. His nose had stopped bleeding and was just a little swollen now.

'I'm so sorry I landed you in trouble. When you were only trying to help.'

'Oh, don't worry. It wasn't your fault. It was that stupid drunken idiot's. Can I get you a drink? I expect you could probably do with one. I'm Gabriel, by the way.' He held out his hand and Emma took it. It was smooth and warm. Gabriel. Emma tried out the name in her head. So *that* was what the guy with the conker-coloured hair was called. Because she had been wondering.

'I'm Emma. Um, thanks, but my friend's just gone to get me one actually.' *Did that sound ungrateful*? She looked over hopefully in the direction of the bar where she could see Tara in animated conversation with a couple of lustful boys who appeared to be hanging on her every word (and a whole lot more) with their puppy-dog eyes. Gabriel's gaze followed hers. 'Anyway, *I* should be buying *you* one to say sorry,' she added.

'No, I've told you, it's fine, don't worry.' He smiled at her. An open, reassuring smile. She smiled back hesitantly, her heart still pounding. And that was when she had the feeling that perhaps Tara had been right. That perhaps he did like her. And did she like him? She knew the answer to the question even before she had asked herself it.

Emma glanced across at the bar again. Tara was still talking to the boys. She could really do with feeling the comforting smoothness of a wine-glass stem in her hand right now. And that lovely warm feeling in the pit of her stomach when the wine hits it. As she looked back towards Gabriel again, she caught sight of him fleetingly out of the corner of her eye as he hastily returned his gaze upwards towards Emma's face from the rest of her body. She realised with a start that he had been looking her up and down while her head was turned and a tingle of excitement zipped up and down her spine.

'So, are you from round here then?' His voice was resonant and confident.

'Yeah, I live near here. How about you?'

'No, I'm just down for the weekend to visit an old uni friend. It's his birthday. The one over there, see?' Gabriel pointed towards the table where Emma had seen him earlier. 'That one there with the red shirt and blonde hair. Tim.' As they both looked across towards him, Tim happened to glance up and see them. He waved uncertainly and Gabriel laughed and turned back round to Emma.

'Where did you go to university?'

'York. What about you? What do you do? Are you a student? Do you work?'

Emma felt her stomach lurch. So this was where the fairy tale ended. She was about to get found out. Should she lie? He'd surely take to his heels if he knew the truth.

'Here you go. One glass of white wine.' Tara was holding out a wine glass. Emma had never felt so relieved to see her. She felt like hugging her.

'Thanks.' She took a grateful swig from the glass, Gabriel watching her all the while.

'So aren't you going to introduce us?' Tara looked indignant.

'Tara, this is Gabriel. Gabriel, meet Tara.'

'Ah yes, Emma's already told me what a hero you are. Do you make a habit of rescuing damsels in distress? I hope so.' Tara flicked her hair and ran her immaculately painted fingernails through it right down to the very ends so that her hand skimmed the outline of her breast as she did so. And her little ploy worked. Gabriel was all eyes.

He laughed. 'Only the pretty ones.' Emma could feel the blood rushing to her cheeks. She hoped that it was dark enough in the bar for Gabriel not to notice. Tara raised her eyebrows suggestively at Emma, who tried to ignore her, taking another sip of wine.

'You're not from round here, are you?' Tara, the consummate socialite who had clocked all the good-looking guys who frequented Venus over the years and who could spot a newcomer a mile away.

'No, I'm down from York for the weekend. I'm staying with a friend. We're sitting over there.' He motioned towards the table again. 'Why don't you come and join us?'

Tara and Emma exchanged questioning glances. 'Yeah, okay. Why not?' Tara ran her fingers through her hair again.

Nudging each other excitedly and exchanging meaningful looks behind his back, the two girls followed Gabriel across the room. 'Now, no bumping into anyone this time, please. Being hit in the nose once is enough for one evening.' The two girls tittered appreciatively.

When they reached Gabriel's table, he found a couple of chairs for the girls to sit on from a table nearby. His friends looked up from their conversations with mild curiosity, registering the newcomers with a cursory, barely perceptible glance up and down, the girls a little waspishly and the boys with a glimmer of covetousness in their eyes, as they tracked Tara's voluptuous outline caressingly. An expectant hush fell on the group.

'Right, everyone, this is Tara and Emma,' Gabriel said, gesturing to each one in turn. 'Emma is the one who got me into all the trouble.' He pulled a mock stern face at her and she smiled back at him.

'It was your choice to come and intervene.'

'I know, I'm joking. Anyway, I'm glad I did, otherwise I wouldn't have got to meet you.'

Their eyes met fleetingly and she felt her whole body, her whole soul, dissolving helplessly in those deep amber pools again. The wine was working its exquisite magic. It hadn't taken long. These days, she wasn't accustomed to drinking and, with racing heart, she let herself flounder in those delectable pools a little longer this time before she looked away again. And in that look, they both knew. They both knew what the inevitable outcome would be. And that there was no going back. In that exhilarating, swollen moment, there was the promise of so much. A mere moment – nobody else around them would have noticed – a moment like any other of the infinitesimal moments that make up a whole lifetime – a moment was all it took to promise each other the world.

'So, this is Chris, Laura, Pete, Tim, the birthday boy, Jack, Jasmine, Carrie, Max, Steve and Luke.' Gabriel gestured towards each of his friends in turn as he introduced them, and they smiled or nodded or waved at Emma and Tara as he said their name.

'Well, I don't know if we'll remember all those names.' Tara smoothed down her dress as she sat down. 'Happy birthday, Tim, by the way.' She flashed a smile at him, the perfectly white, even smile of glossy fashion magazines.

'Thanks.' He smiled back at her. A bold, reckless, brazen smile. A challenge.

'Yeah, happy birthday,' echoed Emma. The two girls were sitting next to each other, with Gabriel at the other side of the table.

And then the hum of conversation started up once more, Tim and Tara throwing shamelessly flirtatious glances at each other while Tara struck up conversation with Chris, who was sitting beside her, and whose eyes kept dropping inadvertently to her ample cleavage. Tara was eating him up for breakfast.

As they were sitting on opposite sides of the table, it was difficult for Gabriel and Emma to talk to each other, apart from in general, group conversation, but over the course of the evening, in the dim half-light of the crowded room, and as the beer and the wine liberated the deepest recesses of their bodies, they would catch each other's eye now and again and speak volumes to each other. Volumes of unquestionable, overwhelming desire.

And then after what seemed like hardly any time at all, everyone was suddenly getting ready to go. Chair legs were scraped against the sticky wooden floorboards of the room and almost-empty glasses were flung back against open mouths and drained and slammed back down on the table. There was mention of heading back to Tim's house. Emma could feel Tara pulling at her arm. 'Are you going to come?' Her eyes pleaded with Emma. No prizes for guessing why she wanted to go. Emma could smell Tara's perfume as she spoke. It was the same one she always used to wear, but mixed with the smell of alcohol, Emma found its scent a little sickly now. Her head was beginning to throb.

'I'd better go,' she whispered to Tara. 'My mum will be wondering where I am. And I need to get back to Sophie.'

'Aw, come on. It will be a laugh. Your mum wouldn't mind. Sophie will be asleep, won't she?'

'You're both welcome to come too, of course.' It was Tim. He was looking questioningly at Tara. Gabriel stood beside him.

'No, I need to get back actually. Thanks anyway.' Emma could feel her head spinning now that she was standing up. She touched the back of a chair to steady herself.

'Oh, go on. Can't you just come for a short while?' Gabriel this time. And there were the eyes again. Emma was tempted. Very tempted. But she knew she should get back to Sophie. She might wake in the night and need her. And more than that, she couldn't face a barrage of well-intentioned questions from her mum if she stayed out half the night. She couldn't be bothered to explain herself. No, she must go. She would never see Gabriel again anyway. He lived too far away, for a start. And even if she did, he would surely soon lose interest once he found out about Sophie. There was no point. And besides, she was starting to feel a bit the worse for wear. She hadn't drunk that much in ages.

'No, sorry, I really need to go.'

Gabriel looked crestfallen. 'OK, if you must. How will you get home? Do you want me to call you a taxi?'

'Don't worry, it's OK, thanks. There'll probably be one outside anyway.'

'Well, let me come with you to find one.'

'No, it's fine, honestly.'

'But I insist.'

'Well, OK then. Thank you.'

Emma called out goodbye to the others. Tara had linked arms with Jasmine and they were both laughing hysterically at something or other, as if they were the best of friends. Emma didn't know whether Tara's college friends were still in the bar or not.

'Have fun.' Emma smiled at Tara.

'I'll text you tomorrow.'

Emma and Gabriel made their way back through the bar. It wasn't quite so busy now. The bolstering effect of the wine had worn off a little and Emma suddenly felt shy again now they were alone and she no longer had Tara at her side.

As they emerged out of the door, Emma gestured up the road past the pedestrianised area. 'There's a taxi rank just up there.' It felt good to be outside again, out of the claustrophobic bar. The music sounded tinny now. A ghostly echo of itself. The air was still warm and breathless. The sun's splendid pink orb had not long set on the summer evening, emblazoning the horizon with its exquisite hues before the sparkling, refreshing curtain of the night had fallen irrevocably on the town, but the street where they stood was suffused with the gentle glow from the street lights and shop windows.

They walked along beside each other awkwardly in the direction Emma had indicated, unsure what to say to each other.

'So when do you go back to York?' Emma ventured, finally.

'Sunday afternoon. I'm back to work on Monday.'

Emma was about to ask Gabriel what he did, but changed her mind at the last moment, in case it would prompt him to enquire again as to what she did too. Not that it mattered. She had resigned herself now to the fact that they would never see each other again.

'Oh right,' she said instead.

Silence again, apart from the ominous click clack of Emma's shoes on the pavement again and the barely audible creak of Gabriel's trainers. Then a peal of laughter coming from somewhere behind them.

'Can I see you tomorrow?' Gabriel blurted out at last.

Emma was caught off guard. 'Well, I…' she faltered. Her mind was in a spin, as she desperately sought an answer.

Before she could think of one, however, he was grabbing her wrist. Not roughly, but urgently. They had both stopped in the middle of the pavement. She was turning to him questioningly, but he was already there at her mouth, driving his tongue between her lips. Any reservations and potential excuses that had been whirling round in her head just a moment ago had all at once subsided and were fizzling away into the starry night as she found herself surrendering to his kiss. An acknowledgement to herself of what she had been craving all along while she had been sitting opposite him at that table, telling herself that it could never be.

Gabriel cupped her face to pull her closer and they carried on kissing, exploring each other, oblivious to anything else around them, as if they were in another time and place. Their own time and place where nothing else mattered. Where there was no past and no future, only an immaculate, sempiternal present. When they finally drew away from each other, and after Gabriel had pressed his lips to hers again, firmly, caressingly, almost as an afterthought, he took her hands in his and looked at her.

'Well? Can I?' His tone was pleading, almost desperate.

'Yeah, I'd like that.'

'When? Where?'

Emma hesitated for a moment. Her mother was in the salon till six on Saturdays. She would have to ask her to look after Sophie again.

'Eight? Shall I meet you at Tim's? Where does he live?'

'Mill Street. It's on the edge of town.'

'Yeah, I know it. What number?'

'25, but wouldn't you rather meet somewhere more central? Or I could come and pick you up from yours if you want.'

Christ, no. 'No, it's fine. The bus goes that way.'

He kissed her again. 'Well, if you're sure then. Let me give you my number just in case.'

She took her mobile out of her bag and keyed in the digits as he said them. He watched her with languorous eyes. Then, after kissing her again, fervently, insatiably, he took her hand and they walked towards the taxi rank a little self-consciously. A couple of taxis were waiting.

'You're sure you have to go?' His eyes searched hers.

'Yes, I must.'

'Well, I'll see you tomorrow then. Eight o'clock. Tomorrow is going to feel like the longest day ever.'

She smiled. And he was drawn to her lips again, gently parting them with a kiss that was lingering, unfinished, unfulfilled, that hung quivering in the torpid night air. A promise of Elysium.

Heart racing, Emma opened the door of the taxi and got in. 'See you tomorrow.' She pulled the door shut behind her and, as the taxi drew away, watched Gabriel walk back the way they had come, getting further and further away until he was nothing more than a silhouette that was finally absorbed into the night.

Her mother was in bed still flicking through one of her magazines when Emma got home.

'Did you have a good time?' She yawned.

'Yes thanks.'

'How was Tara?'

'Oh, you know, the same as ever.' Emma smiled. 'Was Sophie OK?'

'Yeah, she was fine. I gave her a bath and then she fell asleep having her bottle.'

'Thanks for looking after her.' Emma decided to wait until the following day before asking her to babysit again.

'It was a pleasure. I'm glad you enjoyed yourself.'

'Night then.' Emma stooped to give her mother a kiss on the cheek.

'Night, darling.'

Emma lay in bed. And the last thing she felt like was sleep. She lay in a swoon. Her heart was turning somersaults. It felt like it would burst. Her head was still pounding, but she hadn't felt this happy in ages. She could still see Gabriel, hear his voice. She could still smell him, taste him. She felt like shouting out his name. But instead she whispered it into the darkness. She relived every detail of their evening together; the encounter in the bar, the looks and the kisses. Most of all the kisses. She wondered what he was doing now. He would be at Tim's with the others. Was he thinking of her, too?

There was no going back now. She loved the way he made her feel and yet they hardly knew each other. She knew that she had to see him again. There was no question about it. She had to feel this happy again. She would tell him about Sophie when the moment was right. She would cross that bridge when she came to it. *If* she came to it. And then there were certain things she would never tell him. Things that she could never tell anyone.

When sleep finally took hold of her, for once she didn't have her usual nightmare. Instead, she dreamed of him. She dreamed that they were lying together on a deserted beach with the sun beating down on them and a soft breeze rippling the hairs on their naked bodies and in their ears, the soothing swish of the waves lapping a golden shore. He was fondling her all over with his fingers and his tongue and his lips, and her whole body was aching for him. At the moment he was finally about to enter her, her perspective suddenly changed and she was looking down on herself from above, like one of those near-death experiences that some people talk about having had on the operating table. She was up there with the sun looking down from the cloudless firmament. Only she found she wasn't looking at herself. She was looking at Tara. It was Tara's perfectly-formed face that was underneath Gabriel's and that was smiling up at her serenely, indifferently, as Gabriel's pelvis rose and fell, rose and fell on top of hers.

CHAPTER 4

The heatwave that had plunged the country into a state of lethargy for the past couple of weeks continued to show no signs of letting up. Following a fitful sleep, Emma woke to yet another stiflingly hot day. Recalling the previous night, she felt a tingle of excitement run down her spine at the prospect of seeing Gabriel again that evening.

'Would you be able to look after Sophie again this evening, Mum?' Emma, her back to her mother, tried to sound as casual as she could as she popped the toast out of the toaster.

'Are you off out again then?'

'Uh huh.' Emma took a knife out of the drawer and plunged it deep into the butter.

'With Tara again?'

'Yep, we've missed each other.' Deception came easy these days. There had been too much of it lately. But she couldn't be bothered with all the questions. The questions about Gabriel and last night. The questions that tonight would bring. It wasn't that she thought her mother would object, although she might, perhaps, consider it her motherly duty to warn Emma about taking things steady and being careful. Indeed, she would probably be pleased that her daughter seemed happier than she had been in a long time. But she simply couldn't be bothered to head off an enthusiastic barrage of rapid-fire questioning about something that for the time being, felt like it should be private. So she decided that for now, at least, she would keep it to herself. Another small secret wouldn't make any difference.

'Yes, of course I don't mind. I was going to pop round to Sue's to have a glass of wine or two and watch that film that's just come out on Netflix. Oh, what's it called? You know, the one with Diane Keaton and Jane Fonda in it.'

'*Book Club*?'

'Yes, that's it. Well, anyway, Sue can come here. It won't make any difference.' She noticed Emma's brow had furrowed ever so slightly. 'And don't worry, I won't drink too much.' She chortled to herself.

Sue was their next-door neighbour, mother of three grown-up children, one of whom had married and moved away last year, another who had recently moved to London to start a new job, and the youngest who had left a few weeks ago to work on a cruise ship for a year. Having been used for years to a house filled with the noise and mess and work produced by her own children and numerous friends of theirs who would turn up at the door, Sue was finding it hard adjusting to her new-found state of inactivity and solitude – also, her husband was a fireman and worked unsociable hours – and she was not averse to drowning her sorrows now and again with Emma's mother, who was always ready with her own set of sorrows that needed drowning. The last time Sue had been round, following an evening of rowdy, cacophonous singing along, and even dancing, to an Abba album which had been turned up loud enough to wake the dead, and a previously sound-asleep Sophie, Emma had come down to the living room to find the two women slumped on the sofa, their arms round each other's shoulders, both sobbing inconsolably as if someone had just died, and Emma had been the one who had had to escort a teetering, tearful Sue back home.

There was no text from Tara that day despite her promise of the previous evening. Emma wasn't surprised. Tara was a law unto herself. She wondered how things had gone with Tim last night and whether Tara would be seeing him again that evening or whether she had already had her fill of him and was on to the next unsuspecting man now. After spending the day looking after and trying to entertain a particularly grouchy Sophie, who was finding the excessive heat hard to cope with and had finally succumbed to a late afternoon nap, Emma showered and got ready to go out, her stomach full of fluttering wings again. She worried that she and Gabriel might not find each other so attractive now that they were sober, or that she wouldn't know what to say to him, but when she tentatively rang the doorbell of Tim's house shortly after eight o'clock, her heart in her mouth, and Gabriel came to the door to open it, the instant surge of desire for him she felt all over again almost overwhelmed her. Catching a pleasant, faint whiff of aftershave as she stood there on the doorstep feasting her dazzled, hungry eyes on him as if for the first time, it seemed to her as if that moment had been frozen in time. As if in slow motion or as if she was underwater, she could hear the sound of voices talking and laughing with each other inside the house and the murmur of a radio or a television. She couldn't make out which.

'You look nice.' Gabriel ran a hand through his hair nervously.

'Oh, thanks.' Emma shrugged off the compliment.

'I thought we could go out somewhere rather than staying in with this noisy lot.' He motioned inside. 'If that's OK with you, of course.'

'Yeah, sounds good.'

'Um, I took the liberty of packing a little picnic. I thought maybe we could go and eat it somewhere quiet and private. It's not much, just a couple of things. That is, unless you'd rather go back to Venus again, of course. Or somewhere else.'

'A picnic sounds a lovely idea. I'd like that. Thank you.'

'Come inside a minute. I'll just go and grab everything.'

Emma stepped into the hallway and Gabriel disappeared into the kitchen. It felt a little cooler inside. On the floor near the doorway to the kitchen, where the old black and white tiles were the smoothest and most worn, a patch of pale, multicoloured light caught Emma's eye, where the rays of evening sunlight struck the ground after passing through the rectangle of coloured, patterned glass above the front door. The sound was a radio, she decided. It was coming from upstairs and so were the voices. She recognised Tim's. *And was that Laura's?* Her mind was distracted. She was finding it difficult to focus on one thought. There was the sound of water running. Someone having a shower perhaps. And the muffled noise of a hairdryer.

'Here we are.' Now the clink of bottles knocking together and the rustle of plastic as Gabriel reappeared carrying a couple of carrier bags and a picnic rug under one arm. 'Tim let me borrow it.'

'Here, let me take it.' He handed it over. She wasn't sure if it was their skin that touched as he gave her the rug or just the hairs on the back of their hands, but it felt as if a surge of electricity was zipping through her body. She recoiled, not from any disgust, but because the sensation overpowered her for a second. And yet she was already craving it again.

Gabriel pulled the door shut behind them and they set off towards the river, their hearts swelling with nervous anticipation and the sun pummelling their backs, casting tall, spindly shadows that stretched their silhouettes like chewing gum in front of them. Now the smell of a barbecue reached them as they strode purposefully past the rows of red brick houses, and then the sound of a telephone ringing, through an open window. It was a summery Saturday evening like any other for most people. They were doing normal summery Saturday evening things. No one who happened to glance in their direction as they passed them on the street would have imagined the sense of momentousness that was being felt at that moment by this boy and this girl, who looked like any other young couple enjoying that summer's evening.

As if each led by the same magnetic force, as if they both knew what was going to happen and were powerless to resist it, they headed away from the street, down the leafy narrow path that led to the ornate iron bridge where they lingered for a moment under the low-hanging, emerald branches to observe a couple of swans and their brood of grubby-looking cygnets glide silently away in single file up the river. Then they continued along the path, which soon turned to a dusty track that skirted fields of barley, the scalloped lines of the rooftops still visible in the distance along one edge. The sounds of civilisation, the voices, the traffic, had long since faded away, although the faraway wail of a siren cut through the stillness for a few moments, until it, too, finally faded away little by little to nothing. Here the noises of the town had given way to the chirruping of the skylarks, which swooped up and down, skimming the ears of barley, then rising high into the air. Now it was just them and the skylarks and the barley; immense olive-green fields of it, flecked crimson here and there with poppies like splashes of blood, stretching up, up, up to the horizon where they met a boundless, sparkling expanse of azure.

As she walked, Emma let her free hand brush over the ears of barley, the tender, pale-green husks gently caressing the lengths of her fingers as they flexed slightly before springing upright once again.

A flash of dazzling green as it rode the invisible waves, laughing impudently at the world with its strident call, a woodpecker soared over the barley towards the grove at the foot of the hill they were descending. At the bottom, they took the fork that led into the wood. Inside, it was dark and smelt of moss and the air was refreshingly cool. Shafts of sunlight pierced the canopy of branches above them, setting the humid ground ablaze with brightness here and there. Not far inside the wood was a small grassy glade where a cluster of foxgloves grew in the sunlight that had pooled there, splashing the ground lilac, and it was here they headed.

Emma unfolded the picnic rug and together, they spread it out on the grass, pulling at its corners and smoothing out the lumps. And they sat down facing each other in the dappled shade next to the towering foxgloves, with the buzzing of the fidgety bees on the flowers in their ears and the butterflies deep within their bellies as fluttery as the ones that flitted beside them, delicately probing the flowers with their long tongues as they sipped the sweet nectar.

Gabriel took from his bag some olives, some crisps and a bottle of white wine. He poured some out into two plastic cups, handing one to Emma. They knocked their cups together obediently, each taking a sip as they eyed the other diffidently, smiling uncertainly at each other before hurriedly looking away again. Gabriel held out the shining olives to Emma, and the bag of crisps, into which she reached. The crackle of the bag seemed intrusive in the stillness and the noise inside her head as she munched on the crisp deafening. They spoke little, about nothing in particular, the gaps in the conversation hanging conspicuously in the hush of the summer's evening, making them both feel an unnecessary pressure to fill them with things to say.

But, little by little, the wine that slipped down their throats worked its age-old magic, loosening their tongues and their inhibitions. It emboldened them so that they held each other's glances for longer, let a hand linger on an arm or a leg, edged a little closer together on the picnic rug without even realising they were doing so.

They both knew where it was going and how it would end. And they savoured each exquisite step of the journey, knowing that this exploration, this beautiful, shining, new experience could never be relived, that there would never be another here and now.

And before long he was leaning in towards her, his slightly-open mouth drawn towards hers as if they were two magnets. And there they kissed, in the clearing in the woods amongst the lichen and the foxgloves and the bees and the butterflies, but it could have been anywhere because they were no longer aware of their surroundings. It was just them. That was all that mattered. Their hands began an exploration of each other's bodies, first feeling outlines through clothes and then fumbling to get underneath them. Emma drew a sharp intake of breath as she felt his fingers touch the bare skin of her breasts for the first time and then descend to creep underneath her skirt. And later she felt the tickle of his warm breath and of the light covering of stubble on his upper lip as his tongue followed where his fingers had gone before.

There was a desperation, a hunger in their need for each other, driving them forward irresistibly, but not hastily. For both of them, the journey to the end was as important as the end itself. And when he at last took her, there in the clearing of the woods amongst the lichen and the foxgloves and the bees and the butterflies, with his faded jeans and grubby trainers discarded carelessly in an untidy heap beside the picnic rug, he didn't do so recklessly. He was devoted and unselfish. And as Emma lay half-on and half-off the picnic rug with her hair strewn out about her head on the grass, she noticed the tiny beads of perspiration on his forehead as he kissed her and the smell of him and the smell of the mossy ground filled her nostrils as they lost themselves in each other. And it felt for both of them as if there was nothing else in the world except this.

It was unlike the handful of sordid encounters that Emma had experienced before. This was meaningful. It was sublime. It was perfect. And for those few fleeting moments of blissful happiness, there was nothing but the present. Her past had been temporarily separated from her present and so no longer defined who she was. Her present, her happiness was for once untainted by her past.

Afterwards, Gabriel rolled over onto his back and Emma turned towards him, wrapping her arm over his waist. He slid his arm beneath her head and she nestled into him, resting her head on his chest as he stroked her hair gently.

'You're beautiful, you know.' His voice broke the stillness of the glade.

'No, *you* are.'

'And what we just did was beautiful too, wasn't it? It was special. I've never felt like that before.'

'Really? I find that hard to believe. A good-looking guy like you, you must have had your fair share of girlfriends, surely.' She rolled onto her front and propped herself up on her elbows, cupping her face in her hands, looking at him questioningly.

'Well, I guess there were a few at university, but no one very serious. Anyway, you can talk. I bet you've never been short of admirers.'

'Well, there were a couple of boys at school, but no one I ever cared about. And I doubt they cared about me either. That's the trouble when you hang out with Tara. It's like you're invisible. No one really notices you.'

'Well, *I* noticed you.'

'Only because I caused a scene. I think just about everyone in the bar noticed me last night! For once.'

'But I noticed you before that.'

She laughed dismissively. 'You're just saying that.'

'No, seriously, I noticed you as soon as you walked through the door into the bar. Even though the room was full of people, it was you I noticed. So, you see, you're not invisible. It was like you walked through that door for a reason.'

'Well, it was lucky I gave you an excuse to come and talk to me then.'

'I didn't need an excuse. I would have come and found you anyway.' He leaned towards her to plant a kiss on her lips.

'Oh, you *are* a romantic, aren't you?' She smiled.

'I don't see you complaining.' And he kissed her again, more urgently this time, pulling her on top of him, their bodies finding each other again. And like two pieces of a jigsaw that slotted together perfectly, they made love again, there in the clearing of the woods among the lichen and the foxgloves and the bees and the butterflies, in the clearing which was now suffused with a warm pink-orange glow as a fiery, fuchsia orb sank slowly beneath the top of the hill until it was just a gleaming slither peeping over the horizon for a moment before at last disappearing from view to shine on other lands far away, leaving behind a swash of pink and ruby clouds spilling across the sky.

In the rosy dusk, they gathered up their things and sauntered hand in hand back out of the wood and up the hill, following the track that led them back into town again. Here, it was still alive with traffic and the comings and goings of people happy to be outside in the refreshing night air.

'So what now? Where do you want to go?' Gabriel gently tucked a roguish curl of Emma's hair behind her ear.

Emma looked at her watch. Quarter to ten. Her mother wouldn't expect her back for a while yet.

She shrugged. 'There's always Venus I suppose.'

'But it's so noisy in there. You can't have a proper conversation without shouting.' Gabriel raised his eyes for a moment, as if in thought. 'It would be the same whichever bar or club we went to. Maybe we could pop in, though, and try and find Tim and the others. I'm sure he said they were going there. I could get his key and we could go back to his. I'm sure he wouldn't mind.'

'Yeah, OK, that sounds good.'

'Then we'll be able to have some peace and quiet.' He leant towards her and brushed his lips against hers.

As they approached the bar, they could see through the huge expanse of glass window that it was heaving with youngsters, as it always was on any Friday or Saturday evening. Inside, they wove their way through the bar, in and out of the usual groups of people chatting and flirting. Emma felt a bit out of place carrying the picnic rug under her arm and normally, something like that would have bothered her, but not tonight. Tonight, her heart swelled with happiness as she followed Gabriel across the crowded room.

Tim and his friends were sitting at a table tucked away in a corner at the far end of the bar. Emma noticed Tara straightaway, whose pretty blonde head was flung back in laughter which rippled unmistakably over the music and the voices like the babble of a brook, and who was draped round Tim's neck like a scarf. Tim was laughing too, his eyes turned covetously towards her. A look Emma had seen men give Tara a thousand times before.

The laughter subsided as Emma and Gabriel approached the group, all eyes fixed on them with interest.

'Hi guys. You remember Emma from last night, don't you?' Gabriel gestured towards her.

'Hi everyone.' Emma suddenly felt shy, as the object of everyone's scrutiny.

Tara waved to her. Her eyes were looking a little glazed and Emma could tell by her gestures and her movements that she had had too much to drink. 'Hi darling. Are you going to join us?' She was looking at Emma with her beautiful glazed eyes. Emma didn't know why, but she suddenly felt sorry for her.

Hurriedly, guiltily almost, she brushed the unfamiliar thought away. 'Well, no, we weren't planning to actually.'

'Can we borrow your key, Tim?' Gabriel cut in.

'Yeah, course. No problem, mate.' Tim fumbled in his trouser pocket. Tara was still draped around him, making it difficult for him to sit up straight to reach further into his pocket and he shrugged her aside slightly, forcing her too to sit up straight again reluctantly as he struggled to find the key. He found it finally and held it out to Gabriel.

'Thanks Tim.'

'No worries. What's the matter? Are we not good enough for you now?' Tim was smirking.

'No, course not. We just want a bit of time alone, that's all.'

Tim winked back at Gabriel. 'Ah right, I see. Well, have fun both of you, won't you? Don't do anything we wouldn't.' He nudged Tara, who smiled lazily at them. 'Tara and I might be turning in ourselves soon. Won't we, babe?' He turned to Tara questioningly whose response was to lunge at him, kissing him lengthily and unashamedly. There were raised eyebrows and sniggers from the rest of the group. Emma and Gabriel waited awkwardly, unsure whether the conversation was finished and whether to leave the bar now, which, looking back on what happened next, Emma wished they had done. Having finally extricated himself and looking pleased with himself, Tim winked again at them both. 'Just thought I'd warn you. I wouldn't want to walk in on a couple of naked bodies in my living room. Well, I guess it would depend whose they were.' He laughed.

'Anyway, you'll probably be gone by the time we get there, Cinderella.' Tara's voice cut through Tim's laughter like a knife.

'Well, I don't know about that. I don't know how much longer I can wait after you've just kissed me like that.' Tim was still laughing as he turned to Tara again.

But Tara was looking at Emma with those beautiful, glazed eyes again. Those beautiful, cold eyes. Emma suddenly knew what was coming and was powerless to do anything about it. 'But won't you need to get back to Sophie soon, Emma?' She smiled at Emma as she said it.

'Sophie? Who's Sophie?' Gabriel turned to look at Emma.

But before she could think of anything to say to ward her off, Tara was answering, her voice drooling and silvery so that Emma wasn't sure whether the pain that she was about to inflict by what she was announcing to the group was unintentional and the result of being drunk, or a spiteful, calculated insult because she was jealous of Emma's good fortune. 'Sophie is her baby. I thought she would have told you about her. I'm dying to meet her. I bet she's just as cute as her mum. What d'ya reckon, Gabes?'

It felt as if the blood had suddenly drained all at once out of Emma's head and was being pumped at a nauseating speed round the rest of her body by her heart, which had started to pound so forcefully that each quickening beat seemed to reverberate through the whole of her torso. She felt as if a dozen pairs of eyes were boring into her again as a stunned hush descended on the group, broken only by Tara, who exclaimed in mock consternation, 'Oops, have I just said something I shouldn't have? Silly me,' smirking inanely all the while.

'Come on, Emma, let's go.' Gabriel tugged at Emma's arm and led her away from the table. His countenance was crestfallen and embarrassed, but something in the gentleness with which he pulled her away and the fact that he was doing so at all, left Emma with a modicum of hope, despite the fact that her heart was still hammering against her chest as if it was desperate to get out and all the happiness that had only seconds ago been spilling out of it had now gone.

Neither of them spoke as they wove their way back out of the bar. Emma felt as if she was suffocating in there, as she squeezed between people who were smiling, laughing, seemingly carefree, and who were oblivious to the turmoil inside her. They at last reached the doors, which belched them out indifferently, stunned and reeling, into the warm, quiet night. The night felt like a buffer, as if it might be capable of absorbing all her shock and anxiety. As she happened to glance up, she noticed that a handful of tiny stars had come out, pinpricks of light barely noticeable through the glare of the street lamps.

They walked a couple of hundred metres down the street before Emma blurted out, 'I'm so sorry. I should have told you. I was going to tell you. I was just waiting for the right moment. And that certainly wasn't it.' She smiled at him weakly.

'I know, it's OK. I'm just a bit surprised, that's all. I would never have guessed. How old is she? Sophie.'

'Three months.' Emma stated it like it was a question, her intonation rising slightly at the end, waiting for Gabriel's reaction.

Emma heard him swallow. 'Is that all?' She felt grateful to him for taking all this so calmly, for not raising his voice, for not making this harder for her than it already was. For keeping his pain to himself. 'And the father?' Nonetheless, it seemed to her as if his voice quivered slightly as the question hung, suspended, in the darkness. A question that needed asking, although its answer was dreaded.

Emma took a big breath. Gabriel deserved the truth, even though it would hurt them both if she told it. 'Well, I don't really know… I mean, I do know, but I can't remember his name. It was just once, at a party. I was drunk.'

'Oh I see.' He was looking at the ground, scraping a metal ring pull from a can of drink that had been discarded against the ground with the tip of his trainer, letting what she had just said sink in. The noise was setting her teeth on edge. She felt the urge to fling her arms round his neck to try and get some of the pain that she was inflicting to permeate her. And to make him stop that noise.

'So does he know?'

'No. I've never had anything to do with him since that night. I can't even remember what he looks like.' She looked down at the ground. He was still dragging the ring pull along the pavement. *For God's sake, please stop doing that.* She swallowed, trying to force some saliva into her throat and her mouth. They were so dry. God, she could murder a drink of water.

'Don't you think he'd want to know?'

'I don't know. Doubt it. But how would I tell him anyway? Even if I wanted to? I wouldn't know how to find him.'

'But surely someone at the party would remember who you were with that night even if you don't. There must be some way to track him down.'

'Oh I dunno. I'd rather forget all about that night.' Her voice tailed off into the night. 'Anyway, I guess that's put you right off now.'

'Well, to be honest, it might have put me off if I'd known before last night, but now I've got to know you a bit and after the evening we've just spent together, it has just left me wanting more.' He kissed her gently before continuing. 'Yes, it's not the best news I've had all night, but it could be worse. I mean, it's not like you've killed anybody or anything, is it?' Something was squeezing her heart. So tightly that she couldn't breathe. She was choking, suffocating in the breezeless night. Like a fish out of water, desperately, uselessly gulping in air. Her heart was racing. Her palms were clammy. But she had to keep calm, keep calm. *Don't let him see.*

He was still talking, but she didn't know what he was saying. She could hear his voice, but it sounded so far away. It sounded muffled, as if she had her head under a pillow. She needed to get a grip. 'It doesn't really change anything as far as I'm concerned, as far as we're concerned…' she could hear him saying. Then, 'Are you all right? You look really pale. Do you want to sit down?'

He led her to a nearby bench. He tucked the same capricious curl behind her ear again. 'Are you OK?' The concern in his voice grated in her ears

Emma made a last, supreme effort to compose herself and took a deep breath. 'Yes, yes, I'm fine. It must just be the shock of what's just happened. I didn't intend for you to find out like that. I can't believe Tara just came out with that in front of everyone.'

'I think she was pretty wasted, wasn't she?'

'Yes, but even so…'

'Oh well, she's saved you the job of telling me. At least everything's out in the open now.' He stroked her hair again.

'And you're still here. I thought you wouldn't want anything more to do with me.' Her voice was breaking a little. From the shock. With relief.

'I'm still here. And I'm not going anywhere.' He kissed her. A couple of teenagers glanced at them as they sauntered by.

'Come on. Let's go back to Tim's, shall we?' He took her hand and they started to walk down the street, the booming beat of the music in the bar becoming fainter and fainter behind them.

CHAPTER 5

Gabriel came to stay at Tim's again the next weekend. And the following few weekends. He took Emma out to dinner a handful of times and they would sit at a table overlooking the river where they would watch the late summer sun set on another glorious, golden day, gradually turning the water from pink and orange to a shimmering inky blue flecked here and there with twinkling smudges of light and a quivering, misty slither of a moon. He would caress her hand affectionately across the table as they gazed at each other, starry-eyed, heedless of the waiters who bustled frantically to and fro with their heavy, precariously-arranged trays, the patches of sweat on their shirt backs growing gradually larger, hair plastered to their foreheads.

They would go to the pub or go shopping together or to the cinema. And for more picnics. They even drove to the coast one Saturday, Sophie bundled into the back seat of Gabriel's car, where they ate fish and chips sitting in the grassy sand dunes, squinting towards the snowy crests which bobbed up and down like fairground horses prancing to the music of the waves as they smashed onto the fine shingle, while the wind blew the thistledown clouds across the sky and the sun made everything sparkle.

These first weekends together were the happiest Emma had ever known. Years later, she would look back on them, in her album of images, those old, familiar, well-thumbed postcards inside her head that she would flick through with a pang of nostalgia in her heart, and all those dusty memories would have the backdrop of the summer. The endless blue and yellow days, the dusky, damask evenings that still throbbed with the heat of the day, the smell of barbecues and of skin that hasn't stopped tingling from the caress of the sun. The lazy drone of insects. Long, beautiful halcyon days. Near-perfect days. The heady excitement of getting to know each other, the tingling anticipation of seeing each other. She longed for Friday to arrive again as soon as she had said goodbye to Gabriel each Sunday evening. And the weekdays seemed to last forever. She would ache for him all over. To see him, smell him, feel him again.

And the nightmares were becoming less frequent and slightly less terrifying.

Emma had felt a little nervous about Gabriel's reaction the first time she had wheeled Sophie up to the front door of Tim's house, but she needn't have worried. Far from showing any signs of awkwardness with her, he tickled her under the chin and had her chuckling right down to her little round belly within seconds of meeting. He was a natural. And Sophie loved him and would beam at him and reach out for him to hold her.

'Come and stay with me for a weekend in York. I'm fed up with saying goodbye every Friday and Saturday night. And besides, I bet Tim would be glad to have the house to himself for the weekend for a change. Otherwise I'll have to start paying him rent soon. It would be wonderful to sleep next to you and wake up next to you. Please say you'll come. I'll bring you breakfast in bed.' His tone was pleading and so were his melted-chocolate eyes.

Emma laughed. 'Is that a promise? Anyway, what about Sophie?'

'She can come too, of course.'

It was another boiling hot Sunday afternoon. They had stopped for an ice cream and were sitting on a bench in a park near Tim's house. Filling their ears were the playful shrieks of carefree children on holiday, for whom back-to-school Mondays were still just a speck on a distant horizon. For Gabriel and Emma, though, the by now familiar Sunday afternoon dread of their forthcoming separation was overshadowing their last few hours together, making them feel so melancholic that it was difficult for them to make the most of this precious time together. The prospect of saying goodbye to each other had become just as painful for them as the act itself, throwing all the time leading up to it into the deepest gloom.

'But where would she sleep?'

'Haven't you got a travel cot or something?' Emma shook her head. 'Well, order one and get it delivered to my address. I'll pay for it. Choose whichever one you like.'

'But you can't do that.'

'Of course I can. It's fine. If it means I get to sleep two whole nights with you.' He leaned forward to kiss her mouth softly.

'Well, I can't guarantee you'll get a whole night's sleep with this little monkey around.' She smiled down between them at Sophie in her pushchair who was reaching with her clammy little palms towards their dripping cones.

Later that evening Emma and her mother were sitting in the living room. Emma was curled up in the armchair with a magazine and her mother was stretched out on the sofa, laughing at the television, her head resting on a cushion. The reflection of the flickering colours on the screen danced in her mother's eyes and on her face. When the adverts came on, Emma looked up from her magazine.

'Mum.'

Her mother was grimacing at the television. 'God, that advert's so annoying, isn't it?' That was what she said every time she watched it. 'Hmm? Sorry, what were you saying, darling?' She turned to face Emma.

'I've got a boyfriend.' It felt odd saying it. Like she was talking about someone else.

'Well, that would explain why you've been out so much lately then.' She said it without any emphasis anywhere so that Emma wasn't sure whether she intended it as a criticism or not. They were both silent as the next advert came on. 'So? Aren't you going to tell me who he is then?' Her mother smiled encouragingly.

'I met him that first weekend I went out with Tara, remember? He was in the bar we were in. Actually, he kind of came to my rescue. You see, I knocked into this drunken idiot and made him spill his beer all over himself and he had a go at me. Gabes, Gabriel, stood up for me and the drunken idiot ended up punching Gabriel in the nose.'

'Goodness! Poor boy. Was he OK?' Sounding only mildly concerned, her mother glanced at the television as the programme she had been watching came back on.

'Yeah, he was all right. Had a bleeding nose for a while though.'

'And all because he was trying to help you. Sure you're not just going out with him because you feel bad about what happened?'

'No, course not, Mum. I really like him. I've never felt like this about anyone before.' Emma ran her nail back and forth over the raised pattern on the arm of the chair.

'So where's he live? Round here somewhere?'

'No, he lives in York, Mum. He went to university there and now he's working there.'

'York? That's a bit of a way, isn't it?'

'Yeah, I know. He's been staying at a friend's in town at the weekends so we can see each other.'

'Oh I see.' Her mother shot another glance at the television and chuckled obligingly as canned laughter rippled out of the speakers.

Emma was still rubbing the lines on the armchair up and down with her nail. 'But he can't keep doing that. His friend's probably getting a bit fed up with him being there every weekend.' Emma wasn't sure whether her mother was listening to her or to the television.

'So I suppose the next thing you're going to tell me is that you're going to stay at his at the weekend?' Her mother swung round to look at her. So she *had* been listening to what Emma had been saying.

Emma swallowed. 'Um, yes, you're right. That *was* what I was about to tell you actually.' She stopped scraping the lines on the armchair, inadvertently switching to running the fleshy part of her forefinger along the beaded edge of the cushion next to her bare feet. 'Is that OK?' She watched her finger move along the cushion edge without looking up to meet her mother's gaze.

'Well, it will have to be, won't it? I can hardly stop you going, can I? You're nineteen, after all. So what's going to happen to Sophie? You know I can't have her. I'll be at work most of Saturday. And for heaven's sake, I hope you weren't thinking of asking your dad to have her. He wouldn't have a clue. And besides, I expect he'll be far too busy with his bit of skirt.' She raised her eyes and shook her head dismissively.

'Her name's Camilla, Mum.'

'Yes, I know. Camilla. Hmph. What a name. Who does she think she is? Bloody royalty?'

'She didn't choose it. Anyway, I think it's a nice name.'

'You would.'

'She's perfectly nice. I met her a couple of months ago when I went over to see Dad. She's not posh at all.'

'Well, no, I don't suppose she can be if she's shacked up with the likes of your dad. God knows what she sees in him. How on earth did they meet?'

'She works at the estate agent's that Dad found his flat through. Anyway, I wasn't planning to ask Dad to look after Sophie. She's coming with me.' Emma picked up the cushion she had been playing with and wrapped her arms around it.

'Oh, so Gabriel knows about her then?'

'Course he does. They've met plenty of times. He's great with her.'

'So Sophie's met him several times. Why have you kept him a secret from me then?' Her mother sounded offended and Emma suddenly felt slightly guilty.

'Oh I dunno.' Emma shrugged. 'Just been waiting for the right moment, that's all.'

'Did you think I wouldn't approve?'

'No, it wasn't that. I guess I was waiting in case nothing came of it.'

'Well, I hope you're being careful, Emma.' Her mother's tone was far too patronising.

Emma raised her eyebrows, groaning. 'Mum…'

'Mistakes can easily happen, as you well know.'

'Yes, we're being careful. I'm not stupid, Mum.'

'Well, you obviously weren't very sensible the last time. So what does he do anyway, this new fellow of yours?'

'He's in IT. Works for Microsoft.'

'How old is he?'

'Twenty-four.'

'And is he good-looking?' Her mother smiled expectantly.

'Well, obviously *I* think so.' Emma smiled back coyly.

'So how will you get to York? On the train?'

'God, Mum. What is this? Twenty questions? Yes, on the train.' Emma sighed loudly.

'Will you be able to manage Sophie as well? And all her stuff?'

'Yes, it will be fine. Gabriel will meet us off the train.'

'It's fair enough that I want to know where you're going and who you're staying with. I *am* your mother. You'll feel the same about Sophie one day when she gets all independent. I just don't want you to come to any harm. Anyway, darling, don't get me wrong. I'm really pleased for you. You should have told me about him sooner. You'll have to bring him here one of these days so

I can meet him.' She smiled again at Emma. A warm, heartfelt smile that made little curved creases appear at the edges of her mouth. They were always there when she smiled properly. That was how you knew if she was really smiling or just pretending.

'Yes, I will. Thanks Mum.'

Emma's mother finally turned back round to watch the television again. The programme she had been watching had finished now, but a new one had started and it was one of her favourites. The colours flickered in her eyes again, a miniature television programme playing in each eye. Emma nestled deeper into the armchair and turned over the page of her magazine.

CHAPTER 6

She could see him sitting on a metal bench on the platform as the train slowly clank-clunked into the station. He was wearing his jeans and his battered trainers again. He was screwing up his eyes, shading them with his hand, trying to block out the evening sun which was low in the rosy sky and glinting off every shiny surface, trying to spot her through a smeary window of the train. There, right there. A moment. Another vignette to store away in her head. Click. A precious snapshot taken unwittingly by her brain to be pored over wistfully another day, the details of which would gradually elude her memory more and more over time no matter how hard she would try desperately to recall them. Her heart skipped a beat at the sight of him. It was as if she had forgotten over the last few days they had spent apart how attractive she found him. Even though she had thought about him, imagined him, almost constantly, it was as if seeing him right there in front of her on the platform suddenly made him seem more tangible, more credible. He was there; he was no longer in her head. He was real, he was beautiful, and he was hers.

She stood up, gathering all her belongings and fastening Sophie into her pushchair, which she had left at the far end of the carriage by the doors. She struggled off the train, heading towards Gabriel. But he had already spotted them and was striding towards them, eyes shining, cheeks a little flushed. Click.

Click. More upside-down snapshots on her retina that her brain would lovingly invert and imprint in her memory. She caught only intermittent glimpses of him, between the bobbing heads of the commuters who filed purposefully in a great herd towards the exit with their drab suits and their laptops.

And then there he was, right before her, sweeping her into his arms. She nestled into him and everything fell back into place. What she had been at pains to evoke in her head when they were apart, as if they were the most important things in the world, all the little things that made him special, the scent of his aftershave, the breadth of his chest, the contours of his face beneath her hand, were suddenly and reassuringly familiar again.

They drove back to his house, the latent desire burning up inside them as, side by side, one of them would place a hand on the other's thigh, or gently caress the other's cheek, each fizzing inside like fireworks about to explode. Sophie fell asleep in the car and remained asleep on arrival at Gabriel's house so they gently carried her inside before Gabriel seized Emma's hand and led her up the steep wooden staircase to his bedroom where they at last crumpled with relief onto his bed.

They spent another blissful weekend together and found it wonderful both to fall asleep at night and wake up in the morning beside each other. Gabriel was as good as his word and brought Emma breakfast in bed both mornings. He showed her the city – the Shambles, where they jostled with olive-skinned tourists who babbled away to each other in words Emma and Gabriel didn't understand as they traipsed in and out of the gift shops that lined the narrow, cobbled street with its beamed, overhanging houses, and the imposing minster with its numerous Gothic spires jabbing at a gleaming blue and white sky. They did all the usual things tourists do. They took an open-top bus tour and a boat trip along the river where the water and the sunshine made everything shimmer and sparkle; they had tea and cake at Betty's and climbed to the top of Clifford's Tower from where they could see the sharp red and grey edges of the city's rooftops give way to the rolling green moors far away in the distance.

And then of course after that, after their first sweet taste of privacy and of being accountable to nobody else but each other, it was only natural that Emma and Gabriel wanted more, and so Emma finished up visiting Gabriel most weekends. Then, one Sunday morning, having just woken up, as they lay in bed listening to the muffled sounds of the city slowly rousing itself outside the window, the gentle hum of cars and the ripple of voices, Gabriel stretched his arm round Emma.

'Sunday already.' He sighed.

'Yeah, I know. The weekends always go so quickly. And then the weeks seem to last forever.'

'Well, it doesn't have to be that way, does it?'

'What do you mean?'

'Well, you could always stay here, you know. Move in with me, Ems. You've got nothing really to get back for, have you?'

'My mum.' Emma sounded indignant.

'Oh, come on, Ems, you're a big girl now.' He was stroking her hair. God, she loved it when he did that. 'You can't stay at home forever. Wouldn't you like it if we were together all the time? No more goodbyes?'

'Well, yes, of course I would. You know I would. It's just that I'd be a bit worried about telling my mum, that's all. You know, after everything that's happened.' The duvet had slipped off her legs and Emma reached down to pull it back over them. 'With my dad leaving and everything. And she'd miss Sophie like mad.'

'I know, darling. I know you'd feel bad, but you can't live your life for *her*. It's *your* life. And she knows that too. Surely she'd understand. And of course you'd still visit her.'

'Well yes, I suppose so, I suppose you're right. I guess it would be nice; I mean it would be wonderful. But it would be a bit lonely when you're at work.' Emma smiled as she ruffled Gabriel's hair.

'No lonelier than when you're at home and your mum's at work. And anyway, you've got Sophie. You could come and meet me at lunchtimes. And there's loads of stuff to do in York. You wouldn't get bored.'

'But I don't know anyone apart from you. What about my friends?'

'Pffff. If you mean Tara, she's not worth worrying about. She's a rubbish friend. You've said so yourself.'

'Yeah, I know. You're right. She is.' Emma grimaced.

'And anyway, she can come and visit, or you can go back to your mum's to see her. If you're that desperate to see her. It's not a million miles away, is it?'

'No, you're right. It's only a two-hour train journey away.' Emma leant towards him and kissed him. She grinned. 'OK, let's give it a go. I'll break it to my mum and get all my things packed. How about I move in next weekend then?'

Gabriel hugged her. 'How exciting! Ems, I know we're going to be so happy! I'll drive down on Saturday and pick you both up.'

And so it was all decided. Emma broke the news to her mother that evening when she got back. Her reaction was as Emma had expected. Tears of frustration and self-pity, and disguising the fact that *she* didn't want Emma and Sophie to go for selfish reasons by telling her that it was too soon to move in with Gabriel.

'It will save us a fortune in train fares. It makes sense, Mum. Anyway, you were *married* at my age, remember?'

Her mother stifled a sob. 'Yes, but I'd known your father for two years before we got married. And besides, look how *we've* ended up.' Emma sighed to herself. Oh God, why had she brought that up? The final straw. The thought of her husband scarpering and shacking up with another woman. That wound was still very raw and Emma watched, almost fascinated, as her mother's lips crumpled and the tears started welling up again in the corners of her streaky eyes before cascading one by one, along with most of her mascara, down her mother's blotchy cheeks.

'Look, just do it then. Move in with him. You have to make your own mistakes, Emma. But don't say I didn't warn you when it all goes pear-shaped. It's a lot for him to take on, you know, a child that isn't his. He might not always feel the same as he does now about things.'

'Mum, this decision isn't irreversible, you know. I can soon move back here again if things don't work out.'

'Yes, you can, but not before you've had your heart broken.'

'Oh Mum, don't be so melodramatic. You have to take chances in life, you have to make decisions. Sometimes they might be the right decisions, sometimes they might be the wrong ones, but you just have to go with what feels right at the time. And this does feel right, Mum. I've never felt like this before.'

'Exactly, you've never felt like this before. You've never been in love before. You're young and inexperienced and naive. But let me tell you, it won't always feel like this, you know. Things change. Circumstances change; people change.'

'Well, thanks a lot, Mum. You certainly know how to put a dampener on things.'

'I just don't want you to turn round and say to me one day that I didn't warn you, that's all. Anyway, you go and live your own life. You go and have fun and don't you worry about me here all by myself missing my only granddaughter growing up.' She let out a hiccupy sob before continuing. 'Her first words, her first steps. Don't you worry, I'll be all right.' She wiped under her eyes gently with the edge of a wet forefinger.

Emma threw her arms round her mother. 'Mum, don't be like that. We'll come and visit you, I promise. And you can come and visit us whenever you like. You make it sound like we're going to Australia.'

'You'd *better* come back and visit, darling. Oh, I'm going to miss you both.' Emma could feel her mother's chest shudder with silent sobs as she hugged her. 'You'd better tell your dad that you're going, I suppose.'

The next day, after her mother had left for the hairdresser's, Emma took the bus into town and walked the rest of the way to her dad's flat. She didn't think he'd be that bothered about her moving in with Gabriel. It wouldn't make much difference to him, after all. They hardly saw each other these days.

His van was parked outside. Her father opened the door of the flat.

'Hullo love. Come in, come in. And you've brought my gorgeous little Sophie to see me.' He tickled her under the chin again with his rough, hairy finger. There was grime behind his nails. There always was. Oil and grease and gunk from pipes and filters. He repaired broken appliances like washing machines and hoovers and dishwashers. Relied on other people's misfortunes to make his living.

Emma followed her dad into the small lounge and sat on the sofa. She put Sophie down on the floor, casting a surreptitious glance at the carpet either side of her. But it looked as if it had been hoovered recently. Probably Camilla.

'Cup of tea, love?'

'Yes please, that would be nice.'

Her father disappeared into the kitchen. She heard the click of the switch on the kettle and the clink of mugs and the opening and shutting of the cupboard door.

Emma looked around the lounge and noticed that there were new curtains at the window. Expensive-looking ones. *Were they silk?* Sophie had rolled over to the coffee table and was summoning up all her concentration to pull at the overhanging page of a newspaper that lay open on the low table. With a final tug, the newspaper slid on top of her, plunging her into sudden stale-smelling semi-darkness and, too surprised to cry, she flailed her legs and arms uselessly beneath the grubby pages like a beetle that had fallen onto its back. Smiling, Emma lifted the paper off her, patting the pages back neatly together inside the cover and replacing it on the table. She picked Sophie up and propped her up in the corner of the sofa next to her, where she proceeded to claw at the tassels of one of the cushions.

'So, how are things with you, love?' Her father set a too-full mug of tea down on the coffee table in front of Emma, slopping some of it over the top and onto the coaster. 'Never mind, only a teeny bit. Better not tell Camilla.' He smirked and winked conspiratorially at his daughter.

'Oh, fine. Sophie's into everything. Rolling everywhere now. Can't take my eyes off her for a second. We've had to get a stair gate to go at the top of the stairs.'

Her father nodded. 'Oh, right.' He took a noisy slurp of his tea and emptied his mouth again with an audible gulp.

'Just to be on the safe side. You know.' Emma pulled the cushion away from Sophie, who was yanking at its tassels violently now. 'See what I mean?' She rummaged in her bag and presented Sophie with a couple of her toys.

'But you wouldn't be without her now, though, would you?' Her father leaned across from the armchair to stroke Sophie's head and Emma thought to herself how it was less than a year ago that his world had come crashing down when she had told her parents that she was pregnant. Babies have a habit of doing that once they've come out, of making everything all right, of smoothing things over, Emma thought. Without even having to do anything. She was pleased, anyway, that her father seemed a lot more cheerful these days, even if it was at the expense of her mother's happiness. Camilla seemed to be having a good effect on him whatever her mother thought of her.

'I've got some news, Dad.'

'Well, that's funny. So have I.' Her dad took another sip of his tea, sucking in more air as he did so.

'Oh. Fancy that.' Emma's mind had already started to whirr. *New job? New house? Were he and Camilla going on holiday?*

'You first, love.'

‘Oh, OK then.’ Emma inadvertently picked off a bit of fluff from the sofa, brushing it away with her hand. ‘Um, well, I’ve met someone.’

‘Good for you, love. So long as he’s good enough for my daughter.’ Her father smiled proudly.

‘He’s wonderful, Dad. At least I think he is and so does Sophie.’

‘What’s he do then?’ Her father looked at her through a wispy veil of steam over the top of his mug and stopped blowing at his tea for a second. The answer to this question meant a lot to him. Emma knew that it would be as important to him as the answer to whether he was a decent bloke or not or whether he was already married.

‘He’s in IT, Dad. Works for Microsoft.’

Through the steam, her father’s face creased into a wide grin. ‘Well, well. Does he now?’

He chuckled. ‘Maybe he can fix my computer for me then.’ Her father nodded at the laptop sitting on the table in the corner of the room. ‘Got some stupid bug. Right pain in the arse. Can’t do my bills properly. Got to handwrite them at the moment. Bloody nuisance. Give me a washing machine to fix and I’ll get that up and running in no time, but haven’t got the foggiest about computers.’ He scratched his head and tutted. ‘Bloody nuisance.’

‘Thing is, he lives in York, Dad.’

‘Got his own house there, has he?’

‘Yes, he has, Dad.’

‘How many bedrooms?’

‘Two.’

‘Renting or his own?’

‘It’s his own, Dad, but…’

Her father butted in again. ‘Ah, that’s good then. Got his foot on the ladder already. Sensible lad.’ And then, as an afterthought, ‘What d’you say his name is, love?’

‘Gabriel.’ Just saying his name made her heart flutter.

'Gabriel? Thought that was a girl's name.'

'No, that's Gabrielle, Dad.' She enunciated the last part of the word.

'Are you sure? What about the angel Gabriel then?'

'He was male, Dad.'

'Oh well, if you say so.' Her dad scratched his head again, his forehead furrowed. 'Could have sworn angels were female.'

'Well, *my* Gabriel's definitely a man, Dad.'

'Oh, is he now?' Her father gave a raucous, filthy chortle that started him off on one of his coughing episodes. He looked across at Emma, who was managing a half-hearted smile. 'Sorry, love. What am I like, hey?' He did a final splutter, patting his chest vigorously.

'That's the trouble. Anytime I want to have a laugh, sets me off on a blinkin' coughing fit. Must have another go with my Nicorette patches. Camilla keeps having a go at me about it. Especially now with…' His voice tailed off suddenly.

Emma felt like she had been punched in the stomach. 'Especially now with what?' It came out as barely more than a whisper.

Her father cleared his throat again, for once looking bashful. 'Well, that's what I was going to tell you, love. Camilla's pregnant.'

Almost a year ago, she had dropped a bombshell by announcing to her father the very same thing and now he was announcing it to her. Now she was on the receiving end. Her father was maniacally digging at the grime under his fingernails. That's how you could tell he was feeling anxious or uneasy.

He looked up at her, but his fingers were still going nineteen to the dozen. He wasn't even excavating now, only going through the motions. 'Well, aren't you going to congratulate your old man then?' He attempted a smile.

Emma swallowed. She suddenly felt overwhelmingly hot although all the windows were open. *This is what one of Mum's hot flushes must feel like*, she thought. Minute beads of perspiration were gathering in between the tiny hairs on her upper lip. She felt slightly nauseous. Sophie was whining and trying to reach over the arm of the sofa to retrieve one of the finger puppets that had fallen out of her fabric book. Robot-like, Emma stood up and walked round to pick it up and gave it back to her. Sophie immediately threw it over the arm of the sofa again. Emma picked it up again and gave it back to Sophie, who let go of it again. She sat back down and Sophie whined louder, rubbing her eyes. Distracted, Emma picked her up and jogged her up and down on her knee, Sophie still reaching across towards the arm of the sofa.

'Well, yes, yes, of course. Congratulations, Dad. Sorry, it's just a bit of a shock. You know.'

'Well, of course. It would be. I can appreciate that, love. I expect you thought your old man was getting too old for all that sort of thing, didn't you? But Camilla's young, you know. She's only twenty-nine. She wants a family and I didn't want to let her down. She might've gone looking elsewhere if I couldn't give her what she wanted. She means the world to me. She's much too good for me, you know. Don't know what she's doing with me, to be honest, when she could have a younger model. And one with far more money too. And I don't want to leave it too late, love. I want to be able to do stuff with the baby. Before I'm lumbered with a Zimmer frame and can't chase it round the park any more.' He forced a laugh. 'I know it must be a shock for you finding out you're going to have a brother or sister now, when you're already an adult yourself.'

Brother or sister. It was like a slap in the face. For some reason she hadn't thought of it like that yet. Even though the fact was staring her right between the eyes, it hadn't yet crossed her mind that she was going to become a big sister at the age of twenty. God, she was stupid. *It* was stupid. *Camilla wants a family? So, what, there might be more? God. And what about Mum? How on earth would she react to the news?* It didn't bear thinking about. *God, this was crazy. When?*

Her thought escaped. 'When's the baby due?' Her voice sounded faint like it had come out of a long tunnel to get out.

'March 19th. We had our first scan a few weeks ago.'

We. How lovey-dovey. How sickly sweet. March 19th. Less than a year older than Sophie. So what would this baby be to Sophie then? Her aunt? Her uncle? So Sophie would be its niece? God, this was ludicrous.

'So who knows about it?'

'Camilla's parents know. And she's told her best friend. But no one else yet. Haven't plucked up the courage to tell any of my mates yet. Don't know what their reaction would be, to be honest. Anyway, your mum needs to know first. Best she finds out from one of us, isn't it? We'd better tell her very soon really. Camilla's beginning to get quite a bump. I was wondering – you couldn't tell her for us, could you?' He started fiddling with his nails again.

'No! I couldn't! Sorry Dad, but I don't see why I should be the one to do your dirty work for you. It's for you to tell her, not me.'

Her father ran his fingers across his stubbly cheek. 'But I don't see her. You see her all the time. And I'm sure she'd rather hear it from you. She'd eat me alive.'

Emma was still bobbing a fractious Sophie up and down on her knee. 'Well, that's not my problem. *You've* got to tell her, Dad. Don't be such a coward.'

'OK, OK, I'll tell her then. I'll pop over one evening.'

'Right, OK. Well, I guess we'd better be going anyway. Sophie's getting hungry.' Emma carried Sophie over to her pushchair which she had left by the front door and strapped her in, much to Sophie's annoyance.

'Bye then, Dad.' He had followed them over to the door. She leant towards him and kissed him on the cheek. The light had gone out of his eyes a bit.

'Bye, love. See you soon then. You'll have to bring your fellow round to meet me and Camilla one of these days.'

Emma smiled at him sympathetically as she turned the handle on the front door. 'Yeah, maybe.' She pulled the pushchair out of the door backwards, Sophie still protesting vociferously.

'Bye, sweetheart.' Her father stooped down towards his granddaughter and jiggled her foot with his hand before Emma turned the pushchair round and started pushing Sophie away down the corridor. She heard the lazy click of the door shutting behind her. She hadn't told her father about moving to York, but it didn't matter now. She hadn't told him a lot of things, but sometimes it was better that way.

CHAPTER 7

Her father hadn't been to visit her mother that week before she had left for York. Emma knew he wouldn't. Procrastinating was one of the few things you could rely on him to do. Or maybe he was still hoping she would tell her.

Gabriel had made it down from York in good time that Saturday morning to pick Emma and Sophie up and after packing up the car until there was barely any room left for them to sit in it, they had driven into town to meet Emma's mother who had arranged to finish work early so that she could meet the young man who was running off with her daughter.

Emma had booked a table at her mother's favourite restaurant and Gabriel had insisted on paying for everybody in spite of her mother's protests. In between attending to Sophie and assembling all the things she would be taking with her to York, she had worried a little about their meeting each other, but she was relieved to find that her qualms had been unfounded as the two of them seemed to get on like a house on fire and she had even managed to relax and enjoy herself.

Although her mother had drunk a couple of glasses of white wine too many and had become a little snivelly towards the end, Emma was relieved that she had managed to hold it together until they dropped her back home afterwards and hadn't ended up embarrassing either herself or Emma. Emma felt a little guilty as they drove away, following emotional farewells, knowing that after waving them all off, her mother would go back into an empty house and dissolve into floods of tears that would flow all the more readily after all the wine. She hoped Sue was in. Moreover, Emma felt guilty knowing that she wouldn't be around to pick up the pieces when her mother found out about Camilla.

Gabriel's house stood at one end of a terrace of red-bricked Victorian houses on a busy road opposite a row of shops. One of these was a bakery and, when Gabriel was at work, Emma had taken to sitting with Sophie in the bay window overlooking his scraggy patch of a front garden, watching people go in and out of it. After a couple of weeks, she got to know at a glance the regulars who would turn up at the same time every lunchtime to buy their filled baguette or roll to take back to the office (the same filling each day, Emma imagined), checking their smart phones as they marched purposefully towards the shop. At moments when there was no traffic passing, Emma could hear the metallic, self-important tap tap tap of their shoes on the pavement and the sound seemed to her as if it filled the whole world for a few seconds before the next car inevitably droned past. And she could spot from a mile off the tourists who would saunter along nonchalantly, chatting and gesticulating to each other and stumbling on the baker's by chance. Then she would watch them through the shop window as they tried to decipher the scrawl on the board on the wall and point at the various fillings, taking forever to choose and infuriating the regulars who pulled out their phones to check the time as, exasperated, they shuffled from one foot to the other behind them in the queue.

And then there were the other people who passed her window, all with their own set of hopes and dreams and fears. She loved her vantage point. It was like watching a play in a theatre, presenting her with an ever-changing vista without any involvement on her part. There were of course many faces that Emma didn't recognise, but then there were also ones which were becoming increasingly familiar to her. The schoolchildren at around quarter to nine and half past three with their uniforms and their rucksacks – the older ones unaccompanied or in groups, trailing their feet resentfully and kicking up the leaves from the cherry trees on the pavement, and the younger ones, holding their parent's hand as they half-walked half-ran to keep up with them, or whizzing ahead on their coloured scooters – and the businessmen and women who would sometimes have to run to catch the bus, which stopped a short distance from Gabriel's house. Emma would will them to catch it before it pulled away, exhaust pipe spluttering, while she watched her passengers, her protégés, clambering up the staircase to look for a seat on the top deck if the bottom was full.

At other times Emma would take the bus herself to meet Gabriel for lunch and they would squash into a crowded coffee bar and munch on sandwiches before pushing Sophie round a nearby park if it was fine. Summer's heatwave had long since come to an end and autumn, russet and amber, with its chilly, foggy mornings and long evenings had finally gained the upper hand with unerring dependability. Afterwards she would sometimes wander round the shops, killing time until Gabriel arrived home in the evening. The shops had once again started gearing up for Christmas and Sophie loved to see the Christmas trees everywhere with their gaudy spangle of twinkling coloured lights and glossy baubles. Emma had also started taking Sophie swimming and had even joined a mother and baby group which met once a week in the church hall up the road, where she made a few friends, although no very close ones.

These were the things that punctuated her new life in York, that gave shape to the monotony of her days while Gabriel was at work. Whereas before, she had longed for the weekends when she would see Gabriel, now she only longed for each evening when they would more often than not simply snuggle together on the sofa watching television. But there can be times when one day feels like a lifetime and sometimes Gabriel would have to work later than usual in which case she would find herself casting anxious glances at the clock, desperate to hear the sound of his key in the front door. They went out in the evenings less now, given the colder weather and the fact that they no longer had anyone to leave Sophie with.

As such, they were watching television together one Tuesday evening when Emma's phone rang. She fumbled lazily for it between the cushions of the sofa. Her mother's number flashed insistently on and off the screen.

'Hi Mum, how are you doing?' She stood up and, so as not to disturb Gabriel, walked out of the lounge into the hallway, where she sat down on the bottom stair.

There was silence for a moment on the other end of the line followed by a huge intake of breath. Then the words gushed out in a primeval-sounding howl so that Emma could barely understand what her mother was saying. Not that she needed to. She knew what this phone call was about already. It was the one she had been dreading. She reached through the balusters to pull the lounge door to, to block out the consolatory sound of the television.

Her mother drew in breath again, apparently taking time to try and compose herself before beginning once more. 'Kevin's wife, June, came to get her hair cut this afternoon.' Sob. 'You know the one I mean, don't you? Dad's old school friend. Not Kevin at the garage, the other one. They came round for dinner a couple of years ago.' Sob. 'Do you remember? I did them that lasagne that got a bit caught round the edges and you were helping me cut off the burnt bits in the kitchen while they were chatting with your dad in the lounge.' Sob.

'Yes, yes, I know the Kevin you mean.' Emma tried not to sound impatient.

'Well...' All her utterances were punctuated by sobs and loud sniffs. 'June came in to get her hair cut and we were chatting and she asked me what I thought about Camilla.' Her mother blew her nose loudly.

'Well, I thought she meant what I thought about her in general so I said she seemed a bit up herself and said I didn't know what she was doing with an old layabout like your dad.' She sniffed violently and hesitated again as she tried to compose herself to get the story out whose ending Emma already knew.

'Then she said, "No, I mean about the baby." She didn't mean to hurt my feelings. I swear she thought I knew. Then I said, "What do you mean?" And then her face flushed red as anything and she wouldn't look me in the eye. She was all flustered and apologetic and said she thought I knew. Well, of course, I did know then, didn't I? So there it is, your dad and Camilla are having a baby on all accounts.' She started blubbing again.

'God, what's he thinking?' Emma tried to sound surprised. She couldn't let her mother know that she already knew.

'Nice of him to tell me. Always was a bloody coward.'

'So how do you feel about it, Mum?' *God, what a stupid thing to ask.*

'How do you think I feel?! I know he's free to make his own choices now, but it hadn't crossed my mind for a second that he'd go and do a thing like that. I'm shocked and I'm hurt that he didn't have the decency to tell me himself. Fancy letting me find out like that! It was so embarrassing as well. For me and for June. She could see she'd put her foot in it but it wasn't her fault.'

'Oh Mum, poor you. Have you told Sue?'

'No, she's staying with Becky at the moment. She's just had a baby.' The word set her off crying all over again. Typical. Becky was Sue's eldest daughter, the one who had recently got married.

'Do you want me to come down?'

'No, no, you're all right. I don't want to put you out.' Her mother's voice sounded strained.

'It's fine, Mum. It's no trouble. I don't mind. It would be nice to see you anyway.'

'Well, if you're sure. Thank you, darling. It's very good of you. I'll pay the train fare then.' The relief in her voice was evident.

'I'll get the train back tomorrow. Can you pick me up after work?'

'Yes, of course, darling. Just let me know what time.'

'See you tomorrow then, Mum. Take care. Love you.'

'Love you, sweetheart.'

So it was that the following day Emma and Sophie took the train back where they stayed with her mother a couple of nights. Although her mother was, unsurprisingly, still feeling hard done by, drowning her sorrows each evening over several glasses of wine and at times demanding more of Emma's attention than Sophie, Emma was happy to be back home with her and returned to York that weekend feeling unexpectedly revitalised, and eager to see Gabriel again.

Their lives, and the routines that sustained them, carried on as before. Christmas came and went. Gabriel had time off work and they all spent a couple of days over Christmas with Emma's mother who seemed at pains to reassure Emma that she had got over her distress. Or at least she was putting on a brave face. Emma didn't see her father. She was still annoyed with him for not telling her mother about the baby and he made no effort to contact her either, doubtless too busy playing happy families with Camilla.

On Boxing Day, Gabriel took Emma and Sophie to stay with his parents, an event that Emma had been secretly dreading. They had a big house in the country set in acres of land and for them, life was all about horses, Range Rovers and keeping abreast of their social engagements with one fashionable family or another. Although they made an all-too-obvious effort to make Emma feel welcome in a material sense, their relations with her were frigid and strained and she couldn't help feeling that she was being constantly judged and that she was poles apart from the kind of young lady they had in mind for their son. She wondered whether Gabriel had only told them about Sophie at the last minute out of necessity and whether they even knew that they were living together as she and Sophie were given one of the guest rooms to sleep in. The only times when she could truly relax and be off her guard were when she and Gabriel, accompanied by the family's two bounding Labradors, would wheel Sophie, her little rosy face the only evidence that there was somebody under the bundle of blankets, along the bleak, windswept country lanes, their cheeks smarting from the cold and their ears full of the screech of the hungry gulls, but most of the time she felt like she didn't fit in and as if her staying was an inconvenience to the rest of the family. She was relieved when their visit finally came to an end and they could return to the sanctuary of Gabriel's house and she could at last be herself without feeling that it was inadequate.

Then, a couple of days before the end of one of the most eventful years of Emma's life so far, Gabriel surprised her by instructing her to pack her things and the following morning, drove them all to the airport where they got on a plane for Paris. They stayed in a charming little hotel in Le Marais off Place des Vosges, where they ate still-warm croissants and pains au chocolat in bed that Gabriel had got up moments earlier to buy from the ivy-clad boulangerie next door, whose enticing smells wafted up through the window of their room which looked over the cobbled street. Although cold, the days were clear and sunny so that they strolled in the Jardin des Tuileries and by the river and along the Champs-Elysées with its stunning display of lights which had Sophie mesmerised, and its scent of roasted chestnuts, stopping now and then to warm up with a hot chocolate or a crêpe. They went up to the top of the Tour Montparnasse from where they enjoyed a crystal-clear view of the city, its illuminated avenues splaying out far below them like the spokes of a bicycle wheel and on New Year's Eve they watched, arm in arm, as the fireworks splattered their trails of colours behind the Eiffel Tower, as if one of the artists at Montmartre had flicked a giant paintbrush all over the sky and the Seine.

At the end of February, a new girl, Manisha, joined the mother and baby group Emma attended. She was Mauritian and had recently moved to England after her husband, who was a consultant and also Mauritian, had been offered a job at the hospital in York. She had a beautiful little girl, Lydie, who was six months older than Sophie. For some reason, maybe because Emma still seemed a little lonely and lost herself, Manisha would always seem to gravitate towards her and they would spend time chatting together over cups of coffee while the babies amused themselves with toys. Manisha spoke excellent English and after a few weeks, she and Emma became firm friends. She and her husband lived only a couple of streets away from Gabriel's house and so the two women started seeing a lot more of each other. It was as if they had both needed each other without realising it. They would open up to each other, unburdening their hearts of things that troubled them, sharing secrets of their pasts. Emma found that she could talk to her about things that she couldn't talk to other people about, although there were some secrets that were so terrible that she felt obliged to keep them locked away forever.

Thus, she told her about how she had met Sophie's father and about her own father and Camilla and the baby. And in turn, Manisha told her about how her father had been an alcoholic and had beaten her and her sisters, but mostly her mother, until she was black and blue and how the other members of their family, the grandparents, the aunts, the uncles, had all turned a blind eye to it. Then, one day, Manisha had come home from school to find her father hanging from the big Flamboyant tree in their garden that overlooked the turquoise lagoon, an empty rum bottle buzzing with groggy, guzzling insects lying at his feet on the parched grass. And how, even after all that had happened, she missed her island now – the sunshine and the mountains, the feel of the hot white sand on the beach trickling between her toes as she listened to the Indian Ocean surf endlessly caressing the shoreline, a sound that she used to hear when she lay in her bedroom at night with the scent of the geraniums and the bougainvillea floating in on the warm breeze through her window; and she even missed the Flamboyant trees, with their magnificent blood-red blooms. And how when it rained, it would only do so for a short time before the sun would come out again and make everything sparkle like silver whereas here in York, it could rain for hours on end – horizontal sheets of it slung at you by a cruel Arctic wind and chilling you to the bone. Her husband had been so excited about the prospect of coming to England that she had just got swept along on his wave of enthusiasm and had never quite been able to pluck up the courage to tell him that she didn't actually want to leave Mauritius. And now it was too late.

It was Emma's birthday in March and Gabriel took her to Venice for a couple of days. The spring sunshine felt warm on their bare arms as they pottered about the little back alleyways and sat in cafés eating pizza and drinking wine and watching the world go by. They took the obligatory ride on a gondola through the maze of narrow canals and admired the spectacular facades of the palazzi that rose up out of the Grand Canal as they floated past on a vaporetto. More snapshots, more precious memories. As they leant over the Rialto Bridge, the warmth of the Venetian sun on their backs, watching the gondoliers skilfully negotiate their way past each other and eating ice creams, Emma felt as if she might burst with contentment.

Little did she know. If she had been less naive, she might have realised that the honeymoon period doesn't last forever. That this level of happiness cannot possibly be sustained. Looking back, it was difficult to pinpoint when the cracks started to appear. Tiny cracks that went virtually unnoticed at the time, but cracks all the same. Minute cracks for which it was always easy to come up with a plausible excuse in her head, no matter how many times they occurred, to convince herself that he still felt the same as he had at the start.

Maybe it was that Easter, barely a couple of days after standing on the bridge. Maybe that was when the very first crack emerged. And when the nightmares started becoming more frequent again.

They had left Sophie with Emma's mother while they went to Venice. Easter fell early that year and as Emma's birthday was only a few days before, they had returned from Venice on Good Friday and stayed with her mother for the rest of the long weekend.

On Saturday afternoon, Gabriel had suggested they meet up with Tim as he hadn't seen him for a while and so they arranged to meet at Venus that evening. It felt strange going back there. The last time she had been in there had been when Tara had blurted out to Gabriel about Sophie. She hadn't been in touch with her since then, but when they entered the bar, there she was, clear as day, propping up the bar as if she had never left. It was as if Emma knew she'd be there, right in that spot. Although the bar was packed full of people, Emma's eyes fell on her straightaway. It was as if an imaginary spotlight was illuminating her. That was how it always was.

Tara hadn't seen her. She was in habitual pose, chatting up a small group of boys with her friends from college, all eyes on her, grateful for any crumb of attention she might throw their way. She hadn't changed much. The only thing different about her was that she'd had her hair cut. It was jaw-length now. It suited her, Emma decided. It accentuated the shape of her face and neck. Whereas before, Tara would constantly be flicking her long hair from one side to the other, now she could only run her fingers through it, being obliged to stop at the nape of her neck. Emma wondered when she had had it cut. Before Emma could decide whether or not to approach her, Tara caught sight of her as she turned her head slightly to speak to the boy nearest to Emma.

It was difficult to say in that split second whether Tara looked pleased or annoyed. She seemed to stop in mid-sentence for a second before turning to the rest of the group to say something hurriedly. Then she was making her way towards Emma and Gabriel, any trace of vexation now erased from her lovely face as she smiled her perfect smile at them both, effortlessly making the people in the room step aside for her to pass as if she was Moses parting the Red Sea.

'Hi guys! Fancy seeing you! Long time no see!' She stepped forward to hug Emma enthusiastically, then kissed Gabriel ostentatiously on each cheek, her sleek, satiny hair brushing his face softly as she moved her head from one side to the other.

'We're down for the weekend to see my mum. We're meant to be meeting Tim. You haven't seen him, have you?'

'Yeah, I saw him and a couple of the other guys over there somewhere.' She pointed vaguely towards one corner of the room. She was wearing a pair of skin-tight jeans and a strappy sequined top which showed off her slender arms, which were tanned, even at the end of the winter.

'Your hair looks great.' Emma smiled at her. She felt annoyed with herself that she was being so nice to Tara, that she couldn't bring herself to mention the incident that had happened the last time they had seen each other. It didn't seem as if Tara was going to either. She wondered whether Tara had forgotten or perhaps she had been too drunk that night to remember.

'Oh, thanks.' Tara stroked it with the back of her hand. Her nails were perfectly sculpted and painted with gleaming, bright pink varnish. 'I had it cut last week.' Suddenly Emma felt unattractive next to Tara, who always looked so immaculate, so pretty, so alluring. She took hold of Gabriel's hand defensively.

'So, I heard that you'd moved in with Gabes.' Tara had never called him that before and it irritated Emma. That was what *she* called him.

But still Emma found herself smiling obsequiously. Tara had that effect on you. 'Yeah, I've been there five months now. It's going really well, isn't it, darling?' She pulled Gabriel closer and put her arm round his waist.

'Yeah, it made sense. You know. Saves a lot of to-ing and fro-ing.' Tara was watching him intently as he spoke.

'How's the course going?' Emma asked.

'Oh, I've nearly finished it now. Just a couple more exams then I'll be a fully-qualified beauty therapist. I've already got a job lined up in a salon in town.'

'That's brilliant!' Emma felt herself beaming again.

'Do you want to come and join us?' Gabriel's invitation grated upon Emma slightly. She felt that it wasn't up to him to ask Tara. She wasn't *his* friend to invite.

'Oh thanks. Yes, I'd love to! I'd better just go and tell the others where I'm going.' She disappeared off to the bar again. Emma thought she noticed Gabriel's glance linger a little too long on her retreating figure. Along with most of the other men's in the crowded room.

'You don't mind, do you, darling?'

'No, of course not.' Emma forced a smile.

They eventually found Tim together with Pete and Carrie, two of the friends whom Emma had met before. They managed to find a couple of spare seats at other tables and pulled them across for Emma and Gabriel to sit on.

When Tara appeared, Gabriel pulled Emma onto his knee so that she could have a seat. Emma noticed that Tim seemed a little distant with Tara, who seemed to be trying to avoid his eye, and wondered what had gone on between the two of them since she and Gabriel had left the bar back in the summer.

The friends chatted at length about this and that, catching up on each other's news. About life in York, about Sophie, about Tim's new job, about Pete's recent engagement, which they all toasted. After a couple of glasses of wine, Emma even found herself telling Tara all about Camilla and the baby, which, Emma assumed, was now ten days' overdue, unless her father just hadn't bothered to let them know that Camilla had already had it. And Tara told Emma about her latest string of conquests. As Emma relaxed in Tara's presence, it began to feel a bit like old times again, and what happened last summer went clean out of her head.

Gabriel, too, was knocking back the glasses. They all were. As he chatted with his old friends, Emma thought she caught him a couple of times, at moments when there was a lull in her own conversation with Tara, glancing downwards at Tara's top, once when she was leaning forward, her bare elbows on the greasy surface of the table and her breasts, cupped by the lacy black material of her bra, clearly visible. Emma wondered later whether she had leant forward with the express intention of attracting Gabriel's attention. Whether she had known exactly what she was doing from the very beginning. Probably.

It was Gabriel's turn to buy a round and he gently nudged Emma off his knee so that he could stand up. She sat back down on the chair while Gabriel stretched his legs before heading off in the direction of the bar.

It couldn't have been more than a minute later that Tara announced that she needed to go to the toilet. Emma should have put two and two together there and then. Looking back, she could have kicked herself for not saying that she needed to go too so that she could have accompanied Tara, but her head was fuzzy from the wine and it didn't occur to her at that moment. No amount of wishing can change the past. And even if Emma had accompanied her, would it have made any difference to the final outcome anyway?

Unperturbed, Emma continued to chat with Tim, Carrie and Pete, but after a while, she turned round to see where Gabriel had got to. She scanned the bar and it wasn't long before she spotted his distinctive, bushy hair. He was waiting his turn and there she was, bold as brass, standing right next to him, leaning towards him as she chatted to him in much the same pose as Emma had seen her in when they had first entered the bar that evening. Bending her upper body forwards slightly, giving him an eyeful so that he couldn't help but oblige her and look. She was using every one of her prolific arsenal of strategies to reel him in. Fluttering her thick lashes at him, touching the top of her chest to draw his eyes to it again, laughing ingratiatingly at what he was saying, licking her lips like a cat that knows it has got the cream. And he was being taken in by it all. Emma knew that Tara was making him feel special, singling him out, buttering him up. And he, powerless, or unwilling, to resist, was falling into her trap. She was the black widow spider preparing to devour her mate.

Emma watched, glued to her seat, strangely fascinated, as Tara, smiling, reached over to Gabriel, placing her hand caressingly on his hair. Emma imagined her asking him simperingly whether she could touch it. Gabriel, too, was smiling. He was enjoying being the focus of all Tara's attention and unequivocal flirting. They locked eyes and then he stroked Tara's hair from the top of her head downwards, laughing, letting his hand rest on her bare shoulder gently after it had reached the ends of her hair, and then allowing it to glide all the way down her outstretched arm until it lingered on her hand which was resting on the bar. Emma could see the horrid vivid pink of her nail varnish from where she was sitting. And then after what must have been no more than a couple of seconds, he suddenly took his hand off hers, seeming to remember himself. That was all it was. That was all that happened. But Tara was still smiling to herself after Gabriel had removed his hand from hers because she knew that she had done enough. Enough to set the wheels in motion. And now all that was needed was to bide her time.

Months later, Emma would ask herself why Tara hit on Gabriel when she could have had her pick of most of the men in the room. Was it simply because he was Emma's? Was she jealous of her newfound happiness? After all, her own relationships tended to be flings that rarely lasted more than a couple of months, whereas Emma's was the real thing. Or at least it seemed to be.

Immediately afterwards, Emma was angry. Angry with Gabriel, but mainly angry with Tara, the temptress who had seduced him. In her mind, it was all Tara's fault. Too scared of rocking the boat, of losing him, she didn't mention what she had seen to either of them. She didn't want him to think that she was being overly possessive. But then, after a while, the memory of what she had seen during those few drunken minutes became more and more hazy round the edges and she started to trivialise it in her mind, convincing herself that what she had seen was normal between a couple of friends who had got a bit drunk. Surely not even Tara would stoop that low. Especially after she'd been so nice to Emma all evening. So that was how Emma reasoned away the first crack.

CHAPTER 8

The evening of Easter Sunday Emma's father texted to say that Camilla had given birth to a little boy the day before. On Easter Monday, slightly reluctantly, before they headed back up to York, they called in at his flat to meet Emma's new brother.

It was the first time that Gabriel had met her father and Emma was relieved that he got his name right and, although chirpy and in fine fettle, didn't make any wisecracks about it. He made them a cup of tea and crashed about in the kitchen hunting for an apparently elusive pack of biscuits that Camilla had suggested he get out, then bustled around Camilla and his new son, Jack, and straightened the line of blue greetings cards on the windowsill before plonking himself down with a loud, contented sigh on the sofa beside Gabriel. Although Camilla was all smiles with them and tried to seem welcoming, they could tell she was putting on an act for their benefit and that having visitors was the last thing she felt like doing, the dark circles under her eyes and stifled yawns a testament to how she was really feeling. There was a blue foil helium balloon with a picture of a teddy bear on it tied to the back of the armchair she was sitting in and from Emma's position on the sofa, it looked, Emma thought to herself, as if it was coming out of Camilla's head.

At her father's insistence, Emma was given Jack to hold. Having passed him over, his face brimming with pride, her father hovered excitedly next to her, remarking how they had each other's eyes to Camilla, who concurred in a voice much too high to sound sincere. Emma felt awkward holding the squirming baby and couldn't feel any kind of connection with him. He was just another baby. He didn't look anything like her with his vacant, deep blue eyes. Jack started to whimper and she was glad to have an excuse to hand him back to Camilla and her maternity bra.

Camilla was evidently too tired to bother to conceal the relief on her face when Emma finally announced that it was time they should be heading off for York. Her father showed them to the door, exclaiming enthusiastically how nice it had been to meet Gabriel at long last and what a fine fellow his daughter had landed herself, making Emma cringe slightly with embarrassment, and urging them all to come and visit again next time they were down. Emma assured him that they would, all the while doubting it very much.

When Emma saw Manisha at their group the following week, Manisha, her eyes glowing with excitement, announced to her that she had some news. Grinning from ear to ear, the cinnamon hue of her skin accentuating the whiteness of her teeth, she produced with a flourish a scan photo from her bag which she handed to Emma triumphantly. She had been that morning to have it confirmed that she was three months' pregnant.

Another baby. As Emma ambled slowly back home afterwards, she mulled over Manisha's news and an idea, unbidden, began to creep into her mind. It had never occurred to her before, but maybe a baby might be what was needed to cement her relationship with Gabriel. There was nothing stopping them, after all. He had a good job and it would be wonderful for Sophie to have a brother or sister. She was sure of her feelings for him and had he not told her countless times that he loved her? Perhaps not as much now as he used to, but the mere fact that they were living together (*and had it not been his idea to?*) was surely proof enough that he wanted to be with her. She had no idea how he would react to such a suggestion. They had never discussed the future. Gabriel liked to be spontaneous; he didn't like making plans. But even if he balked at the idea to start with, surely she would be able to talk him into it. She resolved to bring the subject up soon, but it was difficult to find the right time.

What with Gabriel's new project that he had on at the office for a start. He was arriving back home in the evenings later and later. And he was often tired and irritable. They had started arguing a lot. Although Emma reassured herself by telling herself that this was normal in a relationship. And it was only over silly little things mainly. Like the other evening. Emma had rung his mobile and got no reply, as was often the case at the moment because of all the extra meetings about this new project, so she had texted him. He hadn't bothered to check his phone after the meeting had finished. She had only wanted him to pop into the little supermarket round the corner from his office to get some rice to go with the curry she had been busy making that afternoon. She hadn't realised that they had run out until it was too late to go out to buy some herself, Sophie having just fallen asleep in her cot for the night.

So when Gabriel did finally arrive home, they had spent the whole of their precious evening together quarrelling. When Emma had accused him of not checking his mobile, he had retorted that he wasn't obliged to have it switched on just for her benefit and for God's sake, it was only a bit of bloody rice. They could have the curry with chips, or he'd go down the road and get some rice from the Chinese if she wanted. In any case, he didn't really fancy curry anyway. The curry ended up in the bin and after they had got into bed, they both made a point of turning their backs towards each other churlishly and went to sleep without even kissing each other goodnight, which they always did, let alone having sex.

The following morning, however, when the sunlight was leaking through the chink in the curtains and the radio alarm had wrenched them unfeelingly out of sleep, Emma had wrapped her arms around Gabriel and nestled into his back. He had turned over and they had apologised to each other abjectly, reassuring each other of their love for one another (*so he did love her, then*) and they had made love hurriedly, but tenderly, before Gabriel had got up to have his shower before work. Last night was put behind them and everything was sparklingly perfect again.

Even the weather seemed to share her joy as Emma, her spirits dancing like a kite on a breeze, drew the curtains and embraced the as yet unblemished new day that stretched out before her with all its vertiginous promise. The morning was full of the music of the birds in the cherry trees and she breathed deep into her lungs the lemony scent of magnolia flowers drifting in through the open window from the tree in next-door's garden. The sky was dotted here and there with clouds, like lambs frolicking about in a field of cornflowers and the street seemed to be dazzling in the sunshine so that everything looked spanking new and fresh and clean. She could hear Gabriel whistling in the kitchen as he got his breakfast and she smiled to herself.

Later, she took Sophie to the park by the river where they fed the ducks. The ripples on the river kept catching the sunlight momentarily in different places like a million diamonds. Sophie chortled each time she threw a chunk of bread at the ducks, who had waddled over, quacking like a group of old women putting the world to rights, to congregate beside her pushchair, as that is where all the bread landed because she couldn't throw it any further. Each time she tried to lob the bread, the tight golden curls on her head would bob slightly and her eyes would screw up with the effort. They were beautiful eyes, changing colour depending on the light, sometimes hazel, sometimes pear-green, but now amber. Her heart overflowing with serenity and love, Emma kissed her daughter, who would be turning one next week. She and Gabriel were planning to take her to the zoo to mark the occasion.

One of the ducks who was a little bolder than the others suddenly snatched a chunk that Sophie had been clutching in her clammy little fist. She was so startled that it took a few moments for her to cry. Emma unfastened her from her pushchair and took her in her arms to comfort her, feeling her sobs reverberate through her little body into her own and the dampness of her tears soak through her top where Sophie was resting her head on her shoulder. When her crying had subsided, they walked over to an ice cream van parked nearby and bought ice creams. It felt like summer. They sat side by side on a bench in the sunshine and Sophie got ice cream everywhere, but it didn't matter because they were happy and the world seemed like a wonderful place right now. Maybe if Gabriel got home early enough tonight, she would mention the idea of the baby.

Gabriel did arrive back earlier than usual that evening, but then Manisha phoned to ask if she wanted to go round for lunch the next day and they chatted for a bit and then Emma's mother called and was on for ages about Camilla and Emma's father and the baby. Again. She had seen them all that afternoon in town going into Mothercare as she was leaving the salon. It was the first time she had seen them since Jack had been born and she said that it brought it all home seeing Emma's father pushing a pram. And he looked so happy and proud. It made her realise that he had moved on whereas she had not. Not really. Maybe, for all his faults, she had needed him more than he had needed her. There were more tears and more comforting. Afterwards, the evening meal needed making and Sophie needed a bath and then Gabriel dozed off when they were watching television together later on. It didn't matter. It could wait.

A couple of weeks later, Gabriel had to attend a three-day conference in Bristol, which meant that he would have to stay there overnight. Emma decided that she would use the opportunity to go back to her mother's. She even made the effort to text Tara while she was down and they went out for a meal together and hit it off like old times, chattering about everything and nothing and laughing until the tears rolled down their cheeks about their own silly jokes that nobody else would understand, much to the bewilderment of the people sitting at the surrounding tables. It felt good being with her again, having Tara to herself, rather than having to share her with her adoring entourage of college friends. At the end of the evening, Emma made Tara promise to come and visit her in York soon.

Emma missed Gabriel dreadfully while he was away, but he sent her lots of effusive texts – far more than he did normally – and called her each evening from his room before going down to dinner in the hotel dining room and before going to bed, to tell her that he loved her. He sounded as if he had had a few drinks at the bar, but she didn't mind. She was glad he was having a good time. When they were reunited in York afterwards, Emma flung her arms around him enthusiastically and nestled her head into his chest, breathing in his smell that she had been craving, but he seemed a little subdued. When Emma questioned him, he wrapped his arms around her affectionately and apologised, saying he was tired. She let it go.

She wasn't to know, and probably never would, that he was tired because he had been up most of both nights screwing a colleague in his hotel room. Their seedy little affair had been going on for a few weeks when they would meet after work now and again at her flat the other side of York. And his nose had been put out of joint when she had finished it that morning, telling him that she was fed up with being his bit on the side. Although he had grown quite fond of her, this colleague, it was more that his pride had been wounded than his heart. He would get over it soon enough.

CHAPTER 9

Spring marched headlong into another summer, lazy and golden, and while Gabriel was stuck at the office earning money to keep them all, which Emma felt somewhat guilty about, although he insisted that there was no need, she and Sophie were able to take advantage of the warmer days and spend more time outdoors. Days that seemed to merge into each other in an endless, glorious haze of powder-blue skies, crisp shadows, Sophie's laughter and the smell of sun cream. At least that is how Emma would remember it afterwards, even though she knew that there must have also been sunburn, wasps and tantrums, as well as rainy days. She filtered out the unhappy days from her brain, she banished any details that might tarnish the memory of that summer, so that they no longer existed, they had never existed, and she made the memory of that summer into something unsullied and perfect, an exquisite pearl. She wanted to feel the poignancy of that summer and the previous one tugging at her heartstrings. She liked to wallow in the ache that comes of losing forever something that was beautiful and cherished. In the filing catalogue of her brain, last summer would be Gabriel's and this summer would be Sophie's.

Gabriel had bought a small paddling pool for Sophie and they set it up in his back garden, which, though a little poky, was south-facing and a real suntrap and she would shriek with laughter as she thrashed her arms about in the cool, sparkling water, the spray making rainbows in the sunlight. She had learnt to walk now and when she was not playing in the garden, she would toddle along in her sundress and frilly hat beside Emma and they would go to the park or sit by the river or have picnics with Lydie and Manisha, who was growing more and more rotund as each mellow summer day went by.

Emma had finally managed to bring up the subject of the baby, now that Gabriel's project at work had finished and he was not having to work so late these days. It had taken a lot of courage on her part and he had been understanding, putting his arms round her and kissing her, as he told her that he loved her and wanted to be with her, but that there was no rush and he didn't feel ready for the responsibility of fatherhood just yet. Give it another year perhaps. Emma had nodded meekly and refrained from pointing out that since he was already like a father to Sophie anyway, little would have to change, because it was as if she had always known deep down what his response would be.

Perhaps to try and make it up to her, Gabriel suggested a couple of days later that they go on holiday. He said that he had a friend who owned a villa in Spain that overlooked the sea and was off the beaten track miles from any resort, so he arranged for them to go and stay there. Every morning they would half-walk half-slide down the steep, dusty path that zigzagged down the rocky hillside flecked with yellow and purple flowers to the almost-deserted beach where Sophie would play beside them happily with her bucket and spade. Emma would watch from the beach towel she was sitting on, smiling, one hand shading her eyes from the myriad of dazzling, dancing mirrors that the sun was making on the turquoise water, as Sophie and Gabriel ran hand in hand to the water's edge, Sophie shrieking when she felt the cool waves lap over her hopping feet. The handful of tourists and locals with whom they shared the sandy cove must have mistaken them for a proper family. A mother, a father and a daughter.

At the middle of the day, when the sun was so fierce it was almost unbearable, they would clamber breathlessly back up to the villa, Sophie perched on Gabriel's shoulders, to eat under the welcome shade of the pergola, then they would put Sophie to bed for a nap and go to bed themselves, where in the dark of their shuttered whitewashed room, they would slowly make love to the gentle boom of the waves pushing and pulling as they broke unremittingly on the glittering shore below them.

When Sophie woke up, they would perhaps wander back down to the beach or stroll into the nearby town and find a bar where they would cool down with a drink under the shade of a parasol. Later on, they would sit on the terrace of a restaurant and watch a magnificent pink sun, with its promise of another sun-drenched day tomorrow, little by little submerge itself in a silvery, shimmering, amethyst sea, their skin still tingling from its rays of today. Night would envelop the little town, switching on a zillion stars which sparkled like fairy lights all above them as they gazed across at the glowing cluster of lights of the sleepy village on the other side of the bay, whose twinkling reflections stretched out like fingers over a sea that had turned sapphire.

By the wobbly light of a torch that they had found in a cupboard in the villa, they would wander back afterwards in the starry darkness that was perfumed with jasmine, Emma linking her arm loosely with Gabriel's as he pushed a drowsy Sophie back to bed, with a hungry-for-each-other ache in the pit of their bellies as if there were magnets inside them pulling towards each other irresistibly. Once Sophie was in bed, they would fall gratefully, desperately, into their own bed and make love all over again. The holiday was so delightful and Gabriel's affection for her so boundless that Emma almost felt like bringing up the subject of the baby again, but she knew better than to risk spoiling something that was already pretty much perfect.

The revitalising high of the holiday lasted for a few days after they had arrived home, when, cuddled up together on the sofa in the evenings, they would reminisce over a glass of Spanish wine and flick through the holiday photos on their phones, but real life soon muscled in on any dregs of exhilaration that remained from the holiday, their relationship seeming to lose a little of its sheen and slipping back into the mundane once again. Then later, towards the end of July, Gabriel announced ruefully to Emma that his boss had roped him into another big project at work, meaning that he spent more evenings at the office and became tired and irritable again. Often he would return home so exhausted that he would fall asleep as soon as his head hit the pillow and Emma would turn over and wait for sleep to come and when it did, it would be troubled and fitful, with the old nightmares nipping at her heels like a pack of ravenous, slavering wolves.

Emma returned home to her mother's for almost a fortnight in August while Gabriel's project was still on, happily ignorant of the fact that this gave Gabriel free rein to bring his latest bit on the side back to his house any evening after work he wanted and spend whole nights with her.

Emma enjoyed being home with her mother again and Sophie, too, appreciated the change of scene. Emma went out with Tara on several occasions while she was home and on the last evening before she returned to York, urged Tara again to come and visit her soon.

September 24th. Emma would remember it clearly. The date would become ingrained in her memory. The day Tara came to stay in York. The day before her world fell apart.

It was a windy day. Grey and unseasonably chilly. The clouds blew across the sky in banks, leaden and bloated and undefined, emitting a fine drizzle now and again so you weren't sure whether it was actually raining or whether it was just tiny water droplets carried in the wind. She remembered seeing the tired, still brittle leaves that had been swept to the side of the platform whipped up every so often by the eddying wind. Restless leaves. Unfeeling leaves. She even remembered hearing the strident screeches of the four ducks that flew over the station in formation as she was buttoning up her coat against the cold, the one Gabriel had bought her last Christmas. She remembered seeing the arrival time of the train, *her* train, on one of those overhead television screens at the end of the platform. 17:34. She remembered she had a headache, not one of those stabbing ones where you can pinpoint where the pain is in your head, but a dull, persistent one that seemed to fill the whole of the back of her head. It had been there all day. It hadn't been bad enough earlier on for her to take something, but now it was starting to throb and she remembered thinking to herself as she stood on the platform, that she must take something for it when she got back to Gabriel's.

The brakes screeched, setting the nerve endings of her brain on edge, as Tara's train drew in beside the platform. She was the first one out of the fourth door down. Striding forward, leading the other passengers off the train. Knowing which way to go without seeming to look up at the exit signs even though she had never been to York before, without having to stop and scan the platform for Emma. The leader of the pack. Confident, purposeful. Beautiful. Emma noticed a couple of men who got off the train further down caressing her body with hungry eyes, the curve of her hips, the movement of her buttocks in her tight-fitting jeans as she walked, and back up to her hair swishing between her narrow shoulders, wishing they could touch it, or rather, that it would touch *them*, swish across their faces as she straddled them and ground up and down on their rock-hard cocks. Is that what Gabriel wished when he saw her as she walked into the hallway of his house with Emma twenty minutes later?

She smiled at Emma. The smile which lit up her face, that obliged you to smile back, that made you feel on top of the world and made Emma forget she had a headache for a few seconds. The honeyed smile that made Emma feel like she was her best friend ever. The sugary smile of deceit and treachery. They hugged, laughing, and Emma picked up Tara's bag for her. Then they walked out of the exit together towards the bus stop, rubbing shoulders as they caught up with each other's news excitedly.

'Oh, it's so great to see you!' Over-the-top as ever, Tara flung her arms round Gabriel enthusiastically. He had just come out of the kitchen from where they could hear Sophie grizzling. She had stayed with Gabriel while Emma went to pick Tara up.

'And you.' Gabriel caught Emma's eye and raised his eyebrows at her, smirking at Tara's exuberance, as he returned the embrace.

'What's the matter with her?' asked Emma, nodding towards the kitchen.

'Oh, I can't get her to eat her tea. She keeps pushing the spoon away.'

'Here, I'll have a go. Take Tara's stuff into the lounge for her, will you?' Emma gestured towards the large bag on the floor. She turned to Tara. 'You don't mind sleeping on the sofa, do you?'

'No, course not, it's fine.' Well, she wouldn't end up sleeping on it for very long anyway.

Gabriel lifted the bag, pulling a face. 'God, what's in it?'

'Everything to keep me looking beautiful.' Emma knew Tara was only half-joking as she tittered at Gabriel and cocked her head at him like a pretty little budgerigar.

Emma went through to the kitchen while Tara followed Gabriel into the lounge. Later, Emma would wonder whether anything happened in the twenty seconds or so it took them to go into the lounge and reappear in the kitchen. Would they have merely caught eyes and said it all in a glance, just as happened when Emma first met Gabriel in the bar that night? Would Tara have found an excuse to touch his hand, or his arm, as he set the bag down on the floor next to the sofa? Would he have touched her too? So many hypothetical questions racing around her head to which she would never have the answers.

In the kitchen, Sophie sat in her highchair sulking, her cheeks blotchy from crying.

'Hi gorgeous.' Emma kissed her daughter between the curls on her forehead and picked up the spoon that Gabriel had left in Sophie's bowl on the table. She held it out to Sophie.

'No! Don't want it!' Sophie pushed the spoon away wearily. After several futile attempts Emma gave up. Her head was still pounding. She must go and get those tablets.

'How about a breadstick?'

Emma opened the cupboard and took a breadstick out of a packet. She held it out to Sophie, who knocked it out of Emma's hand onto the floor. Emma bent down to pick it up, her head feeling as if it was being smashed between a pair of cymbals.

Gabriel and Tara had appeared at the doorway.

'See what I mean?' Gabriel laughed.

'Oh, I give up.' Emma sighed, unbuckling Sophie and lifting her out of her seat. She set her down on the floor, but instead of toddling off as she usually did, she reached up to Emma.

'Cuddle, Mummy.'

Emma scooped her up. 'Oh, you *are* the end.' She smiled and kissed her again. Sophie rested her head against Emma's chest.

'Oh, she's so cute!' Tara walked over to Emma and stroked Sophie's hair. She turned her head away crossly.

They laughed. 'Yeah, well, not all the time. You've been a bit of a grump today, haven't you, madam? Early night for you, young lady.'

'So, where are we going tonight then, guys?' Tara's tone was casual.

Emma hesitated a moment before responding, forcing herself not to sound indignant. 'What do you mean? What about Sophie? We can't leave her.'

'Oh yes, of course, sorry. Stupid me. And I'd packed my new dress to wear as well.' Tara tried to smile away her disappointment, but she didn't quite manage to eliminate it all.

'Well, I don't mind staying here with Sophie if you girls want to go out somewhere.'

'No, Gabes, don't be silly.' Emma winced. God, she hated it when Tara called him that. 'It's fine, we'll just have a few drinks here. It will be nice. I can't really afford to go out anyway.' She flashed Gabriel another one of her smiles to smooth things over.

'You can still wear your new dress, though,' suggested Emma.

Tara let out a little self-conscious giggle and looked down at the floor demurely so that her long upper eyelashes fluttered like a pair of fans. 'No, it doesn't matter.'

'Oh, go on, put it on for us. You know you want to. Gabriel would like to see it, wouldn't you, darling?' Emma didn't know why she persisted. It was as if she was steering them both into what was to happen later. As if she was daring them to do it. A challenge. A game?

Gabriel shrugged, looking uncomfortable. 'Yeah, I guess so.'

'There you are then. Gabriel wants you to wear it. I bet you look beautiful in it. But then, you look beautiful in anything.'

'Oh, stop it. You're embarrassing me.' Tara giggled again, affectedly.

'But it's true, isn't it, Gabes?'

'Yeah, I suppose so.' Embarrassed, Gabriel ran his fingers through his hair, tracing the outline of the tiles on the kitchen floor with the edge of his foot.

'Well, go on then. What are you waiting for? Put it on. You can go upstairs to get changed if you want. Gabriel will stay down here, won't you?'

Emma looked up questioningly at Gabriel who gave a slight nod in response, shooting her a venomous look.

'Well, all right then.' Tara didn't need much persuading. She was dying to slip it on to show them. To show Gabriel.

'I'll open a bottle of wine.' Emma put Sophie down, who started crying again, before heading for the fridge out of which she took a bottle of wine and three glasses.

Once they had heard Tara go up the stairs, Gabriel sidled up to Emma. 'Why did you have to put me on the spot just then?' he hissed, angrily. 'What was I supposed to say?'

'The truth. That she's gorgeous and you want to see her in the dress. God, Gabriel, you're a bloke, aren't you? Even a monk would fancy her.' Emma felt like lashing out. She was in the mood for a quarrel. She still hadn't taken anything. Her headache was getting worse and Sophie's incessant grizzling was grating on her.

'I don't fancy her. I admit, she's pretty, but I fancy you, not her, darling.' Gabriel slipped his arm around her waist and kissed her cheek as she poured the wine.

'Only pretty? Gorgeous, sexy, irresistible, don't you mean? I've seen the way you look at her.'

'I don't know what you're talking about.'

'Well, maybe you don't even realise you're doing it then.'

'No, I don't. Enlighten me.'

'Well, you know, just looking at her, like all blokes look at her, looking her up and down, like you want to shag her.'

'God, you're talking utter bollocks. I swear to you, I don't fancy Tara. What's got into you tonight?'

Emma suddenly relented. 'Sorry, I've got a splitting headache. God, I wish she'd shut up! She's been a nightmare today. She's so grouchy. You should have gone to sleep when you had the chance this afternoon, silly girl. I knew we'd all regret it later.' Her eyes flashing with annoyance and frustration, Emma looked down at Sophie, who was rubbing her eyes with her little fists and wailing.

Then Emma's features softened. 'Oh, I'm sorry, my angel. Don't listen to me. I'm in a bad mood. I shouldn't take it out on you and Gabriel.' Emma picked Sophie up and kissed the top of her head.

'Go and take something for your headache, darling. Put us all out of our misery.'

Emma smiled and kissed Gabriel. 'Yeah, I will in a minute. Promise.'

They heard the floorboards of the stairs creak again and Tara appeared in the doorway, shifting from one foot to the other like a little girl waiting for an audition, sure in the knowledge that she would be successful, however, all eyelashes again, pretending to be all coy.

Emma couldn't see Gabriel's reaction as she was still standing next to him, but she could sense it. She could feel it in his silence, his stillness. She could almost smell it. She felt sure he was devouring Tara with dilated pupils, lingering in certain places on her body to relish her with lustful eyes, to imagine peeling off the very thing that she was supposedly showing them, showing *him*. What man wouldn't want to unzip the lovely dress worn by the even lovelier woman? For Tara and the dress each embellished the other. The dress was the enticing garnish on the delectable dish, the attractive wrapping paper on the present, skimming its contours alluringly, its only purpose to draw attention to the present itself, its ultimate abandonment in a corner of a room inevitable.

It was a short, strapless dress, which hugged Tara's bust and hips closely, showing off her lean, but womanly figure to perfection, so that there was little left to imagine underneath, although, Emma reflected, there was probably a lot left to imagine underneath for a man. The dress was made of a scarlet satiny material. Scarlet, the colour for a harlot.

'Wow! You look amazing! I love it!' exclaimed Emma, a little too brightly. Gabriel said nothing. He didn't need to. Both girls knew only too well what he was thinking. Emma decided not to push him into a response this time and make a fool of them all. So she carried on. Telling Tara what she wanted to hear, what they all already knew, what Tara had very likely planned all along. 'You're going to make me look like one of the ugly sisters tonight. I'm feeling positively unattractive now in this old top and jeans. Maybe it's a good job we're not going out after all!' She forced a laugh.

'You always look lovely, Ems.' Tara smiled at Emma, but it was an automatic response that came out sounding a little insincere.

'You do, darling. It's true.' Gabriel chimed in obediently, seeming suddenly to come out of his trance.

'Well, I don't feel it tonight, anyway. I'll tell you what. How about we hit the shops tomorrow and you can help me pick out some clothes? I could do with something new to wear.'

'Sure. That sounds great. I'd love to.'

Emma turned to the glasses on the worktop behind her and handed one to Tara and one to Gabriel, taking the third herself and raising it in the air. 'Cheers. It's lovely to have you here, Tara. Here's to a great weekend.'

They all clinked glasses together. 'Cheers,' Gabriel and Tara echoed.

They went through to the lounge where Gabriel sank into the sofa. Tara sat down beside him, crossing one leg over the other so that the one on top, bare, bronzed and brazen, hung tantalisingly close to him, and obliging Emma to sit in the armchair which was positioned near Gabriel's end of the sofa, where Sophie clambered up to sit on her lap. Gabriel reached across and stroked Emma's bare forearm which was resting on the arm of her chair as the three of them chatted and laughed and drank. A statement, perhaps. A way of reassuring her in the face of Tara's insurmountable seductiveness.

After a while, when the sound of their voices had lulled Sophie to sleep against her chest, Emma stood up to take her upstairs to bed. She managed to change her nappy without waking her and gently slid her down under the covers of her cot. She bent over to kiss her cheek and stood beside the cot for a few moments watching her chest slowly rise and fall in the shadowy moonlight. She suddenly remembered the first lonely night in the maternity ward with her daughter, watching her as she was watching her now, but resenting her and wishing that she had never been born. Now she couldn't imagine life without her. The sound of Tara's high-pitched laughing downstairs brought her back to the present abruptly.

She padded softly to the bathroom and took some painkillers from the cabinet, swallowing them down gratefully. Then she clattered down the stairs towards the lounge again, coughing loudly and deliberately as she reached the bottom. She could have crept down silently without giving them warning so as to try and catch them red-handed because she knew in her heart of hearts that it would happen sooner or later, but she still didn't want to believe that they could betray her. So she gave them the chance to show her their innocence, to show her what they wanted her to see and all carry on pretending that it wasn't happening.

Emma would never know if anything happened between Gabriel and Tara while she was putting Sophie to bed, but in the end, it didn't matter. All she was doing was postponing the inevitable. And deep down she knew this at the time. She acknowledged the futility of keeping guard over them, because she knew that if they wanted each other, they would find a way of having each other somehow and in any case, it almost seemed to her as if the wanting was as much an infidelity as the having.

When she walked in, she noticed that Tara had edged closer to Gabriel during her absence. Their thighs were only centimetres away from each other. She had uncrossed her legs and Emma tried not to think about the small dark triangle of space between the front hem of Tara's new dress and her bare thighs. She tried to banish the thought that Gabriel's hand might have been exploring that space moments earlier. As she had stood at the top of the stairs, the house had been silent save for Sophie's gentle snoring, but as she entered the lounge, she heard Tara saying to Gabriel, 'So, how's work going?', the sort of inane, unspecific comment you might pluck out of the air if you were anxious to show that you had been previously talking about something, anything, before you were interrupted, rather than doing what you had been doing.

Both of them looked unflustered, either innocent, or well practised in the art of deceit. It was hard to tell. There was no hurried withdrawal of a hand or slight movement away from each other or flushed cheeks. Not the slightest trace of guilt in their eyes as they both looked up at Emma as she entered the room.

'Yeah, good thanks. Quite busy, quite a few projects on,' Gabriel was replying. He looked up at Emma as she curled up in the armchair again. He smiled his beautiful smile at her. Rather than reassure her, it disheartened her through its poignancy because, like Jesus in the Garden of Gethsemane, foreseeing all that would happen, she knew now that he would betray her. 'Sophie go down all right, darling?'

'Yeah, she was exhausted.'

'Gabriel's been telling me about when he took her into town the other day and she was walking along next to him holding his hand when a lady tapped him on the shoulder and asked him if he realised that his little girl's trousers had fallen down.' Tara squealed with laughter again. It was as if she felt the need to account for their time alone or maybe Emma was just being paranoid now

'I wasn't looking at Sophie, I was just looking where I was going,' Gabriel laughed. 'I had been telling her to hurry up though as she seemed to have been dawdling quite a bit. Now I know why!'

'Poor Sophie.' Tara giggled again.

'More wine?' asked Emma.

'Yes please. I can get it though.'

'No, it's fine, don't worry. I'll go.'

Emma went back into the kitchen, leaving them alone again. A further opportunity for a lustful look or a kiss maybe. An opportunity. Was that all it was?

She returned to the lounge and handed Tara her glass. She sat back down in the armchair and they chatted about this and that, about Tara's new job and about Sophie, about the holiday in Spain, about the time a few weeks previously when Tara had met Emma's baby brother, Jack, for the first time, when Camilla had come in to Tara's beauty salon to get her nails done, until Emma found herself going out to the kitchen again to fetch the bottle of wine so that she could refill Tara's glass once again. By now Tara had got through several glasses and Emma kept topping up her glass every so often so that she could knock back another, knowing all the while that she was adding fuel to the fire and getting rid of Tara's inhibitions, if she had any. Maybe it was so that she would be able to console herself afterwards by telling herself that Tara had been drunk.

Unlike Tara, and, indeed, Gabriel, Emma had only drunk a little. She always liked to be in control of her faculties when she had Sophie with her.

Tara was laughing again, head thrown back against the back of the sofa, the palm of her hand slapping against Gabriel's thigh in a gesture of frivolity, five ovals of pink glossiness next to the faded blue of Gabriel's jeans. Emma couldn't remember what they were laughing about. The sound of her laughter, her cackle, filled the room. It seemed to fill the whole world. It sounded like the cat had caught the budgie.

That was why she didn't hear her phone ringing at first. But as Tara's laughter subsided, the electronic buzz cut through the hilarity. Emma looked at the number. Manisha.

Manisha. With Tara's visit, she had forgotten about Manisha. Manisha, Manisha. The name kept flashing in tiny letters on the screen, urging her to pick up, reminding her of the promise she had made. The baby. But it wasn't due for another week. *No, not now. Surely not now. Please not now.*

'Hi Manisha.' Emma listened to her friend's frantic talking on the other end of the line, punctuated occasionally by little moans of pain.

Snatches of Manisha's words were spinning round her head. 'Please come over.' 'In labour.' 'Parents aren't coming till Tuesday.' 'No one else I can ask.' 'Kaleem at the hospital and can't leave Lydie.'

'Sure, of course. I'll be over in about ten minutes,' she heard herself saying. As she pressed the button to end the call, she thought she caught Tara and Gabriel exchanging glances. A silent pact.

'Really sorry, guys, but I'm going to have to go to Manisha's. I'd totally forgotten about the baby. It's not due till next week and I just had it in my head that that would be when she'd have it. I promised her I'd stay and look after Lydie while she was in hospital. She's got no one else to ask. So I can't let her down.' Emma's voice tailed off. She knew she was trapped. Torn between letting a good friend down in her one hour of need and losing the only man she had ever loved. And still did. And still would. In spite of everything.

'Don't worry, I should be hitting the sack now anyway really,' Tara said. She yawned. 'I've had far too much to drink.' No suggestion of going with her. After all, she could have slept on Manisha's sofa. Tara obviously had other things on her mind.

'Sorry it's happened like this.'

'Don't be silly, it's not your fault. Anyway, we've still got tomorrow.' Tara smiled. Little did she know.

CHAPTER 10

Kaleem got back just before nine the following morning. Eyes bright, a new bounce in his step, his whole demeanour gushing with pride and happiness, bursting to tell an excited Lydie that she had a baby brother. Whistling to himself, he busied himself clearing the breakfast things away at top speed before getting Lydie ready to go to the hospital to see her new brother.

Wearily and with a feeling of impending dread that had been hanging over her ever more heavily like a ball and chain since she had woken at four that morning, Emma went upstairs to collect up the few things that she had hurriedly packed back at Gabriel's the previous evening. Before she had left in the taxi for the hospital, Manisha had told her to make herself at home in the spare room. However, Emma had hardly slept, sordid visions of Gabriel and Tara's entwined bodies spinning in a vertiginous vortex in all the dark, empty places in her brain whenever she had closed her eyes.

In an unprecedented show of exuberance, Kaleem threw his arms around her before she left. 'Thank you so much for coming round. I don't know what we'd have done without you.'

'It's fine. It was no trouble. Lydie's been as good as gold.' She turned to Lydie, who was standing beside Kaleem and holding onto his knee. Their facial resemblance was striking. They had the same aquiline nose and ever-so-slightly pouting lips. Emma wondered if the new baby would too. 'You'll have to bring baby Roshan round to see us soon, Lydie. I'm sure Sophie would love to meet him.'

Lydie looked at Emma between her long, dark eyelashes that almost looked as if they had been artificially curled. She beamed at her and nodded.

'Say goodbye to Emma now then.' Kaleem scooped his daughter up into his arms.

'Bye Emma!' Lydie shouted, opening and closing her palms in a childish wave.

'Bye. See you soon. Have fun with Roshan. I'm sure he'll love his big sister.' Emma turned to walk out of the door. When she reached the street, she called out again, waving to Lydie over the privet hedge that marked the boundary of their front garden. 'Bye!'

Finally, as she reached the end of the hedge, out of the corner of her eye she saw the door close behind her and heard the click of the latch. As she carried on walking away from their house, she imagined the excited preparations going on inside and then Kaleem carrying Lydie into the ward and the two of them sitting on the edge of Manisha's bed, Roshan in his mother's arms and Lydie bending over him, a faint furrow of curiosity shadowing her brow and her huge, dark eyes shining with excitement. Then it was Sophie she was imagining sitting beside Gabriel, bent over a baby that Emma cradled in her arms. His baby.

She walked on, lost in thought. The wind had died down overnight and today looked as if it would be quite different from yesterday. The dew on the grass shone gold in the sunshine and the shadows everywhere formed an identical city. A parallel city that looked as if it should resonate with a metallic ping of hollowness if you tapped it with your fingernail; that might blow down if you breathed too hard, or dissolve into puddles of emptiness if it started to spit with rain or if you cried.

As she turned the corner of the street, she noticed up ahead a small swarm of people in dark suits and dresses, solemn and subdued, gathered outside the little church further up the street. A funeral. It was early in the day for a funeral. For some reason, the hearse was parked on the opposite side of the narrow street and four coffin bearers, backs bent under the weight, heads bowed reverentially, were shuffling out of the church door across the road towards the hearse. One of the four men was a little shorter than the others so that the coffin tilted to one side irreverently.

Emma instinctively slowed her pace, but she realised that unless she stopped walking altogether, she would soon reach the group of mourners before they had loaded the coffin into the hearse. The street was empty otherwise. Ahead of her, one of the women let out a raucous sob that seemed to linger in the air, hovering like a wounded bird above the silent group. A second woman enfolded her in her arms and Emma could hear her say in a low voice, 'He's happy now. He's with her.' A bereaved daughter, perhaps.

The daughter remained locked in the woman's embrace, her body convulsed with sobs that she had perhaps tried to contain during the service and could hold in no longer now that they had come outside. They were standing beside the hearse and taking up the pavement. Emma waited dutifully, awkwardly, for the woman to release the daughter and move aside, but they still clung to each other. So she was obliged to walk round the hearse into which they had just finished loading the coffin, into the middle of the road and in between the rest of the mourners who were spread across the road. A couple of them watched her as she hurried on, embarrassed, head lowered, mumbling an apology as she passed by.

When she opened the door, the silence in the house blared like a trumpet in her ears. It smelt stale and the heavy curtains in the lounge were still closed. The sunlight was pounding on them like drumsticks, making them glow, making them burn. An empty wine bottle stood on the coffee table along with three glasses. One of them was still half-full. It must be her own that she hadn't had time to finish before Manisha called. And there was Tara, stretched out on the sofa underneath the throw, one arm bent under her head, her mouth slightly open, dead to the world. Even then she was still exquisitely beautiful.

Emma put her key down gently on the chest of drawers in the hall and her eyes were irresistibly drawn upstairs. The same seedy glow bathed the landing. She could see from the bottom of the stairs that the bedroom doors were shut. She couldn't understand where Sophie was. She looked at the digital clock flashing under the television in the lounge. 9:55. She would normally have been up a few hours by now. Maybe she had woken early and Gabriel had put her back to bed for a sleep. But there was no sign of breakfast in the kitchen. And there were no toys out anywhere.

Tara stirred in the lounge. She turned over to face the back of the sofa. Even in the dim light, Emma could see that she had a red mark like a scar along her cheek from where she had been lying on her arm. Her breathing settled down again, hushed and regular.

Emma climbed the stairs slowly. She pushed down on the handle of their bedroom, pulling it towards her as she pushed open the door so that it wouldn't make a noise. Gabriel was sprawled across the bed on his back, his lower body on his side of the bed and his head on Emma's pillow on her side. He was snoring softly. The duvet was pulled up as far as the top of his boxers and Emma could see the dark shadow of hair above them. For a moment she was tempted to get in with him. But she should check on Sophie first. She could see the red light of the baby monitor glowing on her bedside table.

She crossed the landing, stepping carefully over the floorboard that creaked, as she had done hundreds of times before. She pushed down on the door handle and the door swung open gently. It was darker in this room because the blackout blind was pulled down, but she could make out the outline of Sophie in her cot. She stepped towards her, her eyes adjusting to the dim light.

Something was wrong. Emma could sense it even before she was near enough to hear Sophie's rasping, shallow gasps of breath and see her tiny chest rising and falling much faster than usual, like a balloon that keeps deflating because the person blowing is not inhaling deeply enough. Emma felt her own heartbeat start to quicken as a sickening wave of dread took hold of her with all the force of a bullet entering her body. She reached down to touch Sophie's cheek. It was burning hot. She touched the little hand that rested casually on top of the covers. The little hand that would often reach up to seek her own. Cold. Cold like it had just been making snowballs. She picked her up, the weight and shape of her body so familiar beneath her hands. Her head flopped forwards like a rag doll's. Like her plastic doll that could cry and laugh, Sophie's eyes flicked open and shut once as Emma said her name, quietly, insistently. They were unfocussed, unrecognising, uncomprehending. She wished she could flick a switch at the top of her back to turn her back on. Or change the batteries.

She was saying her name louder now. She felt like shaking her. She still wouldn't wake up. Then she was shouting *his* name. Screaming it like she was being strangled. She couldn't catch her breath between shouts. Her voice sounded unfamiliar, like it didn't belong to her.

She clasped her floppy doll against her chest and ran out of the room. Woken by Emma's voice on the monitor, he was already there, bleary-eyed, sleep still clinging to him like a ghoul that he couldn't shake off, staggering out of their bedroom door on the other side of the landing, as if his somnolent body couldn't respond quickly enough to what his brain was telling it.

'Call an ambulance!'

He looked at her, at Sophie, trying to take it in. As if he was still trying to establish whether he was properly awake.

'For God's sake, Gabriel, call an ambulance! She won't wake up!' She glanced down at Sophie and his eyes followed hers, confused, disbelieving, almost playful. Her voice was high-pitched, shrill, beseeching.

'But…'

'Just call a fucking ambulance!'

It was as if the penny suddenly dropped as Gabriel scrambled back to his bedside table where his phone was lying. Emma stood on the landing as he dialled the number. Awoken by the commotion, Tara came slinking up the stairs in her satiny dressing gown, her face a question. 'What's up, Ems?'

'She won't wake up!' In the background, Emma could hear Gabriel giving their address, his voice seemingly matter-of-fact, composed, although she could detect its barely perceptible edge of panic as reality tightened its stifling grip. She could feel the tears pricking her eyes now.

'She won't wake up, she won't wake up,' she repeated, her voice unsteady, tremulous, as a rivulet of tears started to spill down each cheek.

'But she was fine in the night.'

'I guess she wouldn't have cried. You wouldn't have heard her downstairs anyway.' The words seemed to stick in her throat as she struggled to catch her breath between sobs.

Tara was coiling the end of her belt around her forefinger. 'I guess not.'

Gabriel had rung off. 'They'll be here in a few minutes, darling. I'd better get dressed.'

'Maybe I should go home and leave you guys to it. I'll just be in the way if I stay.' Tara was still winding and unwinding the belt round her finger. 'You need to be able to focus on Sophie.'

'OK. We'll have to arrange another weekend.'

'Yeah, when Sophie's better.'

'Yes.' Emma's cheeks were wet with tears as they both looked at Sophie, whose body was inert apart from her chest, which was struggling with the effort of breathing.

'I'll go and get dressed and get all my things together then. Take care, Ems. Thanks for having me. Hope you get on OK at the hospital. Let me know how she is, won't you?' Emma nodded, stifling a sob. Tara released her finger from the belt, letting it unravel again. She hugged Emma and stroked Sophie's hair gently, as if she were an ancient china doll that might shatter into a thousand pieces.

Then she turned and started to descend the stairs slowly. When she was halfway down, Gabriel stuck his head round their bedroom door. 'Bye Tara.'

As she swung round to look at him, her hair swished against the satin of her dressing gown and the ghost of a smile toyed with the corners of her lips and flickered around her eyes, those heavenly eyes still heavy with yesterday's smudged mascara, those almost dazzling blue eyes that made you feel special if they were looking at you.

Then he added as an afterthought, 'Just close the front door behind you when you leave. We'll take the key.'

'OK. Bye Gabes.' She turned back round and padded down the rest of the stairs, her bright pink toenails clearly visible in the murky half-light. She disappeared through the doorway into the lounge. Emma heard the door close quietly. The next time she saw Tara, she would no longer be her friend.

They could hear the haunting wail of the siren filling the still-somnolent street, swelling to a monstrous fortissimo as the ambulance approached the house, and from her position at the top of the stairs, Emma could see a hazy flash of neon blue through the semicircle of frosted triangular glass panels, like five segments of an orange, at the top of the front door. The gravid silence after the siren had stopped was broken by a loud rap on the door, which made Emma jump, even though she was expecting it. It all felt surreal, as if it couldn't possibly be happening to her. The barrage of questions the two paramedics were firing at her, their hurried movements as they examined Sophie, had an oneiric quality for Emma, making her feel as if she were simply a bemused bystander, uninvolved in the preposterous, hideous events that were unfolding around her.

Later on they explained to her, gently, deliberately, that it was pneumococcal meningitis. Leading to renal failure. The infection that took hold of Sophie's tiny body and ravaged all its defence mechanisms. Emma couldn't have done anything to prevent it. She mustn't blame herself. Children can go downhill extremely rapidly. They did all they could for Sophie. They couldn't have done any more. The most likely cause was the ear infection that Sophie had had a couple of weeks before. They weren't to know that it would lead to meningitis, were they? Children pick up things like that all the time, don't they?

There were a couple of spots on Sophie's chest when the paramedic examined her. Purple and livid, like tiny pinch marks to start off with. Emma hadn't noticed them before, but then she hadn't thought to check her for spots. She had been panicking too much. And Sophie had her sleepsuit on. *Sleepsuits were awkward to get on and off, weren't they?* The paramedic told her that the spots had probably only just appeared anyway, that she shouldn't feel bad for not noticing them herself. The spots quickly grew in size, soon looking like little bruises, multiplying all over Sophie's body so that by the time the ambulance pulled up at the door of A&E, they had become too numerous to count. They whisked her daughter away on a trolley that seemed enormous, Emma having to run to keep up. On the way to Resus, Sophie started fitting, her tiny body overpowered by convulsions that Emma found too appalling to watch.

She felt useless, stripped of all her status as a mother, as the waiting medical team pounced on her daughter's lifeless body, shouting instructions to each other, stabbing at her fragile, unresponsive body with needles, strewing it with wires, frantically shoving plastic tubes up her nose and down her throat.

She was gripping his hand so hard it left marks on it afterwards. He had driven in the car to the hospital to meet her. The beeping sound of the alarms on the machines was filling her head. It seemed deafening to her, as if that was the only sound in the world right now. They waited near the door and watched wordlessly as the doctors did CPR on Sophie. This was it, she thought to herself. This was as bad as it gets. Critical. Make or break time. She could hear them counting. If she concentrated hard enough, maybe it would bring her back to life. The effort of willing her to stay alive was etched all over the doctors' faces. Faces that over the years had perfected the art of appearing calm in a crisis, but Emma could see the panic desperately struggling to contain itself behind their eyes. She wanted to scream at them that there must be something else they can do, those doctors who were meant to make people better. Earlier on, the nurses had tried half-heartedly to usher them outside the room with a veneer of normality fixed like masks to their faces, but in the urgency of that awful moment, no one had seemed to have either the time or the inclination to turf them out completely and Emma and Gabriel had lingered, mesmerised, horrified, helpless, feeling as if their bodies had turned inside out, watching the doctors fight to save Sophie, as if they were glued reluctantly, but irresistibly, to the most appalling horror movie.

Relentlessly, tirelessly, the doctors carried on for twenty minutes or so pumping Sophie's chest and counting. They did everything they could, but at the end of that time, Sophie still had no pulse and the doctors finally agreed among themselves that it was useless to continue. The bloodcurdling sound of Emma's scream sliced through the subdued atmosphere like a scalpel. Her legs were giving way. They weren't hers. Her body crumpled. It didn't belong to her. She wasn't here. This wasn't happening.

Gabriel was supporting her. He was holding her up, steering her out of the room, like a puppeteer with a stupid puppet on strings that has no will of its own and no control of its own body. There was a nurse holding her other arm, talking gently to her. Emma didn't know what she was saying. They led her into a side room where her body was finally allowed to collapse onto a chair in a heap. The nurse left them. She put her hand on Emma's arm in a gesture of sympathy as she passed her, but Emma didn't feel it. They were alone now. Emma buried her head in Gabriel's jumper. It smelt familiar. She loved that smell. He had his arms round her. He was rocking her from side to side like a baby. She felt safe. She cried like a baby until she was empty, numb. He was still rocking her. She wanted him to carry on rocking her forever.

They let her back in to see Sophie and she sat with her for a while. They had taken all the tubes out of her, but the rash was still there, triumphant and unmistakable, covering every inch of her beautiful body. It had finally got the upper hand. She looked like she was sleeping. She looked peaceful. Emma touched her cheek. It was still slightly warm.

Somehow, he managed to drive her home. They sat in silence, stunned, trying to absorb the shock. Outside it was getting dark. Saturday evening. People were getting ready to go out for the evening. Happy, carefree. Emma watched out of the car window with blank, unseeing eyes. When they got back to the house Gabriel led her like a frail old woman into the lounge. He made her a cup of tea overloaded with sugar.

Tara had straightened the throw on the sofa and opened the curtains before she left. Gabriel shut them again, enclosing them in their cocoon of pain as if they were the only two people in the world. He held her as they sat on the sofa together staring at the walls, uncomprehending. They remained like that for several hours, until the stars had come out and the late-night revellers were returning home, whooping and laughing as they walked past the bay window. She didn't hear them. She didn't hear anything but the diabolical voice in her head telling her that her daughter was dead. But she couldn't believe it. She wouldn't believe it.

They stayed there all night, keeping an unspoken vigil for her daughter. Gabriel played the part of the doting boyfriend to perfection. He was gentle, he was strong. She was a precious object, a fragile antique that had been broken and needed piecing together again with the utmost care. For a while, he fell asleep sitting upright, with his head propped against a cushion in the corner of the sofa and she huddled up against him and slept a few fitful minutes here and there, her eyes unable to stay open any longer.

Dawn broke and the light behind the curtains changed imperceptibly from the mellow orange of the street lamps to the garish lemony light of a sunny September morning. He made her another cup of tea and some toast, as she hadn't eaten since having breakfast with Lydie the previous morning. At his insistence, she forced herself to take a few bites which she chewed painstakingly slowly, like an invalid, without tasting anything.

He opened the curtains and let the acidic, brutal light flood the room. They squinted, their cocoon stripped away, surprised at the existence of another world beyond their own. She closed her eyes, unwilling to contemplate another reality that she knew she would have to face at some point, but the light had been enough to stimulate the cogs of her brain, which had ceased turning the moment Sophie had died, into sluggish activity once again. And little by little, questions began to germinate in her mind, at first formless, but which then took shape as words. She put down her plate and forced a dry chewed-up ball of toast down her throat before speaking.

'Had she not woken up at all before I came back?'

Gabriel looked at her. It was the first time she had spoken since yesterday.

'I don't think so, darling. I mean, I didn't hear her at all.' He cleared his throat and shifted position on the sofa slightly.

She turned and looked at him properly for the first time since the previous morning. His hair was a mess, much more of a mess than usual, the whites of his eyes were bloodshot and dark shadows hung loosely below them. The stubble pricked through the skin around his mouth like tiny pieces of wire. He looked older than she remembered.

But she pounced on him, as if she had been lying in wait, as if she had finally got all her wits about her again. 'What do you mean, you don't think so? You had the monitor on all night, didn't you?'

'Yeah, of course I did. I mean, I was asleep, so unless she had cried, I might not have heard her if she woke up. That's all.'

Emma seemed to reflect on what he had said for a moment before continuing. 'Did you check on her before you went to bed last night?'

He was picking at the bits of wool that had clumped together on his jumper and pulling them off. He stopped, his hand in mid-air, a tiny clump of wool between his thumb and forefinger.

'Pardon?' She could tell he was buying time. She could see his brain frantically whirring behind his eyes like clockwork.

'I said, did you check on her last night before you went to bed?' Her voice sounded impatient, fearful. She already knew what his answer would be, but she wanted him to say it out loud.

'Well, not exactly.' He rubbed his thumb and forefinger together above the carpet, letting the tiny pellet of grey wool fall.

She pounced again. The numbness inside her had subsided a little now and she could feel anger creeping up her spine. She needed answers. 'What do you mean, not exactly? Either you did or you didn't. It's pretty straightforward. So, did you or didn't you?'

'No, I didn't. I'm sorry. There we have it. I didn't check on her before I went to bed.'

'Why not?' Her tone was rising. She needed someone to blame. To take it all out on.

'Well, I'd had a bit too much to drink. You know I did. We all did.'

'Yes, well, *I* didn't, because I never do...' She tailed off. 'Did when I was looking after Sophie.'

'I know, but we didn't know you were going to have to look after Lydie last night, did we? What, was I always meant to stay sober just in case you got a phone call out of the blue saying you had to go out suddenly?' He was struggling to keep his composure.

'No, but how much effort would it have taken to put your head round the door of her room before you went to bed? Were you with *her*? Is that why you didn't look in on Sophie? You *were* with her, weren't you?'

'No, I promise you, darling, I wasn't.' He was looking her in the eye. Unerring, reassuring, unnerving, challenging her not to believe him. 'Not this again, Ems. I already told you, I don't fancy her. Tara went to sleep on the sofa and I went up to bed by myself. You saw us both asleep when you came in yesterday morning. We just went our separate ways. It must only have been about half an hour after you left, anyway. I don't think anything would have happened to Sophie in that short space of time.'

'No, maybe not, but she obviously started to go downhill at some point in the night, didn't she?' Emma shot him an irate glance.

'Well, don't go pointing the finger at me. Maybe you should have thought to take her to the doctor on Friday when she was off her food.'

'Oh, don't be stupid. Are you telling me that every time a baby is off its food, or cries a bit more than usual, it means it's going to get meningitis? How was I to know?' Her voice was starting to crack. Gabriel had touched a raw nerve. She blamed herself partly, and always would, for Sophie's death. Which parent wouldn't? She couldn't keep up the tirade. She couldn't keep up the pretence of being stronger than she was. She was breaking. 'And maybe you shouldn't have had such a lie-in yesterday. It was five to ten when I got back. I remember seeing the time on the DVD player. How could you have carried on sleeping so long without noticing that Sophie hadn't woken up?' Her cheeks were wet with tears. She could taste the salt.

Gabriel continued, relentless. Eager to defend himself, to exonerate himself. 'Well, excuse me for having a lie-in at the weekend. It's OK for you. You get to have one every day of the week after I've got up for work. I couldn't help being asleep, could I? I couldn't make myself wake up.'

They were flinging the blame from one to the other, like stinging slaps in each other's faces, unwilling to admit to being in any way responsible for Sophie's death, the burden of their guilt too ponderous to shoulder alone. 'Well, I just know that there would have been no way I'd have carried on sleeping that long. What was it, over three hours after Sophie normally wakes up? I know that I would have woken up long before then wondering why she wasn't awake yet.'

His features were contorted with spite, with anguish. 'Well, forgive me for not being as perfect as you. Anyway, perhaps you've forgotten, she's *your* daughter, not mine.'

'Was.'

'Oh Ems, I'm so sorry. I shouldn't have said that. Forgive me.' He swept her up in his arms and his jumper.

'It's OK. I shouldn't have been so quick to judge. I'm taking it all out on you when I know you're hurting too.' Sobbing, she buried her face in his jumper in the hope that the pain wouldn't find her.

CHAPTER 11

She should call her mum. And her dad. Let them know. They would want to know. She had said she would let Tara know as well, but she didn't want to tell anyone yet. It would make it seem too real. She didn't want anyone's sympathy. She wanted them to carry on their lives as usual, as if nothing had happened. She didn't want to hear their shock. Wasn't ready to answer their questions. She was too much of a wreck to be coherent enough to tell them. She wouldn't know where to start. Wouldn't be able to get her words out. Later. Yes, she would do it later.

She took a shower. Tried to maintain some sort of ludicrous pretence at normality. She turned the temperature dial right down. She wanted to feel something other than this pain that was gnawing away at her, eating her alive from the inside out. She took sharp intakes of breath and shuddered at the cold water which mingled with her salty tears in the shower tray.

The door into Sophie's room had been wide open when she had come upstairs, just as they had left it yesterday morning, and she had closed it gently, not bearing to look into the darkened room where a rectangular outline of daylight surrounding the curtains begged to be let in, like a dog left out in the cold whining and pawing at the door, waiting for someone to open it, and where Sophie's cot stood, the sheets disturbed from when

Emma, panic-stricken, had snatched her out of bed, the slight indent of her head still on the mattress.

Later in the afternoon, Gabriel announced he was going to bed to try and get some sleep and she followed him, zombie-like, up the stairs. He undressed down to his underwear. She watched him, mesmerised, as if for the first time, then copied him. They lay down side by side in the bed which was still unmade from yesterday. He turned towards her and gently pulled her close, wrapping his arms around her. She could feel him hardening against her and in spite of everything, she wanted him. Her mind was a spinning-top of emotions. She felt guilty for wanting him now; it felt as if she was betraying Sophie in some way, but her body was crying out for him with an urgency that she couldn't ignore, was crying out to feel him inside her driving away all the pain. They made love with a voracity that they hadn't experienced for a long time and which dispelled momentarily all their feelings of guilt at the seemingly sordid thing they were doing. For a few brief moments, they were oblivious to everything but each other, everything but satisfying their lust. When she kissed him, his face was wet, but she didn't know whether they were his tears or her own that she could taste. Afterwards, the guilt started to nip away at her once again like a rat under the covers and she suddenly felt dirty and defiled. She moved away from him and from the wet patch on her pillow, and lay there, staring at the wall, her emotions wrung out, until sleep, tormented and restless, took hold of her exhausted body at last.

When she opened her eyes again, it took her a split second to remember. A split second of peace before all the memories came sweeping back into her head like demons. She wondered how long she had slept. It was still light outside, but it was the orangey, golden light of early evening. She didn't know what time they had come up to bed anyway. She didn't know anything any more.

She lay without moving. Gabriel was still asleep. She could tell by his steady, raspy breathing. She closed her eyes again, trying to shut out the world for a few more moments, trying to shut out reality. She heard a low buzzing sound above her head and opened her eyes. She raised them slightly and there was the fly, brainless, emotionless, uncomplicated. It landed beside her pillow, rubbing its front legs together.

And that was when she saw it. How had she not noticed it before? Glinting in the narrow, citrine shaft of afternoon sunlight that was stretching from the chink between the curtains right to the other side of the bed. Right next to her pillow, where the fly was now skittering.

An earring. With a clear blue stone. It was making pretty patterns on the wall where the light was catching it. Tara's earring. One from the pair Emma had given her two Christmases ago.

She continued to lie there, motionless, watching the fly, watching the earring. Letting it sink in, letting her mind slowly put two and two together. Her mind, that was too sore and too full already to be able to absorb and process further information easily. The first realisation – that Tara had been in that bed – did not hurt as much as it would otherwise have done. It was what she had suspected deep down all along anyway, although she had refused to let herself believe it, desperately clinging onto the hope that Gabriel still loved her and that that would be enough. And what was the betrayal of the man she loved and of her best friend compared to the death of her daughter? It didn't matter now. All that mattered was that Sophie was gone. She couldn't hurt any more than she was already hurting. It was the next realisation – that, in all probability, Sophie had become gravely ill while in Gabriel's care and while he and Tara were screwing each other – that struck her like a stab in the heart. That he must have hardly slept for the first part of the night, which would explain his lie-in the following morning when Sophie's condition was critical.

She lay there for a while, stifled by her feelings and her thoughts, which were indistinct and nebulous. Her mind was racing round and round like a cyclone trying to gain momentum. Now and then an emotion or a memory, from yesterday or from last month, maybe, or from her childhood, which seemed so distant and removed now that it felt as if it belonged to someone else, would resurface randomly, dreamlike and vivid, to the forefront of her mind out of the vertiginous kaleidoscope of forgotten images that she had accumulated over the years. Her emotions were so raw, and so acute, but at the same time, so numerous that her body felt numb, as if it had shut down, unable to take any more. She was hurting so much that nothing felt real any more.

She turned over cautiously so as not to wake Gabriel. He looked peaceful as he slept, his body turned towards her, the arm on top muscular and outstretched as if reaching out for her, his mouth slightly open, his eyelashes long and lustrous in the soft light of a sinking sun. She suddenly felt the urge to touch them, but resisted the feeling lest she wake him, and carried on watching him as if committing to memory the position of every freckle, the shape of his eyebrows, his cheekbones, the expression of his lips. *How could he sleep so peacefully after what he had done?* Part of her still loved him, and always would, but she knew that she could never forgive him, that the spectre of that night could never be shaken off and would forever overshadow any future relationship between them. Without even having to ask herself the question, she knew she had to leave. She knew that she must try to start again no matter how hard that would be. Even though her life was in ruins and she had nothing left. Nothing.

She must leave him. She must pack all her things and go. Go home. Now.

She slipped out of bed and silently slid her holdall out from underneath. She didn't want to wake him, didn't want a confrontation. She didn't want it to end like that. She wanted to remember him as he was now. She looked at him again. Click. Another snapshot right there for the album inside her head. The last one. The one that would have its own separate place away from all the other happy images.

She threw on her clothes that she had discarded on the floor beside the bed and opened the drawers and the wardrobe doors slowly, being careful not to make too much noise, gathering up her clothes in silent armfuls and stuffing them into the holdall. Haphazardly, she took a few of her bottles from the top of the chest of drawers, eyeing Gabriel cautiously as they clinked together. He turned over and settled into a new sleeping position, his breathing clear and uninhibited now.

Quickly, systematically, she collected up all her things that littered the bathroom, the things that said that she lived there too, that she belonged there. Her toothbrush on the sink next to Gabriel's, her shampoo in the shower, her contraceptive pills in the cabinet. Not that she would be needing them now, anyway. She looked around. There was no trace of her now. Only Sophie's things. Her little sparkly toothbrush and toothpaste, her bubble bath in the corner of the bath, a net of bath toys hanging on the side. She left them where they were. Gabriel would have to sort them out. Throw them away. And then the bathroom would be his again. She doubted it would be long before he shared it with another woman and *her* things would be where Emma's had once been.

She padded back into the bedroom. She looked at Gabriel and imprinted the image in her mind again for the last time. Then she bent over him and kissed his forehead gently, like a butterfly skimming a flower, so as not to wake him. She placed the earring on his bedside table so that he would know when he woke up. She picked up her holdall and turned away towards the door. She didn't look back. She had no tears left to cry.

She walked down the stairs for the last time and took her handbag from the floor in the hall where she had dumped it when they got back from the hospital. She left her key on the hall table. Then she opened the door and walked out into the evening. The sun was low in the sky, glinting off the dirty russet leaves on the pavement, making them shiny and gold. She squinted at the brightness without noticing it. She closed the door gently behind her. She heard the latch click. Click.

She walked down the street without seeing, without hearing, without comprehending. She no longer recognised her surroundings. Hers was a parallel world of despair and desolation. There was nothing else but the blackness, the bleakness, inside her own head. Images of Sophie at the hospital kept replaying themselves over and over inside her mind like snatches of a song that you can't get out of your head. Sophie unconscious, with tubes and drips violating her tiny body which was fighting to stay alive. She couldn't remember what she had looked like before. Only two days before. She kept thinking, what if? What if Tara hadn't come down that weekend? What if she and Gabriel hadn't ended up in bed together? What if she'd read the signs the day before when Sophie had been off her food and taken her to the doctor, as Gabriel had suggested when they were arguing this morning? His voice was still ringing in her ears. Grating. Whining. Accusing. Was it all her own fault that Sophie was dead? What if Manisha hadn't gone into labour that evening? Manisha. She would be home now with her perfect family. Home, but not home. But Emma would give anything to be in her shoes right now.

Somehow she ended up at the bus stop and staggered up into the bus when it arrived. Somehow she told the driver where she was going. When he asked her for the fare, she tipped all the change out of her purse and stood there staring at him, uncomprehending, while he took the coins one at a time as if she were an old woman who had left her glasses at home, counting out each coin that he slid into his other hand with his chubby forefinger that had dirt stacked up behind its nail. It reminded her of her dad's fingers. He thrust the ticket into her hand dismissively, shaking his head and raising his eyebrows at her with an exasperated sigh before turning to the next person in the queue.

She stumbled into a seat as the bus set off, clutching the holdall on her lap. It was still unzipped and the sleeve of one of her tops was hanging out. She made no attempt to tuck it back inside or to fasten the bag. Oblivious to the bus's metallic rattle which reverberated through every bone in her body, she stared unseeing out of the grimy window beside her as in a matter of minutes, the familiar streets where she had spent some of the best times of her life sped away behind her in a blur. In her jumble of incoherent thoughts, one was nagging her more than the others at that moment. She wondered whether Gabriel had woken up yet.

CHAPTER 12

It was dark by the time the train reached her stop. In spite of herself, she had been struggling to stay awake on the journey. Her senses were dull and her eyelids kept drooping enticingly as she stared out at the inky blackness, punctuated now and then by the soft, orangey glow of street lights and lit-up houses as the train hurtled relentlessly past towns and villages. It was warm and quiet inside the carriage and with its gentle rocking motion, it felt to Emma as if she were in a giant cradle. The few other passengers around her were asleep or reading or engrossed in their laptops or phones. No one took any notice of the freckled girl with the auburn hair and the empty eyes clutching at her holdall with its dangling sleeve, and slumped against the window as she gazed out into the night. She was protected from the world for a while. She was in an in-between place where the pain couldn't find her.

The chilly night air nipped at her like a savage dog when she emerged, as if out of a dream, from the train. She shivered, realising that she had left her coat back at Gabriel's.

She didn't call her mum to ask her to pick her up. She didn't want to have to tell her there, at the station, in front of inquisitive onlookers casting surreptitious, greedy glances. There were a couple of taxis waiting outside the station and she got into one, mumbling her address to the driver. He smelt of stale smoke and hummed along to the radio as he drove along the familiar roads home.

He stopped in front of her house and she held out a note to him, slipping the change absent-mindedly into the back pocket of her jeans. She stood aside as he reversed into the driveway and sped off back towards the town.

The silhouette of the house loomed ahead of her. Unimposing, unremarkable, built in the same style as the houses on either side of it and the houses either side of those. Everything seemed peaceful, normal, as it should be. There was nothing to indicate that a bombshell was about to be dropped on its occupant. The lounge light was still on and even from the road, she could make out the shape of her mother's head. She must be sitting on the sofa in front of the television.

In the silence, the noise of the gravel crunching under Emma's feet seemed to fill every corner of the night. As she approached the front window, she paused to look in at her mother. She had dozed off, her head lowered towards her chest as if it had toppled off her neck, and her mouth slightly open. Her hands were loose and floppy in her lap, the palms upturned towards the ceiling like a sleeping baby's. Emma could see the slow rise and fall of her chest. She looked vulnerable and for a moment, Emma hesitated and forgot her own grief at the anticipation of her mother's. In the half-darkness, she hesitated at the door, after fumbling to find the key in her bag, poised to insert it into the hole, but unwilling to shatter her mother's peace, reluctant to cause her suffering.

As the key turned in the lock, she pictured her mother waking up at the sound, confused, alarmed, and staggering out into the hall. Emma pushed open the door and there she was, eyes wide, a question.

'Oh darling, it's you.' For a second she sounded relieved, but then all at once she took in Emma's wounded expression, her crumpled bearing, her holdall with the dangling sleeve. The absence of her granddaughter.

'What are you doing here? Is something wrong? Where's Sophie?' Her voice was trembling already, panicky. Rather than reach out to sweep Emma into her arms, as she normally would, she stood back and waited for her to answer, dread clouding her features.

Emma lunged forward at her mother, taking her by surprise so that she was forced to take a step backwards to steady herself, and buried her head in her shoulder. 'She's dead, Mum, she's dead.' Emma's body gave way and gratified, sank to the floor in a heap, her hand releasing the holdall, which thudded onto the carpet beside her.

She clung to her mother's legs like a small child and looked up at her, tears making her cheeks shiny wet. 'Mum, she's dead, Sophie's dead!' She was almost shouting it, as if that would make her mother understand.

Her mother took a moment to respond, to absorb what her daughter was telling her. 'What do you mean? How?' Her lip was quivering and in the space of a few seconds, her breathing had become quick and shallow.

Emma was blubbing like a baby. The pain she had been keeping in during her journey was all spilling over now. Her words came out like hiccups so her mother had to strain to hear what she was telling her. 'They said it was meningitis. It was so sudden. It was horrific. They couldn't save her, they couldn't save my baby.'

She let go of her mother and sat with her knees pushed up towards her chin and her head on her knees, moaning as if in terrible pain.

Her mother sank to the floor and sat down next to her, wrapping her arms around her, as much to seek comfort for herself as for her daughter.

'Oh my God. Sophie, Sophie… How can it be true? When did she…?' She couldn't say the word yet and the question hung in the air apologetically.

'Yesterday. I left her at the hospital. Mum, how could I have left her? She's all alone there. They'll bring her back, won't they? She needs to be here with us.'

'Yes, of course they will. Don't worry about that, darling. Come on, you can't stay here like this.' And she struggled to get up before helping Emma to her feet, and they tottered arm in arm, two broken women, into the lounge, where the television was still blaring, slumping down side by side on the sofa, their glazed, unseeing eyes drawn irresistibly to the flickering screen.

After a few minutes, after their sobs had subsided a little, her mother switched the television off and asked Emma in a shaky voice whether she was ready to tell her what had happened. So Emma told her about Manisha going into labour, about finding Sophie unconscious in her cot, about the hospital, about Tara and Gabriel and the earring. She talked and her mother listened with big, streaming eyes, sometimes leaning over to hug her daughter or to stroke her arm when she struggled to get the dreadful words out.

They stayed there all night, as she and Gabriel had done the previous evening, talking and crying and comforting each other. Now and then, Emma's exhausted body succumbed to sleep as she nestled into her mother, but she would wake up minutes later, her heart pounding and her face drenched with tears. Her mother was always awake when Emma looked up at her, silent tears rolling down her cheeks, each one a bloated, glistening globule full of pain, lost in thought as she stared at the faded school photo of Emma, who was looking sideways at the camera shyly, her mouth smiling but not her eyes, in a gilded wooden frame on the wall opposite. Emma remembered having the photo taken. It was a long time ago. In another lifetime. They had queued up class by class in alphabetical order in the hall. The photographer had hung up a black curtain behind one of those plastic school chairs by the windows, but you couldn't see the curtain in the photo. Instead, the image of her had been transposed onto a grainy blue background with flecks of white that was supposed to look a bit like the sky. You could watch the people ahead of you in the queue having their photo taken. After her name had been called out, she had sat there self-consciously with her hands in her lap, feeling half a dozen or so pairs of amused eyes on her, hearing a snigger from one of the boys who was waiting his turn, and assuming rightly or wrongly that she was the cause of it. Her cheeks were flushed in the photo. She remembered that it was warm in the hall and she had had to keep her prickly school jumper on for the photo, but it could also have been out of embarrassment. She must have looked so ill at ease that, she remembered, the photographer laughed and said to her, 'Cheer up, love, it may never happen.' But it did happen. The photographer fiddled about with his camera and called to her to smile, then started a countdown from three. Three, two, one. Click. The photo was taken. It was weird because on the one hand, it felt like a lifetime ago, but on the other, she could remember all the details as if it were yesterday. And there was the photo still on the wall. A moment frozen in time.

They let her mother take a couple of weeks off work to pull herself together and to help Emma with the funeral arrangements. It was on a Friday afternoon in the church down the road, opposite Emma's old primary school. She had often walked past it with Sophie on her way to the park. It was a fine late-autumn day and the sun glinted off the glossy black hearse that waited on the driveway. There was a keen breeze, however, that sent the clouds racing across the sky and reminded you that winter was just around the corner. As Emma stepped out of the house, a flock of birds flying high above the front garden caught her eye. They were dazzling in the sunshine and each time the flock changed direction, it flickered as the birds' wings caught the light. Her mother had to touch her arm gently to signal to her that the driver was holding the car door open for them and it was time to start the short, slow procession to the church.

It was barely half-full. A handful of relatives occupied the first few wooden pews on either side of the aisle. She, her mother and father and Camilla sat together on one of the front pews.

The cold seemed to emanate from deep inside the wood of the benches and the shafts of sunlight streaming through the stained-glass windows onto the sparse congregation seemed to make little difference to the temperature. Her father and Camilla had left Jack with Camilla's mother. *Thank God.* Emma didn't know whether they had left him for her sake or for his. Or both. She wouldn't have been able to abide the sound of him crying or, worse still, chortling and cooing.

Then in the far corner of the church sitting on the back pew was Gabriel. She didn't know he was there till the end of the service when she noticed him through a veil of tears as they filed out to the cacophonous wheezing of the little organ, behind the tiny white coffin. He was looking at her. It felt as if he was trying to catch her eye, but she turned away quickly, towards the coffin, trying not to reveal her shock.

She didn't see him again after that. He wasn't at the graveside or the wake later. Afterwards, she wished she had looked his way. One last time. She didn't know how he had found out about the funeral, but she knew that coming all that way for her and for Sophie was his way of trying to make amends somehow.

CHAPTER 13

That bleak, grey winter was a jumble of bad days and not-so-bad days that all merged into an indeterminate blur of tears and regret, days when her grief was so raw that it felt as if her heart had been ripped out of her and days when she felt as if she might manage to carry on living after all. The days passed somehow and she got through them one by one, even the blackest when she would feel as if there was no point living any more. Her mother's presence was a comfort to her, but she had had to return to work again and the lonely hours dragged without her. Alone, Emma would sit for hours on end staring out of the window of her bedroom, tears pricking her eyes, the emptiness consuming her. She didn't feel like going out, although her mother had encouraged her to, saying it would help to distract her. She didn't feel ready to face the world yet.

Christmas, the first one without either her father or Sophie, was a wretched, cheerless affair of colourful lights and decorations on the outside and desolation on the inside, a period that, in bringing other families together, only served to heighten Emma's sense of loss. Her mother had invited Emma's grandmother for lunch, as she usually did, after which her grandmother fell asleep in the armchair for the rest of the afternoon with her blanket over her knees, much to Emma's relief, as she couldn't be bothered to make conversation and repeat herself continually while her grandmother twiddled with her hearing aids. As her grandmother dozed and Judy Garland's tremulous voice warbled out from the television to an inattentive audience, Emma couldn't help but imagine how different, how alive Christmas would feel if Sophie was there. She could picture her there, just there next to the Christmas tree over by the patio doors, tugging at that glittery pink angel that would be hanging just within her reach, or exclaiming with excitement as she opened the parcels wrapped in children's paper that would be heaped underneath the tree, or helping herself to the tub of Roses that now sat unopened on the coffee table, as she grinned impishly, eyes shining, dribbling chocolate all down her best dress. This year, it didn't feel like Christmas and nor could Emma believe now that it would any other year.

That winter was one of the chilliest and longest Emma had ever known. The old demons had returned, but now it was often Sophie's face that haunted the cold, endless nights. It was Sophie's face, the minute details of which she struggled, panicky, to recall to memory in the daytime, that Emma would see with terrifying clarity behind the blood-smeared windscreen that still featured in her nightmares. Bleary-eyed, her mother would pad into Emma's bedroom and perch on the edge of her bed, stroking her hair that was plastered to her face with tears. Sometimes Emma, shivering, would cross the landing into her mother's bedroom and they would huddle up together in her mother's bed where Emma would lie awake beside her, listening to her mother's grunts and moans as she battled with demons of her own, and waiting for what felt like an eternity for her mother's alarm clock to rip through the darkness, or, if her mother wasn't working, for a glimmer of anaemic light to sneak around the edges of the curtains.

Slowly, ever so slowly, the sun's rays became strong enough once again to thaw the sheets of ice that had coated the dormant ground for weeks, heralding the advent of spring and of new life and allowing a microscopic seed of hope that had taken root, unnoticed, in Emma's heart, to start to germinate. As it did with unfailing regularity each year, the world was at last emerging, triumphant, out of the darkness towards the light.

Emma started to venture out of the house now and again, maybe to accompany her mother on a trip to the supermarket or to visit her dad, perhaps. Jack was almost one now and would pull himself up onto his knees, tugging at her hand for her to play with him. He always made a beeline for her when she called on them. Her dad laughed and joked that she was his favourite sister. She would tickle him or look at one of his books with him and he would try and grab her mouth between his little fists and kiss it, his mouth wide open and slippery with dribble. It was as if he knew somehow that she was hurting. She didn't mind. Before, she had found his presence distressing because he reminded her of Sophie, but she was enjoying being with him more and more these days.

Even her father seemed more like his old self again. He had been devastated to hear about Sophie's death, perhaps all the more so since he had a young baby of his own now. Quite uncharacteristically, he had sprung into action to offer Emma support, dropping in between jobs sometimes when her mother was at work to check on her and chat with her awhile over a cup of tea. His acute sympathy for his daughter seemed to have made him put old grievances behind him, allowing Emma to hope that he had finally forgiven her.

Camilla, too, made her feel welcome whenever she went to see them, although she always seemed reluctant to mention Sophie's name in Emma's presence. It was as if she was worried that doing so would upset Emma and that she wouldn't then know what to say in comfort.

But Emma had to admit that Camilla had done her father the world of good. He seemed much more contented, more like the happy-go-lucky man she remembered him as a long time ago when she was much younger. Having Jack had been the icing on the cake for him and seemed to have given him a new lease of life. He and Camilla appeared to get on well together and Emma was not aware of any arguments between them, whereas each day had been peppered with them when he had lived back at home with her mother, making all of their lives miserable.

He had created a new little family for himself, of which Emma increasingly felt she was a part. However, she felt guilty for the fact that the more integrated into her father's new family she became, the more excluded her mother must feel.

She never heard from Gabriel again. Or Tara. From time to time she would wonder how he was and would flick through old photos, ones on her phone or ones inside her head. She missed him. She wondered whether he missed her. And whether he had seen Tara since the day Sophie died.

One sunshiny Saturday, when her mother was at work and Emma was round at her father's again and Camilla had exclaimed that it was stuffy and had thrown all the windows wide open for the first time in months and Emma could smell the scent of the crocuses in the garden that all the flats in the block shared as it wafted in on a warm, spring breeze, her father had suddenly piped up out of the blue, 'There's nothing to stop you going to university now, you know, love.'

Although he was right, of course, the thought had never crossed her mind. It was a thought she couldn't straightaway entertain. She felt guilty for even considering entertaining it in case Sophie's death could in any way be construed as a convenience in allowing her to follow the path she had always wanted to follow and her father's longstanding dream to be realised, and more importantly, she was worried about what other people might think.

She was flustered. He had caught her off guard. She pretended to be preoccupied in building a tower of beakers with Jack, her mind all the while struggling hard not to think about what her father had said. 'No, it's too late now,' she mumbled, smiling at Jack as she placed the last coloured beaker on top of the tower.

Predictably, his little chubby hand struck at it, sending it flying. He squealed, delighted, and her father had to wait for the noise of the crashing beakers to subside before carrying on.

'It's not. You'd only be three years behind, love. Plenty of people take a break between school and university. It wouldn't be for another six months. I can totally understand that you might not feel ready yet, darling, of course I can, but you might by then. I know it might seem a bit scary – after all you've been through recently – God, it would be a big thing for anyone – but it might do you good to get away and do something different. It might be just what you need. A fresh start and all that.'

She was rebuilding the tower, Jack bobbing up and down on his knees excitedly beside her. She found the noise of the beakers tapping against each other as she piled them up reassuring. She tried to focus on that sound rather than on what her father was saying. Nevertheless, she heard him clear his throat before continuing. 'Um, I hope you don't mind, love, but I had a quick look at the Bristol website the other day, just out of interest, you know, and it said that they welcome mature students. You'd just have to get in touch with them and find out about it if you were interested...' His voice tailed off apologetically.

Having tried in vain to block out the sound of his voice, she couldn't resist an indignant retort now. 'I'm surprised you haven't done that for me already. Maybe *you* should apply, Dad.'

Her dad laughed. 'Well, I *was* tempted, but I might put the other students to shame with my brains.' He smiled at her, more earnest now. 'I'm not trying to force you to go, love. It was only a suggestion. It's up to you. Of course it's up to you.'

'Oh, thanks, is it really? Well, that's good to know.'

Her father chuckled. 'Nice to see that spirit of yours is still there. Anyway, why don't you just think about it?'

She did think about it. As soon as she sat down on the bus after leaving her father's. She couldn't stop thinking about it, couldn't help herself. Even though she had told herself she shouldn't, even though she felt guilty for doing so. Her father had planted a seed that was insidiously, determinedly growing even now and deep down, she knew, but couldn't yet acknowledge to herself, that she wanted that seed of an idea to take shape. She felt torn in two. One voice was telling her that she would somehow dishonour her daughter's memory if she allowed herself to think about something else while another, just as persistent, was urging her to pursue her former goal. She mentioned it to her mother when she returned from the salon that evening.

'Well, to tell you the truth, I can't say it hadn't crossed my mind already, darling. Of course I'd miss you dreadfully, but it's about what's best for you at the end of the day. And I agree with your dad for once. I think it could do you good. I know what happened to Sophie was terrible and you'll never stop thinking about her, never stop missing her, of course you won't, and nobody's expecting you to, but moping around here forever isn't going to help, darling. You have to start again at some point, even though that might feel like the last thing you want to do right now.'

She could feel the tears pricking her eyes again. They were always there, waiting for her like persistent demons. Tears of guilt, tears of regret, tears of frustration. They would take her by surprise sometimes. Anytime tears. Anywhere tears.

She felt her mother's arms encircle her. Again. She felt safe in her embrace. Protected from the rest of the world. How would she manage without her?

For she knew that they were right, her parents. Even if it was hard to admit it to herself. She knew she should try to move on somehow. Try and put the past behind her. Not forget it, no, never ever forget it, but she must start to believe in a future. A shiny new future full of promise that was waiting right there in front of her, just within her grasp.

CHAPTER 14

And so the decision was made, although since Emma's father had first broached the idea of university, there had never really been any decision to make. Much to his delight, she had been back in contact with Bristol again and had a new, unconditional offer to start that October. Her father prized it as if it were his own. A gleaming medal round his neck. And he made sure that everybody else knew about it.

Given her current feelings of vulnerability, Emma found the prospect of leaving the security of home daunting, despite the repeated assurances of her parents that she would feel emotionally stronger by then. Most of all, she dreaded having to explain to fellow students why she had delayed starting her course. She didn't want to have to watch them quickly try and disguise their shock or to listen to their well-intentioned, blundering, empty words of sympathy. It would make it worse.

She had started working at the supermarket on the edge of town. She would get a lift in with her mother on her way to the salon or get the bus. The work was often monotonous, but university was going to be expensive and she needed the money. She spent half the time on the checkouts and the other half stacking shelves. Emma preferred doing this. She could be left alone and lose herself in her own thoughts. She didn't have to talk to anybody and be all bright and breezy and pretend everything was great. And when she was on the checkout, there was always the fear at the back of her mind that Tara might turn up like a bad penny. She must surely have heard about Sophie now.

There were other youngsters there. Trying to save up for university, like she was. Optimistic, energetic, with a sort of fresh-faced arrogance about them as if they thought they were somehow special, that everyone admired them, was jealous of them because this was just a stopgap for them, because they were on their way up. They were going places. They hung out together conspiratorially, made plans for the evening by shouting to each other across the checkouts and joked too loudly about the other employees behind their backs, with whom they would never deign to converse face to face.

Whenever she could, Emma tried to keep out of their way. They irritated her and she was worried that they might start asking her too many questions, not that it was likely they would take any interest in her, so caught up were they in their own achievements and their own plans. Maybe they thought she was there permanently. She didn't care.

One of the managers, Ian, was always kind to her, apparently finding any excuse to come over for a chat. In the early days, she would always try to find him if he was on duty when she wasn't sure about something, because he was the only one who made her feel as if she wasn't wasting his time and hadn't more important things he could be doing. She noticed that he didn't spend quite as much time helping the others, but maybe that was only because they seemed so full of themselves and gave everyone else the impression that they knew it all already.

When she wasn't at the supermarket, she was either at home or her dad's. He had obtained an up-to-date copy of the Bristol prospectus for himself now – having thrown the last one away – and would pat the empty seat beside his on the sofa, where she would sit with a glazed expression on her face while he pointed things out to her on the dog-eared pages, not remembering that he had already pointed them out to her on previous occasions, exclaiming to her enthusiastically and readily giving his opinions on things whether they were wanted or not. Emma noticed that Camilla would always make some excuse or other and slink out of the room whenever the Bristol prospectus put in an appearance. Emma knew that her dad's fixation with Bristol must irritate her. It irritated Emma too, but rather than spoil his fun, she grudgingly went along with the charade. Emma thought that he must know parts of the prospectus off by heart by now, it was so well-thumbed, and he had turned down the corners of the pages he considered most relevant. He never tidied it away with the other books and magazines on the bookshelf. It was always left somewhere prominent, made to look as if it had been casually discarded on the sofa or in the kitchen somewhere, a potential talking point if any visitors ever came round. He was in his element again now that his daughter was off to university again – and Bristol University, no less, he would always add, nodding knowingly, his eyes glowing with pride.

Feelings of dejection would still get the better of Emma at times and the tears were always there ready to spill over at the slightest provocation. Her nights continued to be plagued with the same old nightmares and her days filled with wistful memories and regrets. The ghosts of her past haunted her present. It was images of Sophie that would play and replay inside her head when she was filling the shelves at the supermarket like an old, over-watched video tape, images whose outlines would become a tiny bit less distinct each time she played them, and she would struggle to fill in the outlines, to fill in the gaps in the pictures like a dot-to-dot book whose pages would always return to being blank each time you opened it. Or sometimes it would be Gabriel. Gabriel lying amongst the foxgloves in the woods, Gabriel bringing her breakfast in bed from the bakery next door to their hotel in Paris, Gabriel waiting for her on the bench at the station, Gabriel asleep in his bed, their bed, the day she left, Gabriel touching Tara's arm in the bar, Tara sitting on the sofa beside Gabriel, wine glass in hand, throwing her head back and laughing. She wondered whether Tara had missed the earring and whether she had guessed where it had ended up. Or maybe Gabriel had told her. Tara. Tara. The name stuck in her throat. If Tara hadn't been there that night, Sophie might still be alive now.

'Hi Emma, how's it going?' It was Ian again.

'Oh, not too bad, thanks.'

'I just came to say you can go on checkouts now if you want.'

'Oh, OK, but I'm fine here actually. I prefer being by myself.'

He grinned. 'Oh, I see, I'd better get out of your way then.'

She smiled at him. 'No, I didn't mean you.'

'Good.' He was still grinning. 'So what are you going to study at uni then?'

'English.'

He raised an eyebrow. 'Oh right. Very impressive.' He ran a hand over his hair. No ring. Emma guessed he must be in his early thirties.

'D'you fancy a quick coffee?'

'Yeah, OK then. I wouldn't mind a break actually.'

There was no one else in the staff canteen. 'What do you want?' Ian walked over to the coffee machine.

'A cappuccino, please.' Her voice sounded echoey in the empty room.

He handed her the steaming plastic cup and inserted more coins to buy himself a drink.

The metal legs of the plastic chairs grated on the floor as they sat down. 'You looking forward to going?'

She shrugged. 'Yeah, I guess so. Still seems like a long way off yet.'

'Have you just finished school then?' His eyes flicked down towards the floor.

She paused for a moment, wondering whether she should open up to him or not. It would be easy enough to lie. But lies had a habit of catching up with you. 'No, I finished three years ago.'

'So what have you been doing since then? Travelling?' She knew he was only trying to be friendly, but the questions were starting to make her uncomfortable. She could feel her forehead becoming clammy, even though the canteen was air-conditioned.

'No, this and that.' She decided to keep it vague.

Ian didn't fish any further. Emma found out over the rest of the conversation that, apart from his three dogs, he lived alone, having split up with his long-term partner a few years ago, who now lived abroad. He said his life was much simpler now that he was free to do as he wished. For instance, since she had left, he had been saving up to buy an Aston Martin, a car that he had dreamed of owning since he used to watch the James Bond films as a teenager. He had finally saved enough and had bought one a couple of weekends ago. He said it was a moment he had been waiting for all his life.

'Oh, right, cool,' Emma managed, trying to sound suitably impressed. 'What colour is it?'

'Dark grey.'

'Nice.'

There was a lull in their conversation for a couple of seconds. The hum of the lights and the low whirr of the coffee machine suddenly sounded deafening.

Ian was pulling at a loose thread on one of the buttons of his jacket. The button looked as if it needed sewing back on.

Still looking down at his jacket, he said quietly, almost under his breath, 'I could take you for a spin in it one evening if you'd like.'

He continued to look down for a moment, then receiving no response from Emma, looked up at her inquiringly. She, in turn, looked away, out of the window, which looked out onto a tiny patch of grass separated from the ring road by a line of conifers. It was starting to rain and some of the cars had put their lights on.

'Well? What d'you reckon?'

She at last looked back at him. He was trying to look unconcerned, but she could see that her response mattered to him. She could tell from his eyes. They were pleading with her, like those of a puppy dog hoping it might be thrown a titbit. In the past, she would have felt agitated, wondering how she should respond, but now, she couldn't be bothered to feel excited or nervous. She didn't know whether he was hoping that this car ride would lead to anything other than friendship or whether she even liked him in that way. Another relationship was the last thing on her mind at the moment anyway. Besides, he must be a good ten years older than her and she didn't usually go for the straight-laced type. Still, he had a friendly face and she could do with a friend at the moment. There couldn't be any harm in it.

'Yeah, OK, why not?'

His mouth spread into a grin. Delight and relief flooded his features in equal measures. 'Really? Great.' His surprise was obvious.

She smiled at him. She liked him. He had a look about him that made you feel a bit sorry for him. But then, maybe she had too.

'So when are you free? How about tomorrow?'

'Yeah, OK.'

'6 o'clock suit you?'

'Yeah, fine.' Her mum wouldn't be back from the salon by then. She worked late on Thursdays. She didn't want him picking her up in his flash car when her mum was there. She might read something into it that wasn't there. Ian was just a friend.

She saw the car turn into the drive. It was one minute past. She had been watching for him out of the lounge window since quarter to. She waved to him through the window and came outside to meet him. The passenger door of the car gleamed in the early evening sunlight as he reached across inside the car to open it for her. Her bare thighs squeaked against the leather of the seat as she sat down, the acrid scent of his aftershave catching in her throat as she pulled the door shut.

'Hiya. You OK?' He turned towards her and smiled. He looked quite different without his suit on. Jeans, polo shirt, the soft waves of his fair hair slicked back, although a couple of rebellious ones had managed to escape around the silver-coloured arms of his Ray Bans. The links on the metal bracelet of his watch caught the light as he shifted the car into reverse.

He pulled out of the driveway, his slender fingers loosely fondling the gearstick as he shifted up the gears. 'So what do you think then? Don't you just love the purr of that engine?'

'Mmm, yeah, really nice.'

'You could try and sound a bit more convinced.' He laughed. 'You're my very first passenger, by the way.'

They drove away from the town and deeper into the countryside, where the hedges were thick with tiny blossom flowers and the smell of the oil-seed rape hung heavy in the air, and where the shimmering fields of linseed rolled away to a seamless, faraway horizon.

She heard him clear his throat. 'Do you want to stop somewhere for a drink? We could find a pub.'

It was a warm evening. Maybe they could sit outside. She suddenly felt as if she had been shut away for months. 'OK, just one maybe. That would be lovely.'

He continued to the next village, passing through a small ford as they approached it. He swung into the car park of a pub. She recognised it. She had been there for a meal once with her parents a few years back. In another lifetime.

He bought their drinks at the bar and they wandered outside to find a table. At the end of the garden was a brook and at moments when neither of them was talking, they could hear its chirpy babble.

'Well, isn't this nice?' Ian sighed and arched backwards, clasping his hands behind his head. The gesture reminded Emma of Gabriel.

'Yes, it's really pretty here.' Emma flapped at a fly as she took a sip of her wine.

She felt relaxed in his company, as if she had known him for years already. She didn't feel the need to pretend she was something she wasn't with him.

The conversation naturally centred around work, their common ground. They eventually got on to the subject of the other youngsters. 'They're full of it, aren't they? We always get them every summer. Think they own the place for a few months.' Ian raised his eyebrows and looked at her thoughtfully. 'But you're not like the rest of them.' She could feel his eyes on her, soft and languorous. It made her self-conscious. She turned to watch the young couple at the table beside theirs. They were holding hands over the table, smiling listlessly at each other as the young man caressed the girl's hand. She and Gabriel used to do that at the start of their relationship when the world was still full of promise and she was enough for him. She looked away again.

'Could I take you out for dinner one evening, Emma?'

The brook gurgled on as she picked up her glass and took another sip of wine. She looked at the couple again. She was laughing appreciatively at something he was saying.

'It's not that I don't like you, Ian, but…'

'Oh, here we go. Don't worry. I know what's coming.'

He looked so crestfallen that for a moment, she was almost tempted to change her mind.

She carried on. 'I'm really sorry, Ian, but it's just that I don't feel ready yet. I've had a difficult year.' She brushed the fly off her arm.

'It's only dinner, Emma.'

'Yeah, I know, but I wouldn't want you thinking that it would lead to something more.'

'No, of course not. It would just be dinner. I promise. Dinner, then I'd drop you safely home again afterwards.' Behind the Ray Bans, the puppy-dog eyes again.

She could feel herself relenting in spite of herself. 'Promise?'

He could feel it as well and smiled at her. 'Promise.'

'Well, OK then. Just as long as you know how things stand between us.'

He nodded. 'Are you free Saturday?' Wasn't it this Saturday evening that her mum and Sue were going round to a friend's for drinks?

'Yes, that should be fine.'

So it was that a couple of evenings later, he picked her up in the Aston Martin again. 'You look nice.'

For the first time since Sophie had died, Emma had put on some make-up. She had dug out one of her old dresses and some heels.

'Oh, thanks.' There was the scent of his aftershave again.

He had booked a table at an expensive restaurant in town, one where she and Gabriel would sometimes eat that first summer when he would come down from York at weekends to visit her.

Ian ordered a bottle of white wine. The room was intimate and candlelit and in the middle of each table was a rose in a slim glass vase. A couple of impressive-looking chandeliers hung from the ceiling, their glass drops reflecting the flickering light of the candles.

One of the students at work had been caught shoplifting that afternoon and this was the subject of their conversation for a while.

'What did he take?'

'A couple of iPads and a phone. Stuffed them up his shirt when he was supposed to be stacking shelves. Got caught on CCTV. Pretty stupid if you ask me. I don't know how he wouldn't have noticed the camera.' The waiter brought the wine and Ian poured Emma out a glass.

'Tom always did like to be the centre of attention.' She took a sip of wine.

'Well, he won't be from now on anyway. And good riddance to him.'

Their meal arrived. 'So what are you up to tomorrow then?' Ian stabbed his fork into a piece of steak that he had cut off. 'Haven't you got the day off?'

'Yes, I have. Shouldn't think I'll be doing much. Might pop over and see my dad. How about you? You working?'

'No, actually, I've got the afternoon off tomorrow as well, but before you start to panic, I won't suggest we meet up.'

Emma laughed. 'What will you be doing then?'

'Not sure. Might go and play squash with a mate. Take the dogs for a walk. That's about as exciting as it will get.' Ian refilled Emma's glass as he was talking.

The last time she had drunk wine had been that night. The night Sophie had become ill. She wasn't used to it. And Ian had only had one glassful out of the whole bottle he had ordered, since he was driving.

Ian got up to go to the toilet. She watched him as he walked over to the top of the stairs in the far corner where there was an illuminated sign saying "WCs" and a downward-pointing arrow. His beige chinos clung a little to his buttocks as he walked. She hadn't really noticed his athletic figure before. His arms brushed his sides slightly with each stride – not in an arrogant "look at me, everyone" sort of way, but in an assured, self-confident manner. She took another sip of wine as she watched him patter down the stairs.

She looked around the room at the other diners while she waited for him to return. They were mainly couples, some clearly relaxed with each other, their gestures fluid and uninhibited, and having plenty to say to each other as they fixed each other in the eye with confidence, and others whose self-conscious, nervous smiles and lowered gazes gave away the fact that they hardly knew each other. She wondered whether it looked obvious to others in the room that she and Ian didn't know each other well, whether they assumed that this was their "first date".

She caught sight of Ian trotting back up the stairs out of the corner of her eye. Although she was tempted to turn to watch him walk back to the table, she picked up her glass and pretended to carry on looking around her instead, in case he was looking at her too.

'Shall we get the dessert menu?' he asked her once he had pulled his chair in again. 'More wine?' He was holding the bottle ready to pour into her glass. She hadn't even noticed that it was empty again.

'Go on then. Yes please. It's going to my head, you know.' She giggled, in mock embarrassment.

They ordered their desserts and finished their meal, Emma polishing off the contents of her glass again. She looked across at Ian as he tried to attract the attention of a passing waiter to ask for the bill. In the candlelight and after a few glasses of wine, she thought to herself that he really was quite good-looking. He caught her eye as he turned back to the table. Rather than look away, she fixed his gaze for a few moments and found that he returned it, bold and desirous. She was the first to look away, her heart pounding against her chest. He picked up the wine bottle and shook the base of it so that she could hear the wine splashing against the sides. 'Here you are. You may as well finish it off before we go.'

Emma rolled her eyes. 'I really think I've had enough.'

'OK, as you wish, but seems a shame to waste it and I can't finish it off.'

'All right then. I suppose another half glass isn't going to make a lot of difference.' She watched him empty the rest of the liquid into her glass. When she had finished, they stood up to leave. The room was spinning. She caught hold of Ian's arm to steady herself. He wrapped his arm around her and she leaned against him as they headed towards the door.

Outside, the light was fading and the lengthening, gossamer clouds were glowing golden in the west. The evening air was cool and she gave an involuntary shiver.

'Here, take my jumper. You're cold.'

'No, don't worry, there's no need.' But he was already taking it off and handing it to her. She put it on. It was still warm and she could smell his aftershave again as she pulled it over her head. It made her feel slightly nauseous. 'Thank you.' She smiled at him.

She took his hand in hers and they sauntered along streets that felt like summer, brushing past young people out for the evening, past lipsticked girls who tottered along in short skirts and high heels, and loud-mouthed, swaggering lads, buttering them up and hoping they might get lucky tonight.

'Feel warmer now?'

She nodded. She knew that he knew that she was putty in his hand. He could have taken advantage of the fact that she was drunk at any point and she knew that he knew that she wouldn't have resisted. But he didn't. He was every bit the gentleman. As good as his word. He really had meant it – dinner, then home. And she liked him all the more for it.

'Emma?'

'Uh huh.'

'Do you mind if I ask you something?'

She looked up at him, half-guessing what was coming.

Although she didn't answer, he continued. She knew he wanted to know. And maybe now was the time to tell him. It might make things easier between them if she did.

'What happened last year, Emma?'

The question hovered over them for a moment in the night air like a tiny hummingbird at a flower before becoming lost among the other Saturday evening sounds. The voices, the traffic, the music blaring out of a passing car's window before it faded away again into the distance.

His eyes were soft with concern as he noticed her hesitation. 'Sorry, you don't have to tell me if you don't want to, if it makes you feel uncomfortable.'

Yes, maybe she should tell him. It felt right. She needed to tell someone. Someone outside her family.

'I had a daughter. Sophie. She was beautiful.' She blurted it out into the night.

He was watching her. Eyes wide, sympathetic. Waiting for her to speak again. They had stopped in the middle of the street and he pulled her gently into the dimly-lit doorway of a shop.

'She was eighteen months old when she died.'

She looked at him, expecting him to say something, but he remained silent, waiting for her to go on.

'They said it was meningitis. It was so sudden. We took her to the hospital.'

He cut in. 'We?'

'I was with someone at the time.' She lowered her eyes.

He nodded, unfazed. 'Sophie's father?'

She shook her head. His features remained motionless. Still no trace of any reaction. 'We took her to the hospital and watched her die.' The tears had taken hold of her now. And so had he. She was crying into his shirt, crying hard, crying like she hadn't cried in a while. Purging herself of all the pain. Her body was shaking uncontrollably with sobs, but he was holding her. Close, secure, protected.

He could have told her then. It would have been the perfect time. If she hadn't gone to pieces on him, if she hadn't lost the plot. If he hadn't had to console *her*, he might have shared his secret with her too. He might have told her that he'd once lost a child too. That he knew what it felt like.

And things might have turned out differently.

After a while, once the sobs had subsided a little, she raised her head from his chest.

'Are you OK?' His eyes were troubled, sympathetic.

She nodded, wiping her eyes. 'Sorry, I've got mascara on your shirt.' She was trying to brush it away. 'I must look a total mess.'

'No, you could never look a mess. Not to me, anyway.'

She looked up into his face. A face full of compassion.

He seemed suddenly to remember himself. 'Sorry, I shouldn't have said that, should I? Forget I said that, Emma. I promised you I wouldn't do anything, say anything like that.'

She raised her face to his and kissed his lips. He pulled away. 'Emma, you're drunk. You're upset. You said you weren't ready for this.'

'Ian, it's fine. I know what I'm doing. I want this and I know you want it too.' She tried to kiss him again, but he turned her head lightly with his hand.

'But you might regret it tomorrow.'

'No, I won't.'

'Promise?'

'Promise.'

He looked at her, his eyes dull with longing. Then he pulled her towards her and kissed her. A kiss that seemed to last forever. He was running his fingers through her hair, holding her head as if she still might change her mind and pull away, but she was kissing him back, hungry for attention, greedy for intimacy. A couple of lads walked past them, jeering. Emma heard one of them wolf-whistle, but they didn't care. They cared only about each other right now.

The wine had emboldened her and she reached down to the clasp of his trousers, feeling his hardness underneath. Still kissing her, he tried to push her hand away. She stopped kissing him so she could speak.

'What's the matter? I thought that's what you wanted.'

'Not here, Emma, not like this. Come on.' He took her arm and pulled her gently, but insistently.

'Where are we going?'

'Back to the car.'

Hand in hand, they walked purposefully back to the street where the car was parked, stopping now and again to kiss each other. He unlocked the car and held the door open for her to get in. He walked round to the driver's side and got in beside her and she was there, reaching for him again, thrusting her tongue into his mouth again, rubbing her hand against his trousers.

He grabbed her hand and moved his head back. 'You've got to tell me what you want, Emma. I don't want you to regret this. I want you to be sure that this is what you want.'

'I *am* sure. It's *you* that I want.'

'But I promised you, Emma. I promised I'd take you home.'

'But I don't want to go home. I want to be with *you*. Please don't take me home, Ian. Not to mine, anyway.'

All the worry that had troubled his features suddenly vanished and they gradually slackened into a smile as he at last allowed himself to believe that he was truly going to get what he wanted, and had always wanted since he had first met her. 'Well, if you're absolutely sure that's what you want.'

'More than anything.'

'OK, let's go back to mine then.'

Their mouths desperately found each other again, before having to be forced apart reluctantly so that Ian could start the engine and head off down the road towards his home, finally satisfied that this was what Emma truly wanted.

CHAPTER 15

Her head was throbbing. She opened her eyes and the throbbing grew worse. She could make out a digital alarm clock on a bedside table and some striped curtains that she didn't recognise. The pale sunlight pulsing through the material hurt her eyes. She turned her head to the other side, gingerly, because it hurt more when she moved it. A dormant figure lay next to her, its breathing slow and relaxed.

Ian.

She shut her eyes again. Oh no. Last night's events came flooding back into her sore, shrunken, shrivelled, dehydrated brain with a whoosh of dreadful realisation. *Oh. Shit.*

She silently turned her head away from him again, back towards the window and the bedside table. Her glance fell on something on the carpet. An open box of condoms. "12 Intimate Feel Condoms". Nearby, a discarded foil condom wrapper, ripped open in the heat of the moment and another one, further away. *God.*

She was gasping for a drink of water, but she didn't want to get up in case she woke him. Ian. She needed to think. She lay there for a while, replaying last night's events over and over in her mind. She had thrown herself at him, hadn't she? God, why had she drunk so much? What must he think of her? What had she been thinking?

She turned back to look at him again as he slept peacefully on his side, turned towards her, the duvet, with its black and white cover, flung off him so that it revealed his toned upper body, his upper leg bent over the top and the other leg underneath. She could see the pulse in his neck, a faint watch mark from last summer on his smooth-haired wrist. She gently pulled the duvet higher over her naked body, tucking it under her chin.

It had all been her fault. Ian hadn't tried it on with her. Quite the opposite. He had given her every opportunity to back off.

She supposed that lots of women might consider him good-looking, but in the cold light of day, she didn't really feel attracted to him. OK, she had done last night, but last night she probably would have found a lot of men attractive whom she wouldn't normally. Last night she had suddenly needed intimacy, but today, he didn't set her heart on fire. Not like Gabriel had done. Damn. Why did she keep comparing him to Gabriel? Would she always compare every man to him now?

But she was still so thirsty. Her throat was so dry and uncomfortable whenever she swallowed. She would just *have* to get a glass of water. She would be *really* quiet. It would only take a minute.

She sat up, wincing slightly at her throbbing head, and swung her legs round carefully. She crept across to the door, sliding Ian's dressing gown off the hook on the back of it and slipping it on as she crept out. It smelt of his aftershave. *Well, it would do, wouldn't it?* Everything that was Ian's smelt of his aftershave. And his aftershave smelt of Ian.

She pattered softly down the stairs into the hall. To the right, the sunlight flooded through the front door. She turned left towards the kitchen door. Slowly, she leant down on the handle. It creaked slightly. She pushed on the door.

Oh no, the dogs! She had forgotten about the stupid dogs. Three hairy faces and three wet tongues and three wagging backsides were suddenly upon her, evidently far more pleased to see her than she was to see them. She tried to herd them back into the kitchen, but it was too late. Four paws bounded up the stairs, followed by another eight, up towards the open door of the bedroom. Emma sighed. Oh well, too late now. She would have to face Ian now. She would have had to face him at some point anyway. She would rather have had a little more time to think things over first, that's all.

Having first tried a couple of wrong doors, she eventually found the cupboard containing the glasses. She ran the tap and gratefully gulped down a glassful as she looked out onto the small, square back garden surrounded by a high wooden fence. A row of towering conifers lined the back fence, giving the garden a slightly claustrophobic feel. There was a ball on the grass that the dogs must have been playing with yesterday. She filled the glass again and drank more water, setting the empty glass down on the draining board. Reluctantly, she turned and walked to the bottom of the stairs. *Right. Time to face the music.*

In the bedroom, Ian was making a fuss of the dogs. As Emma appeared in the doorway, they bounced towards her, all tongues and tails again. She laughed as she bent over to stroke them.

'Hi gorgeous, how are you?' He lay on his side, propping his head up with his elbow. He was smiling at her.

'OK, thanks. Well, got a bit of a headache actually. Don't suppose you'd have any Paracetamol or anything, would you?'

'Yeah, of course. I'll go and get some.' He swung out of bed. His nakedness screamed at her, but, unembarrassed, unflustered, he reached for his boxers, which had been flung with the rest of his clothes in the middle of the floor. She instinctively lowered her eyes, as if she shouldn't be watching, although his naked body had become all too familiar to her only a few hours before, and bent down to stroke one of the dogs, who had rolled onto its back to have its belly rubbed.

'Suits you, by the way.'

She looked up at him as he eased his boxers up, trying her hardest not to lower her eyes from his face. He was nodding over towards her, grinning. She looked puzzled.

'The dressing gown.' He was still grinning.

She touched it. 'Oh, this, right. Yeah, sorry, I borrowed it to go downstairs for some water. I was so thirsty. Hope you don't mind.'

'Course not. Anyway, I'll go and get you those tablets. Come on, you three, you need to go out.' He tapped his hand against his bare thigh, calling to the dogs, who followed him out of the room and thundered down the stairs.

Emma sank onto the edge of the bed, wondering whether to get back in or whether to seize the opportunity to get dressed while Ian was out of the room. She heard the key turn in the back door as Ian let the dogs out. She surveyed her surroundings. Apart from their clothes and the condoms, the room was tidy and clean and bare. There were no ornaments anywhere in the room and no photos. Only a framed print above the bed of an Aston Martin and a large black and white print of an odd-looking bulldog with its tongue lolling out to one side on the opposite wall.

She heard a cupboard door bang shut downstairs. She made up her mind. She would get dressed. She couldn't face lying in bed naked next to him again. At least, not now anyway. He might be expecting more sex now that she had foolishly assured him last night that it was what she wanted. She wouldn't have the heart to tell him that she regretted last night now, just like he had warned her. Hastily, she gathered up her clothes from various places on the floor and slipped off the dressing gown. She pulled on her dress and was still struggling to do the zip up at the back when she heard Ian coming up the stairs again.

His face dropped when he saw her. She felt guilty now. 'You're not going already, are you?'

'I was just getting dressed, that's all.' She smiled at him weakly. Maybe she should stay a little while. 'I just…' Her voice tailed off. She couldn't think of a reason to give him.

'Here, let me help you.' He handed her the tablets and the glass of water he had been holding and finished pulling the zip up to the nape of her neck, gently holding her hair out of the way as he did so.

'Thank you.' Why did he have to be so *nice*? She would never be able to admit to him that she had made a mistake. She wouldn't be able to bear seeing those hurt puppy-dog eyes again. She sat down on the side of the bed to take the tablets. He sat down beside her, but not close enough to be touching her.

'Did you sleep OK?'

She nodded, popping one of the tablets into her mouth and taking a sip of water. 'Yes thanks.'

'Good.'

They were silent for a few moments.

Then Ian took hold of her hand, stroking it softly with his thumb. She felt him hesitate. 'You're not having second thoughts this morning, are you? Like I was worried you might.'

'What? Of course not.' She took her hand away from his and started to stroke his thigh, as if to affirm what she was saying.

'Thank God. I was worried you might have changed your mind.'

'No, don't be silly.' She turned and kissed his cheek softly. It was prickly with stubble.

She looked down again and saw, beneath his boxers, that the stroking was making him hard. *Oh shit.* She hadn't intended that to happen. She was only touching his thigh, for Christ's sake. She stopped the stroking, letting her hand rest on his thigh, but it was too late. He was turning his face towards her and kissing her lips, pushing her backwards onto the bed.

'Ian, stop.' She pushed him away and sat up again.

'What's the matter?'

'I'm very sorry, Ian, but I've got such a bad headache. I don't really feel like it at the moment, that's all. Sorry.'

'No, that's fine, of course. Sorry, I didn't think.' He looked away. Embarrassed, Emma wished the still-unmistakable bulge in Ian's boxers would go away.

'I guess I should think about getting home really. My mum will be wondering where I am.'

'I'll run you back.'

'OK, thank you. If you're sure you don't mind.'

'No, of course not. I'll just get some clothes on.'

She remained sitting on the bed while he dressed. She felt sorry for him again. She felt guilty again.

They sat side by side in the car, solemn and subdued. Emma couldn't help comparing it in her head to the car journey back to Ian's last night, when she had been leaning across to him as he drove, her hands and her lips desperately seeking him. Now she was desperate to get away from him.

Ian broke the silence. 'Nice day.' He cast his glance upwards.

'Yes. Where will you take the dogs?'

'There's a disused railway half a mile away from where I live and I often take them there. Plenty of space for them to have a good run around.'

She nodded, but he was looking ahead at the road.

'Maybe you could come with me one day. Would be nice to have some company.'

'Yeah, that would be good.' She turned to stare out of the window.

Silence again. When they were only a few minutes away from Emma's house, he reached down and took her hand. 'You're sure you don't regret last night?'

'No, I told you I don't.'

'Because I'd rather you told me now if you've changed your mind about me. I'd rather know, I'd understand. You don't have to go along with it all because you think that's what *I* want. You do know that, don't you?' He turned to her and smiled sympathetically, anxiously.

Again, he was giving her the opportunity to back down. She could just say it now. That she regretted it. That she'd been drunk. He would understand. But there were the puppy-dog eyes again.

She didn't want to hurt his feelings. She did really like him. And she liked the fact that he cared about her, that he made her feel special. She was worried that she might lose him altogether if she told him her true feelings. That she might lose a good friend. And she needed him now. She needed his friendship. She just wasn't sure yet whether she liked him in the way he wanted her to like him. But maybe if they just took things a bit more slowly from now on, the rest might follow. Yes, maybe she would tell him that she didn't want to rush things. After all, it was still early days. Very early days. It was still less than a year since she had lost her daughter. And Gabriel.

And so she clasped his hand in both of hers and heard herself reassuring him again. 'Yes, I know. I promise I haven't changed my mind, OK? I promise! So which evening are you free next week then?'

All of a sudden, the tension in his face was gone. His muscles had crumpled into a smile. A genuine, exuberant, delighted smile. Finally reassured again.

'Any evening apart from Wednesday when I have to work late.'

'Tuesday then?'

'Tuesday sounds perfect. I'm looking forward to it already.'

'Me too.' And she was. Wasn't she?

When they approached Emma's house, Ian slowed down, ready to drop her off at the end of the drive, but since her mother's car wasn't on the driveway, he drove up to the front door. Her mother must have gone out shopping. She often liked to go early on a Sunday and arrive at the supermarket just before it opened. To avoid all the crowds, she told Emma. In any case, Emma was relieved that she had gone out, as she hadn't planned what she was going to say to her.

Ian switched off the engine. 'Well, thanks for last night. It was amazing. *You* were amazing.'

Emma felt herself blushing. 'No, thank *you.*' She was turning her bracelet round and round her wrist. 'And sorry again about this morning.'

'No, don't be silly. It's me that should be sorry.'

They both smiled uneasily, uncomfortable at the mention of Emma's earlier rebuff. 'How's your head now, anyway?' He lifted his arm and touched her head fondly, twisting a lock of hair round his fingers.

'Much better thanks.'

'Right, well, enjoy your day off.'

'Yeah, you too.'

They hesitated, both unsure what to do next. She undid her seat belt and bent down to pick up her bag from the floor.

'Bye then.' She turned and reached for the door release, but he grabbed her arm and pulled her towards him, kissing her lips, tenderly but insistently.

He drew back from her. 'Bye. See you at work tomorrow. It will brighten up my Monday.'

She smiled at him, opening the door and climbing out. He waited until she had unlocked the front door of the house, before starting up the engine and turning the car round. She waved shyly from the doorway as he started to drive away and he waved back, smiling. Then she closed the door, hearing the car turn out of the drive onto the road. She climbed the stairs to her room. The door was shut. Emma had left it shut before she went out last night. Maybe her mother had assumed she was still asleep when she had left for the supermarket this morning. Maybe she hadn't noticed that she had been out all night. Maybe, if Emma was lucky, she might get away with it.

CHAPTER 16

Over the next couple of days, Emma saw Ian at work on several occasions, Ian making even more excuses than usual to come and talk to her, when he would smile conspiratorially, his eyes fizzing with a thousand electric sparkles, as if he were bursting to share their secret with the rest of the world. Once, when no one else was there, he even pushed her up against the shelves of tinned fruits in one of the storerooms and kissed her. He invited her to meet him in the canteen for a coffee, hoping to steal a few private moments with her, but there were other people in there and so he had to content himself with merely letting his fingers linger longingly on hers and exchanging meaningful glances as he handed her the steaming cappuccino.

He picked her up on Tuesday evening, as arranged. She told her mum she was going out for a drink with some friends from work and her mum, without looking up from the programme she was watching, had nodded and smiled and said she was pleased that Emma had made some nice new friends. Ian took her to a bar in town where there were businessmen in suits, and leather sofas and classily-dressed waitresses who brought your drinks to your table and smiled graciously at you when they took your order, worlds apart from Venus with its thumping pop music and overexcited youngsters who jostled with each other to reach the bar. She told herself that she had grown out of Venus now and in any case, she wouldn't have wanted to risk bumping into Tara. And Venus held too many memories. No, Ian knew how to do sophisticated and how to make her feel special. He had taken her hand as they had headed towards the bar and she had walked along beside him self-consciously, vowing to herself that she wouldn't get drunk this time.

She had plucked up the courage to tell him what she had been planning to tell him since Sunday morning. That she wanted to take things more slowly from now on because she was still getting over her daughter's death and her emotions were still all over the place. She failed to ask herself whether it was because of losing Sophie that she was reluctant to get close to Ian or because of losing Gabriel. Ian, grateful for any level of commitment from Emma at this stage, thankful for any lifeline she might throw him, had been understanding about it all, as she had never for a moment doubted that he would. Earnestly and good-naturedly, he had assured her that their relationship should progress at a pace with which Emma felt comfortable and she had reached out for his hand appreciatively across the low glass table and leant forward to kiss him. At the end of the evening he had driven her home and they had kissed again in the car, for longer this time, before he had dropped her off at the end of the driveway. He behaved as if Saturday night had never happened now, but they both knew that pretending that it hadn't happened wouldn't make the memory of it go away.

They started to see each other frequently after work. He would pick her up in his gleaming car, his face always a picture of excitement to see her, and he would drive her to a country pub or a bar in town, a restaurant or the cinema now and again. She had told her mum about him now, that she was in the early stages of a relationship, that she was taking things slowly until she was sure about him, until she had got her head sorted out, but she didn't tell her about that first Saturday night she and Ian had spent together. Her mother said she was pleased and that she felt proud of Emma for taking control of her life once again. She seemed to approve of Ian on the couple of occasions when she had met him at the front door, although she had been surprised that he was so much older than Emma.

'How old is he then?' she asked, after Ian had dropped her back home at the end of the evening.

'Thirty-three.'

Her mother raised her eyebrows. 'You're sure he's not married, aren't you?'

Emma groaned. 'Yes, Mum. He got divorced over two years ago. He never speaks to his ex-partner now. She lives in Spain.'

'Well, as long as you know what you're letting yourself into, Emma. I wouldn't want you getting hurt, that's all. Especially after everything that's happened.'

'Ian is a lovely person, Mum. I've never met anyone as thoughtful and caring and kind as he is. I know that the last thing he would want would be to see me get hurt. Seriously, Mum.'

Her mother raised her eyebrows again. Emma wished she wouldn't keep doing that.

'Well, darling, I think you're right to take things slowly, even so.'

They didn't make love again until several weeks later. He had invited her over one Friday at the end of June when they both happened to have the day off and he had made lunch for her. Afterwards, they had taken the dogs for a walk at the disused railway he had spoken about, holding hands while Ian whirled the dogs' leads around in his free hand, laughing as they watched the dogs streak across the fields that were carpeted with clover and buttercups before returning to them, worn out and panting. When they arrived back at Ian's, he had put the kettle on for a cup of tea and she had joked and said that they were becoming like an old couple, sidling up to him in the kitchen and wrapping her arms round him. He had turned to her and kissed her and winked at her and replied, grinning, 'We don't have to act like an old couple, though, do we?', a flash of fear passing over his eyes before he had even finished speaking at the sudden realisation that she might think he was overstepping the mark, but she had kissed him back and one thing had led to another and they had ended up in his bed again.

She didn't regret it afterwards. But then she didn't feel any sort of elation either, as she had with Gabriel. God, there he was in her mind again. She hadn't planned that today would be the day. It just happened. A spur of the moment kind of thing. And she still didn't fancy him really. Not if she was honest with herself. He didn't set her heart on fire. Not like… No, she mustn't say his name. But she greatly admired Ian as a person and they had become remarkably close friends in a relatively short period of time. He filled a gap in her life. Or went some way towards filling it, anyway. And she knew that she filled a big gap in his life too. Only a couple of months ago, they had both still been lost, lonely souls.

It was almost as if she took that next momentous, more or less irreversible step in their relationship for him rather than for her, because she knew it was what he wanted more than anything, and she wanted to make him happy. Not that he ever put any pressure on her to rush into anything with which she didn't feel comfortable. It was almost as if she felt she owed it to him now that they spent so much time together and had got to know each other so well. After all, it was what couples did.

Later, after they had laid together side by side in bed for a while, Ian's eyes shining with incredulity and happiness, like a child who has just been given the most wonderful birthday present, they went out for a meal at the pub in the village where he lived, and she had asked him if she could stay the night and his face had lit up again. She loved to see him happy. Once or twice before, she thought she had glimpsed a flicker of sadness creep over his features, like a cloud momentarily blocking out the sun, which had made her want to throw her arms round him and tell him everything would be all right. He had told her that she didn't have to ask, that of course he couldn't think of anything better than to spend the night with her, and, like a couple in love, they had walked back to his house arm in arm in the twilight and made love in the lounge, and then again later, after they had pulled the covers of his bed over their naked bodies in the stillness of the night. After all, it was what couples did.

One Saturday evening towards the middle of July, warm and balmy, with the sound of voices and laughter and crockery and the smell of food from the restaurant tables on the other side of the street lingering in the motionless air, they ran into Tara. Emma knew it was bound to happen sometime, but seeing her right there in front of her, for real, and not the image she had kept of Tara inside her head, would always have come as a shock to her. One second it was just the two of them, her and Ian, returning to his car after eating in a restaurant in town, holding hands and laughing at something Ian had just said, and then the next there she was. All of a sudden, from round a corner just ahead of them she appeared. Boom. Just like that. There was no warning. No glimpse of her in the distance or from behind, no luxury of a few minutes, even a few seconds, to prepare herself for the impact. They saw each other at exactly the same moment.

Emma's blood ran cold as she recognised her. She wanted to look away, but she was frozen. It was as if with one glance, Tara had turned her to stone. Tara, lovely Tara. *Her* Tara. She hadn't changed since that night. Only her hair was a little longer again now so that it swished over her back like it used to. Flanked by a couple of friends who were hanging on every honeyed, worthless word that passed those beautiful lips. Thinking about it afterwards, playing their encounter over and over in her mind, Emma couldn't remember ever seeing Tara alone. She had always had someone there to flatter her, to pander to her, to egg her on in her endless charade. Because that was all it was. The people around her made her the person she was. Without her audience she was nobody. A nobody like everyone else. And deep down she must have known it.

A trace of a smile hovered inadvertently over Emma's lips for a moment. A preposterous, ingratiating smile. What was she doing? After all that happened, she was smiling at *her*, smiling at Tara, smiling at the monster who had taken Sophie away from her, and Gabriel. Tara had stopped talking and for a split second when they first noticed each other, a look of fear swept over her face before she promptly recovered her composure and, taking in Ian at Emma's side, returned her half-smile with what could only be perceived as a smirk.

Then they passed each other and she was gone. It was all over in a matter of seconds. Back into the town, back into the night and back into the past where she belonged, but in the emptiness that followed, a high-pitched laugh, one that Emma still knew well and could pick out from the hubbub of voices around them, rang out like the sinister screech of a hyena in the darkness. And Emma knew that she was laughing at *her*. Laughing at what she had become now that Tara had taken everything away from her.

On the way back from town, the image of Tara's smirk still lingering, indelible, in her mind's eye and the shrillness of her laugh still echoing round and round her head, Emma paid little attention to what Ian was chattering away to her about as he drove. His voice was just white noise, a sound coming out of his mouth that failed to make any sense to her. Ian, being Ian, had picked up on the fact that her mind was elsewhere and had touched her hand and asked her if everything was all right. She had nodded, fighting back the tears that were prickling the back of her eyes again like tiny needles, but when they had arrived back at Ian's, she hadn't been able to shake off her despondency and he had asked her again and the needles had finally fallen out of her eyes as big, heavy tears rolling down her cheeks and she had ended up telling him all about Tara and he had wrapped his arms right around her and held her close and kissed away her tears and told her everything would be all right.

Later, they had made love and he had told her that she had nothing to worry about now that she was with him because he would always look after her. By the time he rolled over and fell asleep, she had almost forgotten how, earlier that evening, a tiny part of her had felt something a little like shame when she had noticed Tara's disdainful glance fall on Ian, as if she imagined that Tara must be thinking smugly to herself that her former friend had come down in the world a bit since Gabriel. Wasn't all that mattered that Ian loved her and she loved him? Because yes, she reflected, she did love him now. Maybe not quite in the same way as Ian loved *her*, but that didn't really matter. Did it? Even if she always held a little part of herself back when they made love, that didn't mean that she didn't love him. Did it? However, as she listened to Ian's breathing become deeper and slower, she still couldn't get Tara's smirk and her laugh out of her head, no matter how hard she tried to think about something else.

Over time, Emma realised that even though *she* disclosed certain things to Ian about her past that were sometimes uncomfortable to talk about, she didn't really know much about him. Whether intentional or not, his past was firmly locked away inside his own head and if she ever touched on a subject that might be in any way related to it, he would skilfully, almost without her noticing, steer the conversation in a different direction. Maybe he didn't realise he was doing it, or maybe he didn't like talking about himself, but just occasionally, though, she would have the impression that he was about to open up to her, to tell her something momentous, but then he would appear all of a sudden to change his mind and the opportunity would have slipped away and instead, he would talk about work again or the dogs or what they were both going to do on their next day off together.

These days she often stayed at Ian's. She had even started to miss him on the nights she still spent at her own house. Just about everyone at work knew that they were together now. They would turn up in Ian's car together in the mornings, and one of the other students had walked in on them kissing in the canteen once. Of course, the news that they were seeing each other had spread like wildfire through all the staff after that.

July rolled stealthily into an overcast, clammy August and then, all too soon, without her noticing it, the once green and glossy leaves on the trees had seemingly overnight become limp and russet and brittle and began to flutter to the ground one after the other like dying butterflies, marking the relentless passing of the shortening days, and the whirring combine harvester in the field behind Ian's house was throwing up dense dust clouds, coating the windowsills with a thin film as it drove tirelessly from one end of the field to the other, shearing it of its golden tresses and leaving nothing but a coarse, ugly stubble in its wake.

She had never imagined that September would one day dawn and with it, like a damp morning when the grey stretches monotonously from one end of the sky to the other without any holes anywhere to let the blue through, the prospect of university. One by one the other students worked out their last days at the supermarket and their wearisome, frenetic talk was all of packing and new kettles and student halls and freshers' weeks.

Up to now, she had banished the thought of university to the back of her mind, trying to busy herself with her work at the supermarket and with Ian so as to stop it from resurfacing to the front, but now that the start of term was only weeks away, the thought was becoming more and more niggling and increasingly hard to keep pushing away. Ian was the one who raised the subject one warm, drizzly Sunday morning as they lay in bed after lazily making love.

'So when is it you have to go?' She was lying on her side with her back towards him. He was also lying on his side, facing her, pulling her towards him, his arm encircling her waist.

'I haven't got work today, darling, have I?'

'I know you haven't. I was talking about Bristol.'

Although she had already had an inkling that Ian hadn't been talking about work, it felt to Emma as if her heart had suddenly been gripped tightly in a vice, making it beat harder and faster to compensate, 'Oh, right.' She was wide awake now.

'So?'

'Um, beginning of October I think. The 6th, maybe?' She felt a little annoyed with Ian for bringing up the subject just now when she had been enjoying her lie-in, but then she supposed she would have been annoyed with him whenever it had been. 'There's freshers' week before that, but I won't be going to that.'

'Why not?'

'Dunno. Because it's just a week of drinking and being on the pull, isn't it? Guess it's just not my scene. Can you blame me? Would *you* want to do that?'

'No, I suppose you're right. Might be a good chance to meet people though…'

She didn't respond and they remained silent for a few moments. The room was stuffy and she threw the duvet off her upper body. 'Anyway, I'm not sure I want to go any more, anyway.'

The statement seemed to hover uncertainly in the air above them both for a moment like a question before Ian spoke again.

'Darling, what do you mean?'

'What do you think I mean, Ian? I don't want to go any more. I don't want to leave you. What is there not to understand?' She turned over to face him. In the gloom of the curtained room, she could see the furrows on his brow that his eyes were making.

'Darling, don't be silly. What are you saying? You have to go, Emma. Everything will be all right. And you know I'll wait for you, don't you? It's only three years.'

'Only?' Her eyes were wide with anger.

'And I'll come and visit you whenever I can. And we'll still have all the holidays together. You get really long holidays at university, don't you?' He moved his arm along her body and started to twist a lock of her hair through his fingers.

'But Ian, that won't be enough. I miss you when I don't see you for a couple of days. How would I survive a couple of months without seeing you?' She swiped at his hand to push it away as if it were a pestilent fly.

'I thought you'd be pleased, Ian. I thought you'd want me to stay. I thought you might miss me too, but obviously not.'

'Darling, of course I'll miss you. To tell you the truth, I'm absolutely dreading it, but I won't let you waste this opportunity. You won't get it again. You can't work all your life in a supermarket, Emma, like me. You're far too good for that. You could really make something of yourself.'

'Well, I'm very sorry to have to disappoint you, but I've made up my mind. I'm not going.' She glared at him defiantly.

'Emma, don't be stupid. Please think about this. You can't just throw it all away.' His eyes were doing their puppy-dog thing again. She ignored them.

'I have thought about it and I can do whatever I want, Ian. I'm not going. I'm staying with you.'

'Please Emma, don't do this. I know you'll regret it later.' The puppy-dog eyes made a last desperate attempt to make her change her mind.

'I'm doing it. You can't stop me.' She threw the duvet off her side of the bed and onto Ian's and marched into the bathroom where she got into the shower and turned it on full, letting the warm water wash over her face. She needed to get away from the puppy-dog eyes, from Ian and his level-headedness. She knew deep down that what he was saying made sense. She knew deep down that she was panicking and trying to convince herself that the reason she didn't want to go to university was because she would miss Ian too much, rather than because she was too scared to go.

Later that afternoon, he picked her up in his car again on his way back from work. The early-morning clouds had cleared away to leave a warm, fine afternoon, one of the last of the summer, and they took the dogs to the disused railway where they raced about in the distance, inky blotches against a darkening, damask sky. She had been telling him about her trip to the park she had taken with Jack earlier that afternoon, while Ian had been at work.

Afterwards they were both quiet for a while, lost in thought, the conversation from that morning still going round in their heads. Ian kicked at the damp leaves abstractedly, scattering them into the air. 'What if I tried to get transferred to Bristol?'

'What?' She watched the leaves fall to the ground, heavy and ruby and gold. One of them landed on the top of her trainer and stuck there as she walked.

'I could have a word with my boss and see if he thinks it might be possible. Then we could get a house together up there. You would still be able to do your course then, but we would see each other every evening, every night. What do you think, darling? Wouldn't it be the perfect solution?' He stopped and seized both her hands, his eyes shining with excitement.

She was silent for a moment, absorbing what he had said. 'You'd really do that?'

He nodded fervently. 'Of course I would. In a flash. I'd do anything for you, you know that, my darling.' He leaned towards her and kissed her lips as if to substantiate what he was saying.

She turned and looked at the silhouettes of the dogs on top of the hill, their details becoming clearer as the dogs bounded towards them. 'But, but what about the dogs?'

He laughed. 'What do you mean? Well, they'd come too, of course.' His eyes were still bright. They looked amethyst in the evening light as they darted up and down, side to side, scanning her face hopefully for signs that she would accept his proposition.

'No, Ian, I couldn't ask you to do that for me. It's too much.' But her face was already creasing into the first glimmer of a smile; she was already starting to let him convince her that it was possible.

'But you're not asking. I'm the one asking you. It's what *I* want. Look, you were prepared to give up university for me, because you love me, and I want to do this for you. Because I love you. I love you so much, Emma, and, like you, I don't want us to be apart, yet at the same time, I still want you to go to university. This way we can have everything.'

'But Ian, are you sure? It's such a big thing. You really love me that much?' Her smile filled her whole face now. Because she already knew the answer. And there he stood before her, smiling back at her. Relieved, elated, adoring.

CHAPTER 17

'But are you sure that's a good idea, darling?' Her mother opened the door of the washing machine.

'What do you mean? Why wouldn't it be?'

'Well, are you sure you want to be tied to Ian?' As she bent down to empty the contents of the washing machine and load them into the tumble dryer next door, she shot a glance up at Emma, who was frowning slightly as she leant against the doorframe between the kitchen and the utility room, pushing the washing-machine door back and forth with the side of her leg. 'Don't do that, Emma.'

'Why not?'

'Because it's annoying and you're getting in the way.'

Emma stopped and her mother continued to sort out the washing. 'Ian seems like a nice man. I do like him, darling, but what if you make new friends at university? You might want to spend time with them. You might not want to have to worry about him all the time.'

'I don't think I'd be that bothered about making new friends. And anyway, even if I did and we did go out anywhere in the evening or at the weekend, Ian could always come with us.' Emma stooped to pick up a sock that her mother had dropped and threw it into the dryer.

'Hmm, he's quite a bit older than you. He might not want to. He might not quite fit in with university life.'

'Oh Mum, don't be silly. How can you say that when you don't really know him? And anyway, what do *you* know about university life?' Her mother looked hurt and for a moment, Emma felt guilty. 'Look Mum, this is how it is. I love Ian. He loves me. We want to be together. If he comes with me, we can be together. If he doesn't come with me, then I don't want to go. I don't want to leave him, so if you want me to go to university, then you'll have to accept that Ian's coming too.'

'Well, of course, at the end of the day, it's up to you, darling. You're a grown woman now, but I hope you've thought it all through carefully.' She raised her eyebrows at Emma, but then her face suddenly softened and she held out her arms to her. Emma leaned across the washing basket on the floor and laid her head against her mother's shoulder as she embraced her.

'You'll still come and see me in the holidays though, won't you? You won't have anything to come back for now, apart from me and your dad and Jack. You won't forget about us, will you?'

'Of course not, Mum.' Emma closed her eyes and breathed in the scent of her mother. She knew that she would miss it.

Her father came round to the idea more readily. 'Well, love, I can understand that you don't want to go by yourself. After everything that's happened. I expect you're still feeling quite fragile. And that you don't want to leave Ian now. I like him, anyway. Seems like a decent enough bloke. Every time I've met him, he's been very polite. Seems to treat you well.'

They were in the lounge at her dad's and Jack was pulling at her hand, trying to get her to play trains with him. 'Ian's sorted it out with work. I didn't think it would be so easy. He's renting a house somewhere on the outskirts. He's still going to keep his house here. He might think about renting it out while we're away. The house in Bristol sounds great. It's fully furnished and it's got a bit of a garden for the dogs. It's on a quiet street. Only five minutes' walk from a bus stop. We can move in at the start of October. It's all worked out perfectly.'

Her father smiled and put his arm around her. It almost felt like old times. 'I'm glad you're happy, love. If anyone deserves to be happy, it's you.' Emma looked down at the floor. Jack was still tugging at her hand and, more frustrated now, had started to shout at her. Her father chuckled and squeezed her arm. 'I know someone who's going to miss you when you go.'

They had hired a van for all the things they were taking. And the dogs. The Aston Martin was already waiting for them in Bristol. Ian had dropped it off when he had picked up the van the day before. Emma's dad had driven over to her mother's house to wave her off. Along with Camilla and Jack. In a show of unaccustomed civility, Emma's mother invited everyone in for a coffee before they left. Everyone, apart from Jack, perhaps, could sense the tension that hung over them all as they gathered in the lounge with insincere smiles on their faces that looked as if they had been stuck on with glue. Camilla had never been to Emma's mother's house before and Emma thought she looked uncomfortable as she perched woodenly on one end of the small sofa while Emma's mother sat at the other, Emma's father having already claimed his old armchair for himself. Emma and Ian sat facing everyone on the floor as if holding court, while Jack clambered from one person to another, dribbling everywhere because one of his molars was coming through, Camilla explained, as she wiped his chin with the back of her hand and rubbed her hand along her jeans, Emma's mother looking on all the while with unconcealed distaste.

Emma's mother was subdued, perhaps partly because she was dreading saying goodbye to her daughter and partly because Camilla seemed particularly talkative that morning, making her reluctant to risk getting into conversation with her. Even her father seemed at a loss for words for once, never having found himself in the same room as his new partner and his soon-to-be-ex-wife before. He had finally pulled his finger out and started divorce proceedings, which made Emma's mother's mood at that moment even more precarious.

A pang of apprehension mixed with relief gripped Emma when Ian finally announced that they should get going. After dutifully collecting up everyone's dirty mugs and taking them into the kitchen, he came back into the lounge and smiled across at her.

'You ready?'

She could hear the dogs getting impatient in the van. She nodded. Her cheeks were wet with tears before they had even started their goodbyes. No sooner had she wiped them with the back of her hand than they were wet again, as wet as Jack's chin. Here it was at last. The moment she had been dreading all summer. Now that it had arrived after so many months of waiting, it didn't feel real somehow.

Although the prospect of university was far less daunting now that Ian was coming with her, it was still a huge step into the unknown for her, and indeed, for Ian as well. And even though she would have Ian now, she would miss her parents' support, which had been monumental over the past year. She would never have been able to get through it without them.

She scooped a bewildered Jack up and kissed him, tears mingling with saliva, then hugged her father, who whispered in her ear to look after herself and to remember he could be down there in a flash if she needed him, although Emma wondered to herself whether he really would. His breath tickled her ear as he spoke. His eyes welling up, he turned to Ian and said in a shaky voice, 'You're a lucky fellow. Make sure you take good care of her, won't you?' And Ian, slightly embarrassed, had nodded and assured him that he would.

Her mother clung onto her, sobbing unashamedly, mopping a screwed-up tissue at the tiny rivulets of black that turned to a watery grey as they ran down her cheeks. Through her own tears, Emma noticed Camilla hovering at the door of the house uncertainly and once her mother had finally let go of her, went over to her and put an arm round her and kissed her on the cheek a little awkwardly. Then, at last, amidst a chorus of goodbyes, they got into the van and were ready to set off.

They walked to the end of the drive to wave them off, her mother and father and Camilla and Jack, whom Camilla held in her arms, and, as the van pulled away, Emma waved out of her window and shouted goodbye, watching the four figures become smaller and smaller and straining to hear their voices under the noise of the engine until the van turned a corner and they were gone.

Ian took his hand off the gearstick and let it rest on her thigh. 'Cheer up. You've still got me.' He shot her a sympathetic look.

'Yeah, I know.' She put her hand over his and fought to keep the tears in. 'It's just that they've been there for me over the past year and I'm really going to miss them.'

'I know they have, darling, but I'm here for you now. I'll always be here for you. Every step of the way. You can talk to me about anything. You do know that, don't you?' He turned to her and smiled, brushing a tear off her cheek with his finger.

She nodded. 'Yes. Thank you.' She sniffed and smiled back at him, squeezing his hand in hers.

'It's the start of a new life for us now, a new adventure.'

'I know. There's no turning back now.' She leaned over to him and kissed his face. 'I love you, Ian.'

'And I love you, darling.'

CHAPTER 18

They had driven down to look at the house a couple of weeks before. Situated on a sprawling residential estate a short distance away from a main road into Bristol, it had its own small driveway which would be just big enough to park the Aston Martin, once Ian picked it up from the van-hire place where it had been left while they moved in. It should be secure on the drive, he had told her, what with the street light on the pavement right outside the house as well. That was one of the main reasons why he had chosen this house rather than somewhere nearer the city centre and the university. It wasn't just the two of them he had to consider, or even the two of them and the dogs. There was his precious car to think about too.

Admittedly, the back garden was a little cramped for three dogs, but last time they had visited, they had walked along the main road looking for somewhere to get some lunch and had come across a park only ten minutes' walk from the house, with plenty of open space. It would be perfect for the dogs, Ian had exclaimed excitedly, swinging her arm enthusiastically as they strolled along hand in hand, to convey to her his delight that everything was falling into place so well.

Ian had already dropped a few odds and ends off yesterday when he had picked up the van, Emma having stayed behind to pack. When he turned the key in the front door and Emma pushed it open, she was greeted by an impressive arrangement of flowers on the windowsill in the hall. She recognised the blue ceramic vase that Ian used to keep at the back of one of his kitchen cupboards. She squeezed his hand and smiled at him. How organised he had been, she told him, to have bought flowers and remembered to bring the vase from home to put them in! When they climbed the stairs to the bedroom, she found their bed already made up with his duvet from home and covered with real rose petals and chocolates. She had kissed him and told him how lucky she was to have him. Eyes shining with satisfaction, he had sat on the end of the bed and pulled her down beside him, but she had jumped up again, smiling as she wagged her finger at him in mock rebuke and told him that there was too much to do and that there would be time enough for that later. Reluctantly, like a dog with its tail between its legs, he had followed her downstairs and back out to the van.

Relieved not to be cooped up any longer and with noses to the ground, the dogs had eagerly set about exploring their new surroundings as Ian and Emma traipsed back and forth from the van to the house, carrying in all their belongings that would turn this house into their home.

When at last the van was empty, Ian drove it back to the depot a few miles down the road while Emma remained in the house to unpack. Half an hour later, she watched through the lounge window as the car nosed onto the drive. She heard the familiar high-pitched squeak as Ian pressed his remote-control key to lock it. On his way to the front door, he threw a glance over his shoulder back at the car, as if to satisfy himself that it wasn't rolling down the slight incline of the drive onto the road. She had known he would do that. He never left his car without a backward glance and she smiled to herself, thinking how well she had got to know all his idiosyncrasies now.

That night he made love to her tenderly, under the familiar black and white-patterned covers with the soft glow of the street light outside the window eerily lighting up the corners of the unfamiliar room. Afterwards, he stretched out his arms to embrace her and fixed her with a look of such adoration that it made her feel slightly uncomfortable. The orangey light from the window was shining off his face in the darkness. 'I love you so much, Emma. I'm so glad I'm here with you. I wouldn't have been able to bear it if we'd been apart.'

She smiled and kissed him. 'I'm glad you're here, too.'

There was still another day before Emma started her course and Ian his new job. They spent most of it cleaning and shopping for food and loo rolls and light bulbs, unpacking the rest of their belongings and finding places for them all. Making a home together. It felt strange to Emma seeing her clothes hanging neatly in the wardrobe beside Ian's, like a proper married couple's. The last time this had happened, she had been living with Gabriel, but it had always felt to Emma as if it was still *his* house, whereas now, because she and Ian had moved in at the same time, it felt to both of them as if it was *theirs*. Even though Ian was paying most of the rent, she felt as if the house belonged just as much to her as it did to him. She suddenly felt grown-up. Even a little *too* grown-up. It all smacked of commitment. And it was barely a year since Sophie had died and she had left Gabriel. Life had moved on quickly. Too quickly. Life has a habit of doing that. Of creeping up on you when you're not looking. But here she was already, living with another man in another city and about to embark on a degree course. Things had come full circle almost without her realising, but the house was all sorted now. Her clothes were hanging in the wardrobe. Their wardrobe. The Aston Martin was on the drive. Their drive. And her course was starting tomorrow. It was too late now for any doubts.

The following morning Ian insisted on driving her into the city centre before heading all the way back out again to his work, which was five minutes' drive from where they lived on the outskirts. However, she asked him to drop her off down a quiet backstreet near the university because she didn't want any of the other students seeing her get out of the Aston Martin. She didn't want to draw attention to herself. She failed to ask herself whether it might also be because she didn't want them to see her with Ian. Much to his obvious disappointment and feeling as if he were letting her down, he wouldn't finish work in time to pick her up again at the end of the day so she would have to get the bus home, he informed her apologetically.

He arrived home soon after her. She heard the peep of the lock and the key in the front door. The dogs barked. She was looking forward to seeing him again. He flung his arms around her and kissed her. The dogs circled his legs, tails wagging nineteen to the dozen. 'So, how did it go, darling?'

'OK thanks. How about you?'

'Oh, fine. I don't think it's going to be that much different from my job at home really. Tesco's is Tesco's, isn't it? Just a few new faces to get used to, that's all. Anyway, tell me about your day, darling. I've been thinking about you. Did you find your way around OK? Did you make any friends?' He sank onto the sofa and patted the seat next to him. 'Come and tell me all about it, darling.'

So she sat beside him and nestled against him, his arm around her. It felt good to see him. She felt safe again. 'I spoke to a few people on my course, but I'd hardly call any of them friends yet.' Yes, they were nice. No, she didn't get lost. Yes, the lectures were all right. No, it wasn't too difficult. 'We didn't really cover a lot of ground today, anyway,' she explained. She turned her head towards him and kissed him. 'I've missed you.'

He pulled her towards him and held her close. 'Me too. I'm here now, though.'

She suddenly stood up from the sofa and tugged at his hand, cheeks flushed, smiling encouragingly. Suggestively. 'Come on.'

For a second he looked confused, but she was still smiling and there was a glint in her eye that he had rarely seen before. With a start, he realised, joyfully, what she wanted. Grinning from ear to ear, eyes bright with anticipation, ever ready to oblige her, he stood up too and let her lead him up the stairs to the bedroom.

Gradually, they both established their new routines. Routines that intertwined and then parted again, that gave a sense of shape and direction to their days and nights together. Ian soon became acquainted with his new colleagues at the supermarket and quickly settled into the somewhat undemanding responsibilities of his new position, while Emma, despite some initial reticence and nerves, did eventually get to know a few students. There were a handful of other mature students on her course, some a good deal older than her and with families, but the four or five in their twenties tended to stick together. If anyone asked her why she had delayed starting university, she told them she had been ill. It worked. That shut them up. Ian had told her to say it. 'No one will have the gall to ask you about it,' he had added. And he had been right. They hadn't. She had mentioned to a couple of her new friends that she was living with her boyfriend, but none of them had had the pleasure of meeting Ian yet.

As the first few weeks of her course passed, she found she hit it off particularly well with one of the other mature students on her course. Ben was twenty-five and had been working in Madagascar as an English teacher. He had only intended to stay there for a year after his A levels, not anticipating that he would fall head over heels in love with the island and end up staying for six. He said he was finding getting his head down again hard after what had felt like an endless holiday. She loved hearing him tell her stories about his teaching, about people he had met and the animals he had encountered. Animals were one of his passions, he told her, and he had been torn between an English and a zoology degree. She couldn't help feeling glad that he had chosen English.

He made Madagascar sound like the most wonderful place on earth. He even showed her a few photos one afternoon when they were studying in the library that he had brought with him specially. She said she thought she would have liked to have gone to Madagascar with him to see the lemurs and the volcanoes. He laughed and said he would take her there one day. She knew that it would never happen, but she found pleasure in talking about it as if it would. She felt comfortable with Ben because he never asked about her past. It was as if he somehow sensed that she didn't want to talk about it.

He asked her whether she would like to go with him to watch a band play at the student union one evening after lectures, but she had declined, saying that Ian would be waiting for her at home. He had suggested that he join them, but she had explained that it wasn't really Ian's thing. If it hadn't been for Ian, she would probably have been tempted to go, she mused. But Ian *was* waiting for her at home. Kind-hearted, doting Ian who had given up so much to be with her. Yes, she should get back to him, she told Ben, who nodded understandingly and said he would see whether one of the others would go with him.

It was raining as she hurried to the bus stop. She hadn't noticed the rain when she had been sitting in the lecture hall. Emma was finding out that it rained quite a lot in Bristol. The last lecture had finished slightly late and she saw the bus pull up at the stop when she was still at the end of the street. If the lecture had finished on time, then she wouldn't have found it. Not that day, anyway. She might still have been living a lie, but she was bound to find it sooner or later. She started to run. There were still a few people waiting to get on. She might just make it. She ran faster, but her shoulder bag kept getting in the way and she kept having to stop to heave it back over her shoulder.

Umbrellas were obscuring her view of the bus now. Large golfing ones, small foldaway ones, plain black ones, garish coloured ones, but she continued to run, having to move her head this way and that to avoid them. The bus reappeared as she emerged out of a small throng of people. She came to a halt as she watched the last person get on before the bus finally pulled away, its windscreen wipers tirelessly dancing from side to side and its headlights illuminating the rain that was falling in torrents now. The inside of the bus was lit up. Through the front windscreen, she could see the passengers smug in their seats and the driver, grim-faced, peering out behind the frenetic wipers. The windows along the side of the bus were steamed up. Inside it looked warm and inviting. She watched the blurry silhouettes of the passengers go past her as the bus's wheels threw up a thick, grimy spray which splattered across her legs.

Not that it made any real difference. She was already soaking anyway. People nearby were huddling in the shopfronts as they watched the rain lash down, smiling at each other and raising their eyebrows in complicity as they lowered their umbrellas and gave audible sighs of relief. Emma walked over to the nearest shopfront. People shuffled backwards and sideways to make a space for her, but she was on the outside of the group and the rain was falling diagonally, whipping against her body.

The next bus wasn't until another half hour and she was wet and cold. A taxi pulled up next to the bus stop and a woman got out, slamming the door behind her before she made a dash for it to the entrance of one of the flats that were over the line of shops. The taxi waited a few moments, its engine running. Through the rain, Emma could make out the driver fiddling about with something inside. The woman's money or the radio controls, perhaps. The taxi sign on its roof lit up and even before her brain had finished making the decision to do it, she was running to the door and pulling on its handle. If it hadn't been raining, or at least, if it hadn't been raining so hard, then she might have waited for the next bus and she wouldn't have found it. Or if that woman hadn't lived in the flat where Emma happened to be sheltering from the rain, and the taxi hadn't stopped right in front of her. If. If. It was a whole sequence of events that led up to her finding it later that evening, but the first was the rain. Afterwards, she would blame the rain for what happened afterwards. Rain, rain, go away, come again another day. The Bristol rain.

The driver threw her a look of disapproval as he took in her drowned-rat appearance, seemingly worried about his back seat. Emma gave him their address and the taxi set off down the hill, stopping and starting in the rush-hour traffic. It was warm inside the taxi and smelt of salt and vinegar crisps. By the time they pulled up outside the house, it was starting to get dark, but the rain had almost stopped now. Emma noticed that the car was in the drive. Ian must be home. 'Nice motor.' The driver raised his eyebrows at the car and gave out a low whistle as he pulled up behind it at the bottom of the drive. He shot Emma a curious look, as if bewildered by the fact that his bedraggled passenger was going to the house with the Aston Martin parked in the driveway. 'Fifteen fifty, love.'

Emma scrabbled around in her purse. There was only a ten-pound note and a few coppers. In her desperation to get out of the rain, she hadn't thought to check whether she had enough money on her. 'Sorry, I haven't got enough. Would you mind if I just ran in the house quickly to get the rest?'

'Yeah, suppose so.' The driver ran his hand through the bristles of his beard. 'Don't be long though. I've got someone else waiting.'

'No, won't be a minute.' Emma slammed the door shut and hurried towards the house. There was no barking. The dogs weren't there and nor was Ian. He must have taken them for a walk. Damn. She hoped he hadn't taken his wallet with him.

She cast a swift look over the kitchen worktops and in the lounge. Through the window, she could see the taxi driver eyeing up the car. He looked up as she walked past the lounge window and nodded at her.

She ran up the stairs to the bedroom. Ian's wallet was there on the dressing table. He must have put it there when he was getting changed to go out for a walk. She pounced on it with relief, holding her breath slightly as she unfolded it to see whether there was actually any money in it. There were a couple of ten-pound notes at the back and she grabbed one, throwing the wallet back towards the bed as she flew out of the door. It missed the edge of the bed and she heard a soft thud as it fell onto the carpet. She would pick it up when she had paid the taxi driver.

He had his finger inside his ear, twisting it round from side to side and didn't notice her arrive. Emma tapped on his window. He wound it down and rubbed the finger that had been inside his ear back and forth against his thumb a couple of times before he put his hand out to take the money Emma was holding out to him. The finger that had just been in the ear skimmed her hand as he gave her the change and she recoiled slightly. 'Thanks, love. Bye now.' He reversed into the empty driveway next door and accelerated off down the road.

She went back upstairs slowly. She ought to change into some dry clothes. The wallet had fallen upside down on the carpet and some of its contents had slipped out. She bent down to pick it up, as well as the stack of plastic cards that were underneath. The wallet felt soft in her fingers and she could smell the leather. She tried to push the cards back behind the thin leaf of leather on one of the sides of the wallet where she knew Ian kept them, but they wouldn't go in. Something was stopping them. She slid her thumb and forefinger down behind the leaf. She had been right. She could feel something there. A small piece of paper or card. Her thumb and forefinger closed around it and pulled. A tiny dog-eared square of blank white card. It didn't look like much. But no, it wasn't card. It was photographic paper. She turned it over. And there it was. The Photo. That was how she found it.

Her immediate instinct was to drop it and it fluttered down onto the carpet again. She dropped onto the bed. Her head was spinning and she felt as if she couldn't breathe, as if there was something heavy squeezing her ribcage. Her mouth suddenly filled with saliva and she knew she was going to be sick. She stood up and staggered across the landing to the bathroom. She felt so dizzy she could hardly walk. It felt as if there were invisible forces pulling her in every direction apart from the one in which she wanted to go. She flipped open the toilet seat and it slammed against the cistern. She heaved her guts up into the bowl a couple of times.

The stench of vomit was overpowering and she stood up, reaching across to the window to throw it open. She closed her eyes, letting the chilly evening air rush over her, even though she was already frozen, even though her body was trembling with cold. Still feeling dizzy, she tottered back across the landing, using the walls on either side to help her balance. Warm, warm. She needed to get warm. She peeled off her wet clothes, leaving them in a sodden heap on the bed. As she couldn't see her own dressing gown anywhere, she slipped off Ian's with her finger from the hook on the back of the bedroom door. It smelt of his aftershave, but she had got used to the smell now. She pulled it tighter around her, her upper teeth clattering against her lower ones violently, her muscles quivering with uncontrollable spasms as her body struggled to raise its temperature. She lowered herself back onto the edge of the bed and bent over gingerly to pick up the photo again.

She could still vividly remember everything about it as if the last time she had seen it had only been yesterday. The grey V-neck jumper, the crisp white collar, the red and grey striped school tie. That crooked front tooth that protruded very slightly over his bottom lip as he smiled at the camera. The eyes, bright and wide with concentration, as if trying hard to please the photographer. That lock of thick hair that had been combed across his forehead and looked as if it didn't want to go that way. Not three years ago. Three long years. So much had happened since then. *Was it really only three years?* It felt as if she had been keeping her secret for a lifetime. She had almost succeeded in convincing herself that she might be able to find some way of living with it after all. That she might be able to put it behind her somehow. And that her guilt and her remorse might not overshadow every single one of her actions and her thoughts for the rest of her life after all.

There it was. The face of her nightmares staring her out, daring her to look away. She had never thought she would see it again. Not like this. Not face to face, as it were. She had seen the photo a few times after the accident. That very photo. She hadn't *not* been able to see it. It had been splattered all over the front pages of the local papers, it kept popping up on the regional news. Her mother and father had shaken their heads at the television and murmured to each other as they sat in the lounge, her mother on the sofa, her father in his armchair. Uncomprehending. Disbelieving. 'How could anyone do that?' 'That poor child.' And, 'How terrible for his parents.' And she had had to leave the room and sit it out in a cold sweat in her bedroom until she had regained her composure and felt able to hold it together once more.

Those days, those weeks, those months afterwards had been almost unbearable. Trying to deal with the burden of her guilt alone, constantly living in fear in case her secret was discovered. Reliving those awful moments. The events of that night. *That* night. The night of Megan's party. The night she got pregnant. The night she got drunk. The night she decided to drive home when she knew she was over the limit. When she knew she should have slept at Megan's – as many of the others had – or phoned for a taxi. But she hadn't stayed at Megan's. She had just wanted to get home. That boy was still there. Sophie's father. And all she wanted was to get away from him now that the high from the drink had worn off. She regretted having had sex with him and she didn't want to be anywhere near him now. And she didn't have money for a taxi. It was stupid. She could have asked one of her friends if they would lend her some. She was sure that someone would have done. Why hadn't she asked someone? Why? The question would always plague her.

So she had driven home. Yes, she had driven home. Of course she had known that she shouldn't, and if she could turn the clock back… God, if she could turn the clock back. *If only* she could turn the clock back. It was about half one. It had started to rain. Bloody rain. The day had been hot and sultry and the odd boom of thunder was starting to growl in the distance. The wind was getting up. It was only ten minutes back to her house. Ten minutes. Megan lived in the next village and there was a long road lined either side with trees between her village and Emma's. No houses. Just trees. It was a sixty-mile-an-hour limit along that road because there was nothing there. No one ever walked along there, especially at half one in the morning. For a start, there was no pavement. She didn't feel drunk any more. She felt fine. Just a little tired, maybe. And she was driving at the speed limit. Or sixty-three, sixty-four perhaps. Yes, definitely no more than sixty-four.

It was totally straight, the road, apart from one sharp bend in the middle. She hadn't known someone would be there, just round the bend, a couple of metres from the left-hand edge of the road, had she? You wouldn't *expect* someone to be there, would you? Not at half one in the morning. She braked. Yes, she had definitely braked. She remembered the noise. The screech. But the screech of the brakes only happened at the same time as she heard the thud. The thud as he bounced off the windscreen like a rag doll, all arms and legs until the head struck the glass right in front of her face. How had it not broken the windscreen? She had braked as she hit him, not before. There hadn't been time. There had only been time – a fraction of a second – to register that it was a human form that she was about to hit. She couldn't have done anything. She wouldn't have been able to stop. Even if she hadn't been over the limit. It wouldn't have made any difference. But the police might not have seen it like that. She had panicked. She had felt the wheels go over his body, crushing any bones that were still intact. It had felt like driving over a speed bump. And even then, she had still been braking. She remembered still hearing the screech as she was going over the speed bump.

And then she remembered checking in her rear-view mirror that there was no sign of approaching headlights around the bend, and driving home. Yes, she just drove home. Not as if nothing had happened. No, of course not. She wasn't *that* callous. She had been wracked by guilt ever since, hadn't she? She couldn't remember anything about the rest of the journey home. She remembered feeling surprised that she had arrived home in one piece as she pulled up onto the drive. And she remembered slinking in through the back door and being grateful that her parents hadn't bothered to wait up for her. They would surely have noticed her distress otherwise and she would never have got away with it. She could hear her dad snoring through their bedroom door as she crept past to her bedroom and shut her door silently.

Thankfully, the car didn't seem to have suffered any damage from the impact. And when her parents had heard about the accident on the news, her mother had commented, 'You would have come along there wouldn't you, on the way back from that party? What time was it when you came along there?' And she had said twelve forty-five to cover herself. Too drunk and too busy getting off with each other, her friends wouldn't have remembered what time she left. 'You must have just missed it then. They reckon it happened about one forty-five.'

She looked at the photo again. And the boy looked straight back at her. As he always would. Stuart Smith. That was his name. Smith. A common enough surname. There must be so many Smiths in the world. Her heart suddenly did a belly flop. No, surely not. It couldn't be. Ian didn't have any children. He would have told her. *Wouldn't he?* Anyway, Ian's surname wasn't Smith. But then, Stuart might have taken his mother's surname. There was no reason why not. But then again, if Stuart wasn't Ian's son, then what was his photo doing inside his wallet? Had he been his nephew? A godson, perhaps?

Her mind was racing to fit the pieces of the jigsaw together. Three years ago. Ian was thirty-three now so that would have made him thirty at the time of the accident. The boy had been nine at the time so that would mean that if Ian was his father, he would have had him when he was twenty-one. That would work. Ian said he split up with his partner three years ago. The boy had been wandering alone in the road in the middle of the night because his parents had been rowing. Screaming at each other, the neighbours had said. They reckoned that it must have woken the boy up and that he must have become frightened and panicked and run out of the house. The parents hadn't noticed he had got out of bed and left the house until the police had knocked at their door later that night. The pieces were starting to fit together.

She was going to be sick again. She ran to the bathroom and threw up, sinking to the floor beside the toilet and letting her head fall like a dead weight into her hands. The wind had caught the window and it had blown wide open. The bathroom was freezing. Her body was still convulsed with spasms as she trembled, but she didn't notice how cold she was any more. She stayed like that for a while, stunned, shivering, praying that she might have got it wrong.

'Emma?'

She nearly jumped out of her skin. Ian stood at the bathroom door. *Fuck.* She had completely forgotten that Ian would be coming back soon. How many minutes had she been sitting there like that? Five? Twenty? More?

'Are you OK?' His cheeks were flushed from his walk, his eyes soft with concern. She looked away. She couldn't look him in the eye. She had killed his child. How would she ever look him in the eye again if it was Ian's son she had killed?

The room must still stink of vomit. Even with the window open. She hadn't flushed the toilet. She watched as his glance hurriedly took in the toilet and the window. It was blowing a gale in the small bathroom. His eyes returned to her, now taking in the dressing gown and wet hair and tormented face that all the blood had drained out of. Shit. Shit, shit *shit.*

'Emma, what are you doing? What's going on?' He looked scared now. She could see the rise and fall of his chest. His breathing was becoming shallower, faster.

'It's nothing. I'm fine. Really.' She pushed her damp hair off her face in a ridiculous, futile, last-ditch attempt to regain some composure.

A look of realisation suddenly seemed to sweep across his face and a faint smile toyed with the corners of his mouth. *God, why was he smiling?*

'You're pregnant, aren't you?' It came out like a statement rather than a question, but she could tell it was a question from the way his eyes were frantically scanning her face for any sign of a response.

Fucking hell. If only it were that simple. 'No. No, Ian, I'm not.'

His face fell and anxiety clouded his features once more. 'So what is it then? Are you ill?'

She shook her head.

'For fuck's sake, Emma. What is this? Some kind of sick guessing game?'

All of a sudden she remembered the photo that she had left on the bed. She needed to put it back before he noticed it. 'Will you get me a drink of water, please?'

He nodded. 'Yes, of course, but afterwards you can tell me what all this is about.' He made as if to turn out of the bathroom towards the stairs, but something must have made him glance across the landing into the bedroom opposite before he did so. Maybe it was her heap of wet clothes on the end of the bed. Maybe it was something else that caught his eye before he headed downstairs to fetch her drink.

'What's that on the bed?' He strode the short distance from the landing to the bed. Emma held her breath and waited. Her heart was thumping against her chest as if it wanted to get out.

'What have you got that out for?'

She was watching him across the landing. As she cowered on the bathroom floor, quaking with cold and with panic, he marched back towards her, holding the photo out in front of him accusingly for her to see. But he didn't need to show her. She already knew what he had found.

'I needed some money to pay for a taxi. It was pouring down and I missed the bus. I didn't realise that I hadn't got enough money until we got home. I dropped the wallet and it fell out.' She craned her neck to look up at him from the floor. His temples were pulsing furiously. She took a deep breath. 'Ian, is this your son?' Her voice was tremulous. His subsequent nod of assent was dreadful. 'Why didn't you tell me you had a son?' It was almost a whisper.

'I don't know, I don't know. I don't like talking about it. It hurts too much.' He was shaking his head as he turned over the tiny photo and moved it closer so that he could see it. 'I *did* have a son, Emma, but I don't now. Not any more.' She watched as the tears started to trickle slowly, steadily, down his cheeks. So many tears. Too many tears. 'He died three years ago. He was nine. It was a hit and run.' His voice quivered as he spoke the dreadful words.

So her suspicions had been confirmed. Stuart Smith *was* Ian's son. The room was spinning again. It was going way too fast. She felt sick again and she couldn't catch her breath. It felt as if she were suffocating. She could hear a loud whirring sound like a spinning top in her head and it took her a moment to realise that Ian was speaking to her again, let alone to make sense of what he was saying.

'Anyway, why would you have assumed that it was my *son*? Emma? What's the matter? Please tell me what the matter is. Are you all right? You look terrible. Is it the photo?'

He was staring at her, his eyes boring into her, waiting for her to answer.

'Yes, it must be! It's something to do with the photo, isn't it?' He squatted down next to her, thrusting the photo under her nose, but she turned her head away to the wall.

'Yes, it is! I know it is. You found the photo and it has obviously affected you in some way.' He was silent for a few moments, turning things over in his mind. 'I didn't tell you about Stuart because I don't like talking about it. I'm sorry, Emma. I should have done. I'm not very good about talking about stuff. I keep it bottled up.' He glanced up at the open window. 'God, it's freezing in here, darling.' He stood up to reach over to the window and pull it closed before lowering himself to kneel on the floor beside her. 'But surely you wouldn't have reacted so violently just because you thought I might have a son. And anyway, you didn't *know* it was my son, did you? It could have been someone else. A godson, a nephew.' His eyes darted this way and that, trying to make sense of what was happening.

He was silent once more and she waited. She knew that it was only a matter of time before his brain arrived at its terrible, inevitable conclusion. 'Unless...' He turned to her and she lowered her eyes to the floor. 'Unless you know something about the accident!' He grabbed hold of her head roughly and pulled it up so that she was facing him, but she found that she was still unable to raise her eyes to meet his.

'Emma, look at me!' He shouted it, making her jump, at last provoking a reaction from her. She raised her eyes to meet his for a split second, long enough to see that his were boring into her, eager for answers now. Then her glance returned to the floor.

'Emma, why won't you look at me?' He was still shouting, but there was a whining, imploring note in his voice as well, leaving her in no doubt of his increasing desperation to get to the bottom of it all. She could hear one of the dogs barking downstairs. Ian's shouting must have set it off. She wished he wouldn't shout.

'Oh my God. No, please, God, no.' It was little more than a whisper, floating above their heads like a wisp of invisible, deadly vapour. He groaned and sank his head into his hands. Then, as if doing so required him to make a monumental effort, he raised it again slowly to look at her. 'It was you, wasn't it?' She could hardly hear the words, he said them so quietly. She was still looking at the floor, but she could see him staring at her out of the corner of her eye. And she could feel it. She wished he wouldn't keep looking at her like that. Downstairs, the dog had stopped barking.

'I said, it was you, wasn't it?' She felt him grab hold of her shoulder and start to shake her, but still she wouldn't look up. 'Yes, it was near your house that it happened. It all adds up. It was you, wasn't it?' The dog had started barking again. She wished it would shut up. And she wished Ian would whisper again. Her head was pounding. It was hurting. *He* was hurting. He had started shaking her again. 'It was you, wasn't it?' He was screaming it in her ear now.

He grabbed hold of her face again, pinching her skin between his fingers as he pulled her head round towards him. 'Just fucking look at me, Emma. Just fucking tell me it was you.' A second dog had started barking now.

As if there was a great weight bearing down on her eyelids and with what felt like a Herculean effort, she raised her eyes at last to his. She nodded slowly, barely moving her head at all, but it was enough. He had seen. That was all the confirmation he needed to know that it was she who had killed his son.

He released her face roughly, shoving it away from him as if he never wanted to set eyes on it again, and lowered his head into his hands, lifted his knees up towards his chin and started rocking backwards and forwards and moaning in a low voice as if in the most atrocious pain. 'No, no, no.'

'Ian, I'm so sorry, I'm so very sorry. I can't tell you how sorry I am.' And then the tears started falling. Bitter, swollen tears that had waited a long time to fall. Tears of pain, tears of grief, tears of unspeakable regret. Her whole inside felt raw as if it was being seared all over by a red-hot iron. At that moment she felt as if she was crying about everything she had ever cried about. Tara, Gabriel, Sophie, Ian, Stuart. She felt as if she would never stop crying. She felt as if she would cry for the rest of her life. And that she deserved to.

Without changing his position, Ian lifted his head from his knees to look up at her again with bloodshot eyes. The colour had disappeared from his cheeks and his face looked drained of all its vitality. 'Tell me what happened.' He spoke through clenched teeth. She couldn't tell if he was angry or defeated. Or both.

'OK.' She tried to hold back the tears, but they kept coming. Purging her soul. Unburdening her heart. She took a deep breath and started trying to tell him, her voice trembling, her body convulsed with sobs and shuddering violently with cold still and with shock, about the party and about the bend in the road and about coming across Stuart just round the other side of it, how she couldn't have done anything to stop or to avoid him. He was there, just there. She held up her hand in front of her face to show him how close the boy was. Stuart.

'But why didn't you stop afterwards? How could you have just left him there? My boy, my precious son?' His tear-filled eyes were searching her face. Disbelieving, uncomprehending.

'I was over the limit.' She looked down at the floor again through her tears and muttered it under her breath, as if saying it quietly might soften the blow.

'Over the limit?' She lifted her head, watching him digest this piece of information.

'How much over the limit?' He was starting to raise his voice again.

'I don't know. A couple of glasses. Three? Four? I don't know, Ian. But I didn't feel drunk any more. The feeling had worn off by the time I drove home.'

'Worn off? Oh, so you thought that was OK, did you?' His yelling was hurting her ears again.

'No, of course I didn't. I knew I was wrong to drive home. I took a risk, a stupid risk, and have paid the price ever since.'

He cut in. '*You've* paid the price. What about me? What about Nina? What about Stuart?' His eyes blazed with anger. 'What about Stuart, Emma?' The dogs were barking frenetically downstairs.

'I know. I know I caused unimaginable suffering, Ian. And I can't tell you enough how sorry I am. I will always regret what I did, Ian. I know I should have got a taxi. Or stayed the night at the party.' She looked at him, trying to hold his glance, but having to hang her head in shame.

'But you didn't. You thought it was OK just to get in the car and plough into someone.'

'Ian, I've told you. I wouldn't have been able to stop. It wouldn't have made any difference whether I was over the limit or not.' She tugged at the collar of Ian's dressing gown to dab her wet cheeks with it.

He carried on, without listening to what she was saying. 'Just to plough into a nine-year-old boy, *my* beautiful nine-year-old boy, and drive away as if nothing had happened.'

'Ian, it wasn't like that.'

'No? What was it like then?' His eyes were bulging out of his face like some kind of gruesome reptile and his cheeks glistened with tears.

'I panicked. I wasn't thinking straight. All I was thinking about was being over the limit. I didn't think about the consequences at the time, about the effect it would have on his family. God knows I've thought about it since, Ian. Not a day has gone by when I haven't thought about it, when I haven't regretted what I did that night. It will haunt me for the rest of my days. That's my punishment. That's what I deserve.'

'No, Emma, what you deserve is to go to prison and then to fucking rot in hell. That's what you deserve.'

He screamed it at her demoniacally, his parting shot before she heard the slip of his socks on the stairs carpet as he pattered down, followed, a couple of minutes later, by the heavy thud of the front door, the sound of which reverberated through the house for a second. Then the squeak of the remote control and the slam of the car door and the sound of the engine jumping to life.

She didn't know how long she remained like that on the bathroom floor in Ian's dressing gown with its damp collar. When she could bear the cold no longer, she stood up and padded across to the bedroom. There was no sign of the photo on the landing carpet. Ian must have taken it with him. Out of the bedroom window, she could make out a few faint stars far away in the distance. The clouds had all blown away now. She lifted the duvet and got into bed, shivering. The sheets felt cold, in spite of Ian's dressing gown. She lay there in the darkness waiting for Ian.

Somehow it felt like a relief. To have told someone finally after keeping her secret for so long. Even if it was the dead boy's father whom she had told. But, in a strange, macabre way, she also felt glad for having got her share of answers too. That she had solved the last clues of the puzzle. That the boy had some kind of identity in her mind now and that she had at last been able to say sorry to someone. That she might perhaps have some sense of closure. What happened next was up to Ian.

He didn't come back that night. Or the following one. Emma didn't go into the university. There would have been no point. She wouldn't have been able to concentrate on anything. And besides, she wanted to wait for Ian. To be there when he arrived home.

It was about half past two the next afternoon when the dogs started barking and she heard the slam of the car door and the squeak of the remote. Through the lounge window she saw him get out of the car and look back at it before slowly walking up to the front door. She had half-expected a police car to have been following him home, but no, to her relief it was just Ian. She heard the key turn in the door and held her breath and waited. He appeared at the lounge doorway. 'Hi.' He passed the back of his hand over the stubble on his chin.

'Hi.' She looked up at him, too nervous to force a smile, trying to gauge his mood, but his expression was blank.

He walked over to her and sat down next to her on the sofa, not so close that their bodies were touching, but near enough for them to have easily reached out to touch each other if they had wanted. Her heart thumping, she waited for him to speak.

'Are you OK?'

'Uh-huh. You?' She wondered where he had been. Where he had been sleeping. In the car? It was hard to tell. He looked worn out. Done in.

'Yes, thanks.' He was fingering the metal links of his watch strap. 'Emma, I've been doing some thinking.'

'Uh-huh.' She felt sick with trepidation as she waited for him to pronounce her fate.

'I want to try and put all this behind us.'

What? What's he saying? Has he gone mad? She was staring straight ahead of her at the picture on the wall opposite. The one of the stupid bulldog. Ian had moved it down to the lounge after making a collage of photos of the two of them and of the dogs, which he had put in their bedroom.

She turned to him, eyes wide, incredulous. 'What do you mean? How would we do that? Have you forgotten that I killed your son? That's always going to be there between us. In the way. How would you ever forgive me for that? I know *I* wouldn't.'

'Well, I'm not you, am I?' He shifted nearer to her and took her hands in his awkwardly, as if for the first time.

'I know, but I don't think there could be many people in the world who would forgive someone for killing their child.' Her head was throbbing. She hadn't even realised that she had a headache until now.

'No, probably not, but you didn't do it deliberately, did you? You said yourself that nobody would have been able to stop in time. Stuart was just in the wrong place at the wrong time. It was my fault. Mine and Nina's. We shouldn't have been shouting like that. Not when Stuart was in the house, anyway. We were shouting so loudly we woke him up. And we should have realised that he had left the house. We didn't even realise he wasn't there with us until the police called round to the house after the accident. He had walked over a mile from the house and all the time he was walking out there all alone in the dark, I thought he was in bed. So what sort of parent does that make me, Emma?' His eyes flashed with anger. 'I've never been able to forgive myself for not checking on him that night, for screaming so loudly at Nina that I didn't even hear him come down the stairs and open the front door.'

He had started to cry. Bloated, silent tears rolled down his cheeks and she put her arm round him without thinking. An instinctive reaction. 'But you didn't know that was going to happen, did you? You didn't know he was going to walk out of the house and get run over. All couples argue. It's perfectly normal. Don't blame yourself, Ian. Please don't blame yourself. It wasn't your fault. It was nobody's fault. It was an accident.' She wasn't sure whether she was trying to reassure Ian or herself.

She was crying too now and she wiped at her eyes with the edge of her finger. They had edged closer together on the sofa without realising. She laid her head on his chest and he encircled her with his arms. She could hear his heart beating. Constant. Regular. All of a sudden, she felt exhausted. 'I was worried about you.'

'I've come back. I'm here now. You don't need to worry any more. I love you, Emma. I can't live without you. I've been turning it round and round in my head and I think I can forgive you. I know that you're a good person. And I know that you would have stopped if you hadn't been over the limit. It was only because you panicked. I would probably have done the same. Yes, you were wrong to drive when you were over the limit, but we've all done stupid things in our time. You didn't mean to kill him. It was an accident.'

He gently moved her head off his chest and pressed his lips against hers. They tasted of tears. Then he moved his face back from hers and looked at her, his eyes overflowing with tears and with love. She looked down self-consciously, smiling slightly. She was still finding it difficult to look him in the eye. She wondered whether she would ever stop finding it difficult. In time, maybe. She couldn't believe that he was prepared to forgive her just like that and for a moment, she remembered Gabriel and what he had done. What Gabriel had done was nowhere near as heinous as what she herself had done, but she still hadn't been able to forgive him. And yet here was Ian, kind-hearted Ian, ready to forgive her. How could he find it in his heart to be so magnanimous?

For a moment she wondered whether she might have been half-hoping that Ian *wouldn't* forgive her, because she doubted whether their relationship could ever go back now to how it was. She almost wished that he had finished with her, thrown her out, punished her. After all, it was no less than she deserved. She wasn't sure whether she could live with his forgiveness, whether she could forgive him for forgiving her, senseless as it seemed. Although she loved Ian, she had never quite managed to love him the way he loved her and maybe deep down she had always been waiting for something like this, something that would make Ian finish with her, because she had got herself in too deep now to try and get herself out of this relationship. So now she would have to try to live with his forgiveness. She would have to try to love him like he loved her, to deserve his love and be the woman he wanted her to be. Because she had told him her secret now and it mustn't go any further than Ian. She suddenly felt trapped.

He stood up and pulled at her hand. 'Come on, my beautiful Emma. I want you to know how much I love you.' Obediently, she followed him into the hall and then behind him as he climbed the stairs, still holding her hand, casting glances down at her over his shoulder and smiling through his tears. She smiled back at him because she knew it would please him. And because she knew it was her duty now to please him.

And so they made love under the black and white duvet again. The one they had made love under so many times now. The one they had made love under the first night they had spent together when she had been drunk. The night before the morning when she had been afraid to admit she had made a mistake.

And she tried to pretend to him and to herself that she wanted to make love to him again now. Even though she was finding it hard to believe that he still wanted her, that he was making love to her, his son's killer, with such longing. He kissed her and she kissed him back. Like she couldn't get enough of him. Even though inside she was screaming for him to stop. Even though she found the intensity of his love for her oppressive.

CHAPTER 19

The next day it was as if for Ian everything had returned to how it had been before. As if she had never found the photo. And the craziest thing was that neither of them ever mentioned it again, although for Emma, at least, it was always there at the back of her mind. Always in the way, invisible but glaringly obvious.

At university the following week, Ben asked her if she wanted to go back to his flat one evening after lectures to see the rest of his Madagascar photos. Emma shook her head dolefully. 'No, sorry, Ben, I can't. Ian will be waiting for me. I have to get back to him.'

He smiled easily at her. She liked it when he smiled. It seemed to light up the room. 'That's OK. Some other time then.' But somehow she doubted there would be another time. She knew that Ben would eventually give up asking because he would always get the same reply.

She would have liked to see the photos. For Ben to show them to her. The photos of a place far away from here. But she had to get back to Ian. He would be waiting for her. Looking forward to seeing her. They would have their evening meal together. Maybe watch some television. Then go to bed and make love and kiss each other goodnight. Because it was what couples did.

And she might lie awake beside him for a while in the strange orange half-light under the black and white duvet going through another photo album, flicking through the well-thumbed pages of photos in her head of Sophie and of Gabriel. Photos that seemed as if they were from another place that was far away from here. Another time. And she might cry herself silently to sleep. Then she would wake up tomorrow morning and Ian would roll over and wrap his arms around her and tell her that he loved her and she would pretend everything was all right again.